CW00376729

DAGGER OF ASH & GOLD

K. ELLE MORRISON

PROLOGUE

We woke early the next morning, not that we slept much through the night due to Althea waking several times screaming Cornelius' name. Talos was up and walking on his own by six o'clock, healed from his battle with Lawrence. He didn't remember much of our escape, at least as far as I could tell. He had few words to share so early in the morning. Althea paced the small space of the motel as I called for a taxi to pick us up and take us to the nearest vehicle rental. Traveling by car was less risky but would take us twice as long to make it back to Cinder.

I waited outside the motel door for the taxi to arrive, the others waiting inside close to the window for my signal. The sun had begun to rise over a line of trees and cast golden light on the near empty road out front. Althea should be on her way to her honeymoon right now, she and her husband should be blissfully wrapped in each other's arms. But instead my friend was glassy eyed and worn with reliving her horror of a wedding day every time she closed her eyes.

When the taxi arrived I peered to the driver through the

passenger window, he was mortal from what I could tell. He asked for my name

"Olympia," I said and he nodded as he hopped out of the car to open the rear door to load any bags we had.

Which we had none, we had escaped with nothing but what was on our backs. The small bag I had grabbed with my laptop, phone, and wallet had come in handy. I had a chance to send Zaida and the others a quick message that I was headed back home but needed to speak to them when I was secure. I hadn't checked my messages and wouldn't until home in the off chance they had put some type of trace on my electronics. I doubted they had been so smart, or was more sure that they had been foolish enough to believe we wouldn't have escaped to infiltrate my belongings.

I stopped the driver and let him know that I was the only one with a bag and that we were ready to leave. He jumped back into the van and I knocked on the door and watched the parking lot as Talos exited the room and swiftly got into the van, followed by Althea, then Amil. I waited for them all to be in the van before settling in myself next to Amil in the middle seats. Talos and Althea took up the back with Althea lying down with her head in Talos' lap. She'd not said a word while awake but Talos didn't seem to need to hear her words to know what she needed. He had given her his jacket to wear over her ripped wedding dress. The bottom shredded from running through the manor and then fighting sleep over night.

The driver silently drove us to the nearest rental dealership that was open, one Fata employee sitting behind the counter rifling through paperwork and clicking a keyboard. She only briefly looked up to us and set a clipboard on the counter as I approached.

"We only have two SUV's available and you'll need to pay extra to have it returned from Cinder." She hummed boredly.

"Thank you, either will be fine." I signed the document with an alias and a card matching the name.

She eyed me over her thin reading glasses, then to the large Incubo, Amil, next to me. Snapping her gum, she thought better than to say something cheeky and handed over a copy of the paperwork then keys to a large SUV that was parked on the side lot. She pointed the way and went back to her duties. Amil was not thrilled with this arrangement, he wanted us to take separate vehicles but I didn't want to bring too much more suspicion to us if we could help it.

Althea and Talos waited on the side of the building out of sight while Amil and I checked the vehicle to be sure it was clear of any obvious obstructions. When we deemed it clear, Talos took a once over before inviting Althea into the back row of seats. She darted out of the shadow of the rental building and laid across the seats. Talos sat in the passenger seat and Amil offered to drive the first few hours. I got into the middle row of seats and laid down as well to try and get some sleep. As long as we drove the speed limit and staying within the confines of traffic laws, there shouldn't be any reason for us to stop until we needed to switch drivers.

Sleeping in the backseat of a car wasn't unfamiliar territory although it had been many years and I was much taller than the last time I had curled up into a lumpy car seat. One of the last memories I have of my birth mother was when she had told me to wait for her in a car she had stolen while she made the exchange with Mr. Blue. A large sum of money for whatever she deemed more worthy than her only daughter. Mr. Blue had woken me up from sleeping in the back seat and had promised me that I would never have to consider a vehicle a home unless I chose it. He pulled me out of that car and saved my life, a guardian for the weak and unwanted.

It wasn't long before I had fallen asleep, the sound of the

road lulling me until my eyelids were too heavy to keep open. I dreamed of being back in Cinder, of Ms. Green in the kitchen of Banner House 216. Of my siblings running combat drills. And of my penthouse home that looked over my small piece of the city.

CHAPTER ONE

The absent sound of the engine woke me up as Amil opened the driver side door and took a moment to stretch. I sat up and looked out the window to see we were still somewhere rural at a gas station between Arta and Cinder. Talos opened the passenger door and raised his arms over his head then rolled his neck. He looked into the car and gave a nodded silent request to accompany him into the gas station convenience store. Looked back behind me to see Althea asleep across the seat and made sure I closed my door quietly as not to wake her.

The bell above the door clinked as I opened it and took a few steps inside, peering around to see the tall Incubo who had beckoned to me. An older Mortal man sat behind the single check out count counter reading a magazine, unaware of the deadly patrons who had just entered his store. The short aisles filed their way towards chilled drink fridges where I spotted Talos' head pop up from where he had been leaning down to grab a drink

I joined him at the glass doored chillers and grabbed a bottle of water for myself and an armful more for our companions.

"Thank you, Isa. I haven't said it yet but I'm eternally grateful and indebted to you for getting Althea out alive." His eyes traveling along the many candy and snack wrappers on the racks next to us.

"I'd like to say 'you're welcome', but if it weren't for you I wouldn't be standing here. Lawrence—"

"Let's call it even then, shall we?" He gave me a weak smile that didn't reach his dark eyes.

Before I could say any more, he turned and walked away to retrieve snacks for the rest of our trip. I watched him for a moment before grabbing a few things for myself. None of us had eaten much since the morning of Althea's wedding, we'd not discussed it but a sense of being too stressed to eat seemed to be the tone of our trip. We would be in Cinder soon enough, stopping and risking being seen at a restaurant was foolish.

I placed the bottles of water and snacks on the counter and reached into my bag to pay but before I could find my wallet, Talos appeared at myself and set his items down with his credit card. The teller didn't pay us any mind, he hardly looked up as he rang up all the items and put them in a brown sac. When the receipt printed and the man finally looked up to hand it over, terror washed over his features. Talos gave him a wink and a smirk as he picked up the bag. The corner of my mouth pulled up as I rolled my eyes at the interaction that had given Talos some humor and followed him out, the teller's eyes intent on us as we went.

Back at the car, Amil was finished filling the tank and Althea was sitting up in the back seat. Talos sat in the middle row of seats and took out a candy bar to hand over the seat back to her. Amil held out the keys to me to take.

She offered him a small smile of thanks and sat back, his oversized suit jacket swallowing her up. I handed back a few water bottles as Amil plopped down in the passenger seat. He looked to the back window and his features changed suddenly dark and defensive.

"We need to go now."

I glanced back but saw nothing but acted on his instinct and started the car, throwing it in drive quickly and getting back on the road in the direction that Amil's hand was pointing me from low in his seat.

"The gas station employee was watching us and talking to someone on the phone. We probably have about thirty minutes to find an alternate route before we're caught up with whoever he had contacted." He took out his cell phone and began looking at a map on the screen.

I looked up to the rearview mirror and saw no suspicious vehicles. I caught sight of the back of Althea's head as she watched out the window, her hands gripping the seat. Talos was looking down to his phone with one hand stabilizing himself against the roof of the van.

"Turn off here, we'll take this exit and take a few back roads for a while." Amil gestured to the nearest exit for me to take.

The side road was several yards away from the main highway, but less visible through the trees and miscellaneous buildings and homes. We eventually found the Main Street of the small city we had been approaching before our stop at the gas station. There wasn't much to see, a grocery, a few restaurants, and the homes of locals. We didn't stop to investigate but found another side route away from the highway to travel down for several more miles.

It seemed that Amil's plan had worked. When we hadn't seen anyone following us about an hour later we decided to get back onto the fastest route to Cinder. Althea and Talos didn't speak much but frequently turned to look out the rear window. Amil fell asleep with his head leaning against the passenger side door, he had slept the least of us all. I was wary to ask Talos to take a turn driving due to his head injury and insertenty of the severity.

After another two hours on the highway we reached Cinder city limits. The sun was setting over my city and I could feel the warm embrace of familiarity wrapped around as I drove past buildings I had seen hundreds of times while living in Cinder. We parked the van several blocks away from my building and I walked Althea and Amil up to the main entrance first. Talos volunteered to stay at the car to look out for anyone who may have followed us. My door man tipped his hat in greeting as he swung the door wide for us to pass by him. He eyed Althea's dress but didn't make a comment, by the look on his face when he noticed Amil and Althea's eyes, he had forgotten all words.

I slipped my key into the elevator lock to take us up to my floor. When the doors opened before us, Althea gave a small gasp. Her eyes drank in all that she could see from the open entryway. She took a deep breath and walked to the couch to sit and stare out the large window overlooking the city street.

Amil took a few steps in and looked around before turning to me and speaking "Bathroom?"

I pointed him down the hall and he inclined his head and gestured for me to follow him. We reached the hall between my bedroom and the bathroom when he stopped and pressed his back to the wall opposite me.

"What's wrong?" I mimicked his posture, but crossed my arms in annoyance.

"What the next move here, Isa? Are we supposed to hunker down in your small apartment like a teenage sleep over?" He rubbed his palms into his eyes before yawning.

"I think we all need a full meal. Stay here and keep an eye on Althea until I get back. I'll send Talos up and then grab some take out."

"I'll go with you." He pushed away from the wall and began

walking back into the living room but I grabbed the crook of his arm to stop him.

"Amil. Stay here. We don't know if someone has followed us here or if anyone was involved here. I'll be fine."

He sighed and hung his head and I didn't wait for him to respond. Althea turned her head to me as I approached the back of the couch and leaned on the back edge of it with my arms extended.

"I'm going to grab some dinner. What can I get for you?"

She laid her head on the back of the couch and looked up to me, her eyes watery and raw from crying and very little sleep.

"Anything would be fine. I actually feel like I could eat just about anything."

I brushed a lock of hair from her forehead and smiled weakly. "The bathroom is at the end if you'd like to shower. My closet is in my bedroom to the left and you can use anything that fits."

"Thank you, Isa." She said, her voice low.

Amil came out of the hall to join us in the living room, I slipped my hand into his as I walked past him and gave him a small squeeze of assurance that I could handle anything beyond this point. When I got into the elevator and got off on the ground floor I stopped in the lobby to let my doorman know that I'd left friends upstairs and that I would be returning with another soon. His eyes mooned and his voice shook when he said "Yes, ma'm."

When I reached Talos, who was leaning against the van and looked to his phone, I peered around us to see if anyone was more than a little interested to see an Incubo casually waiting on the street. Several passersby glanced in our direction but none dared speak or linger. Talos looked up to me from his phone stone faced, "News has finally spread."

He passed me his phone that was open to the local news webpage:

Wedding Massacre!

By Lindle John

It has been confirmed that over forty wedding guests have been found murdered on the Welp estate in Arta late Saturday afternoon. The victims were to attend the marriage ceremony of Cornielus Welp and his fiancée Althea *NAME*. Among the deceased is Cornileus Welp, his father Stavros, and his mother Camilla. The estate will be passed onto the next of kin. The body of Cinder native and father of the bride Pytr *NAME* was also found among the victims but there is no verification that the new bride Althea, has also fallen victim in the attack. There have been no reports on who will be held responsible for this mass murder but police have brought in investigators from Amples to assist in the investigation. If anyone has any information leading to the whereabouts of Althea [Welp], please contact local police non emergency line.

I looked up to find Talos watching me as I read the short article. I read over it one more time before passing him back his phone for him to pocket.

"What does this mean?" I folded my arms to my chest.

"This my dear, Isa, means that Althea and the rest of us by extension, are suspects in a terrorist act." He slid both hands into his slacks pockets.

CHAPTER TWO

I walked Talos into the lobby and to the elevator of my building. I summoned the lift by its illuminated buttons and we waited for the doors to open. He towered next to me, reminding me very much of the first night I'd met him in an elevator not far from here.

"I'm sorry." He spoke to the floor without glancing over to me.

"For what?" I said as I watched the lights above the elevator doors tick off each floor as it descended the shaft.

"I have put you in more danger than I intended." The doors opened and he stepped inside, turning to face me.

"To be fair. That article didn't mention me." I winked as I instructed the elevator to rise and the doors shut with him behind them.

I turned back to the lobby and the door man caught my eye again. He seemed anxious now that three Incubo were tucked away upstairs and I seemed to be leaving them there. I grinned to the floor as I left through the main entrance. There was a Fata owned pizza shop a few blocks over that was my usual stop for fresh brick oven pizza. I turned the corner outside and looked around, I knew that it was unlikely that anyone would find us, even if they had found out where we were going or had trailed the van we had driven, there was no way of knowing where we would be now.

The pizza shop came into view, beings flitted in and out of the front door with companions. Large, flat takeout boxes held up over patrons heads as they passed through the narrow doorway. When I got to the door, a tall being held the door open for me, I looked up to a man with bright white-blond hair and my breath caught.

"Are you alright, miss?" he said kindly.

"Yes, sorry. I thought you were someone else." I shook my head and passed under his arm into the restaurant.

I knew Lawrence was dead. He had to be.

I slit his throat then he was attacked by Talos. There was no way Talos would have left him breathing after what he had put Althea through. But he had survived a stab to the ribs, and my blade across his neck didn't seem to slow him one bit while he attempted to strangle me. If it wasn't for Talos and Amil, he would have killed me before bleeding out on top of my body. I took a deep breath in and slowly let it out as I approached the front counter and put in my to-go order. I wasn't sure how hungry Althea would be or what she took on her pizza so I ordered one plain cheese and one pepperoni pizza with two orders of breadsticks in the hopes that everyone would find interest in something.

I waited in a booth near the counter for the food to be ready. I watched as beings passed by, saw the smiling faces of citizens of my city blissfully unaware of all I had learned in the past few weeks. Did the Fata here in Cinder know of the coupe being staged in Arta? Could something like Althea's wedding happen here next?

All questions that I didn't have answers to but my stomach tossed at the idea of Cinder igniting into a war amongst its residents. My fellow Banners and I would be utilized as contract killers for the top bidders which hurled the image of Argo being auctioned off to the forefront of my mind. I hadn't had a moment to check on the search for Argo by my other siblings.

I pulled out my secure cell phone and dialed Zaida's phone number. It rang once before she answered "We do not shy away from the dark…"

"For we are the shadows," I chanted in reply, "Have you found him yet?"

"Nothing. The location we pinned was cold, they must have left as soon as they ended the call or much smarter than we initially thought and deflected our trace. Are you safe?" She sounded tired.

"Yes, I'm home but I'll be on my way to you tomorrow evening."

I hadn't discussed this with the Incubos I was currently abetting but I'd spent enough of Argo's time away. I needed to help find him.

"Let me know when you're on your way and I'll send you our coordinates. And Isa." She paused to lower her voice, "Come alone. Tension between Incubo and Fata here in Amples is high, best to keep out of it."

With that her line went dead. I sat with the phone in my palm for a moment to mull over her warning. She knew of Talos and the mission I had been on but she may not yet know of the massacre that occurred at the wedding in Arta. She would have no idea that Althea, Talos, and Amil were currently waiting for me to return home with pizza. I pocketed my device and walked towards the counter and to the Fata who was placing a stack of boxes down and double checking orders before calling out names.

"Donovan. Eliza. Thomas." He glanced around at the room flicking his sights to two men standing close to me.

I had given the name 'Eliza' with my order, it was one of

many names that I gave. I waited for the other patrons to take their orders before taking my four flat boxes and heading for the door. I hipped the door open with the hot cardboard flats against my forearms and nodded a thanks to a woman who was kind enough to hold the door fully open for me as I passed her.

The busyness of the shop and the street outside anchored me to the realization that was setting in. I was home but only for a moment.

CHAPTER THREE

When I returned home, Talos was out on my balcony and Amil was resting with his eyes closed on the couch. I looked around but didn't spot Aleatha, "She's taking a shower." Amil spoke out into the room without moving.

"Has she been in long? Should I check on her?" I said as I set the warm boxes down on the kitchen counter.

He shrugged his answer. I looked out to Talos who was inspecting the many vine and flower pots crowding the singular balcony chair. I decided to wait to check on Althea for the moment and went to the open balcony door to lean against the metal frame. If Talos heard me behind him, he didn't turn around to greet me.

"Pizza's here." I stated and waited for his response.

"Your home is lovely, Isa. It suits you very well." He fingered a tendril at the ledge gently.

"Did you expect a weapons vault with a bed in the middle?" I joked.

He turned to me when he spoke again, "I didn't know what to expect to be perfectly honest. As mysterious as my kind is to you, the Banner's are more enigmatic to us."

15

He eased the space between us on the small landing and looked down into my face. His eyes danced with wisps of white opaque smoke as if he were seeing me clearly for the first time. His hand cupped my cheek, drawing my sight and chin up towards him. The familiar pull behind my navel tugged as the thin veil smoldered to a dark grey. Storm clouds invading his pupils as he lowered his lips to hover over mine.

I swallowed hard and waited for his full lips to press against mine. To feel his warm breath brush across the bridge of my nose and take him into my lungs. He hummed a contented sigh "Have I thanked you for saving Althea?"

"I'm not sure." My lips fluttered against the bow of his as I spoke.

"And for saving my life?" He paused, pulled away to catch my sight again, "I will have to find a way to show you how grateful I am."

My knees felt weak at the implied tone in his voice. Moony to the thought of all the ways he could show me his appreciation. The butterflies in my stomach stirred up images of the stolen moments we had shared in an elevator, a brownstone sitting room, the cabin of a train, and the suite of the Welp's manor. It would be so easy to slip back under his potent spell, and be driven down into giving myself over to him in any way he wanted. Pinpricks of my skin still reacted to his slightest touch when the hunger in his eyes bore down to mine. The butterflies in my stomach stirred up images of the stolen moments we had shared over the last month. Flashes of his mouth on my neck and between my legs caught my breath.

"Perhaps you have preferred compensation in mind?" His grin teased against my lips.

A fog rolled over me as the scent of his stale cologne mixed with sweat, and the familiarity of the city around us. I leaned into him and felt a relief in the way his shoulders sagged as he held me close to his chest. Warmth from his body further encapsulated me from the memory of what we had all survived. I wanted to stay in his embrace for as long as I could. To feel his lips claiming mine in the place I had carved out as my sanctuary for so long. Where no one other than my siblings had ever stepped foot. I'd never allowed anyone into my home. My little piece of the Cinder.

For a too brief moment, nothing was amiss. He took that worry away. The same way as Amil had taken away my stress and pain back at the manor when Argo had first been taken. And now Amil was splayed across my couch, possibly witness to what may be conceived as a betrayal to him and our time together. But neither Incubo laid claim to me here in Cinder. None were to say I couldn't have either one of them. Or as Talos had described during our last meeting, they could share me together. A bitter feeling washed over me at the thought of sharing my bed with either or the both of them tonight.

The skin on my arms raised as a cool breeze swept over the balcony, a rush of sound from the street below brought me back to reality. Talos pulled away first and I steadied myself on my own feet and backed away to add to the distance between us. I looked over my shoulder to see Althea had walked down the hall into the living room. She had showered and found a pair of sweatpants and a slouchy shirt from my dresser. Our sight connected for a moment, her watery eyes stricken with the waves of grief she'd been battling with since her wedding day. She glanced to Talos who moved past me to go to her side. He embraced her, not at all the way we had just done, but in a warm encircling hug.

I looked to where Amil had fallen asleep on the couch, his arms crossed over his chest and face towards the back cushions. I didn't wake him but went to the kitchen and took down some plates for us all to attempt a meal. When I turned back to Talos and Althea they had separated and spoke in a hushed tone. I cleared my throat gently before speaking to the room at large, "Would anyone like a drink? I have wine, whiskey and some tequila."

Althea stepped around Talos and joined me in the kitchen. Talos nudged Amil awake before following Althea's lead to the center island where I had set plates down. They both pulled out stools and sat waiting. Amil rose from the couch and stretched with his arms over his head. His warm brown skin peeking out from his raised shirt, the strained muscles there rippled in his movement. He looked at each of us and came to join me on the other side of the counter. I opened each box and slid them closer towards Althea, waiting for her to take a slice or a breadstick. She hadn't eaten much on our trip here, not that I could blame her for her lack of appetite.

Talos watched her out of the corner of his eye waiting for a sign to encourage her or reassure her. She took a slice of cheese pizza and laid it on the plate set in front of her and looked up to me, "You said you had tequila?"

I gave her a smile and quickly retrieved it from the cabinet behind me. Zaida had left about half a bottle from the last time we had spent been together. I also grabbed the whisky and several glasses. Amil took up a couple glasses and filled them with ice and set one in front of Althea. I poured her a half a glass before offering the bottle to Talos who declined with a shake of his head.

Amil placed a cup with ice in front of Talos before clapping him on the shoulder, "Talos prefers vodka, but I've seen him take whisky in a pinch."

Talos gave Amil a half grin and shook his head before glancing to me, then to Althea who nudged the whiskey bottle closer to his hand.

"Enablers, all of you. Fine." He said as he pour himself a half glass of whiskey, "But only if Isa joins us."

"It would be my pleasure." I winked to Althea who gave a weak smile and looked at us all in turn.

Amil poured himself tequila and then poured some whiskey into my glass. He held his glass up and out, "Saluti!"

We all took long pulls at his request.

The first sip rushed down my throat, quenching a thirst but leaving a thick heat in its wake. My chest and stomach warmed and rebelled as I remembered how empty it was. We ate our pizza and refilled our glasses. Sometime later we sat in my living room in front of the blazing fireplace. Althea sat on the floor near the hearth sipping from her third glass of tequila and watching the flames dance against the dim room.

Talos stood on the other side of the fireplace, his gaze moving from the fire to Althea every few minutes as he waited for her to want to start a conversation. Any conversation. He hadn't said anything since our first drink. Amil sat opposite me on the couch, my legs draped over his and his thumb rhythmically smoothing back and forth over my exposed calf.

"Althea, you can sleep with me if you'd like." I spoke softly to not alarm her.

She didn't turn to face me but spoke into the fire, "Thank you, Isa. But I think the couch will suffice. I don't think I'll be sleeping and don't want to keep you awake."

Talos looked to her, then to me. His gaze lingered on my face before he glanced at Amil then back to the fire as if he'd intruded on Amil's claim to me at this moment.

"I'll sleep in here with you then. Amil and Talos can have my room." I gave Amil a slight smile when he looked to me.

"It's a king sized bed. You both can fit." I spoke to Talos when he also turned his attention to me.

They looked at each other. Talos half smiled and shook his head as he took another sip from his glass. Amil laid his head back against the arch of the couch and huffed a shallow laugh.

"Alright, but I'm the big spoon if we cuddle." Amil raised his head and grinned at Talos who gave a throaty laugh.

"As usual then?" He joked back.

I smiled into my glass as I drained the rest of its contents. I set the glass down on the low coffee table and stood up to stretch. The effects of the liquor reached my tight muscles forcing them to loosen with a tingle.

"I'm going to go take a shower. Then we can hang out a little bit, Althea." She looked to me this time and nodded before returning to the flames licking over the faux wood.

I knew I wouldn't be able to comfort her but I could possibly ease her mind enough to sleep. Both Talos and Amil watched after me as I rounded the couch and headed down the hall to the bathroom. I took fresh towels out of the cupboard and set them on the sink and turned the water on to heat as I undressed. Looking at myself in the mirror I looked worn. It had felt so much longer than a couple days that had passed since leaving the manor. I hadn't noticed the bruises around my neck earlier. The dark purple and green smudges wrapped around my throat on both sides from what I could see as I turned my chin from side to side.

I lifted my shirt over my head and could see small cuts and more bruises from Lawrence and the other Fata who had waged war against the wedding guests. I took the rest of my clothing off and dropped the bundle in the hamper. Dirt and blood caked on my pants in patches. I would likely never wear them again and would end up tossing them out at the memory of what they'd seen me through.

Flashes of Lawrence's angry and surprised face hovering over me as he pressed his remaining energy onto my airway. Blood flowing from the slash across his throat, falling all around and on me. His hot rage hitting me from every angle and blocking out every other sensation I had. I closed my eyes against the memory and took in several deep breaths to force myself to remember that my lungs still had access to fresh air. That the sour taste at the back of my throat was just my stomach roiling and not cartilage being crushed under the weight of attack. The smell of his cologne wafted into my nostrils, the warm slick fluid dripping onto my cheeks and arms. Tears began to slip from my eyes down to my chin, breaking on my chest.

I heard the click of the door knob and my eyes shot open to see the outline and faint resemblance of Amil in the steam covered mirror. I turned to face him and his eyes were stormy, his expression mournful but his jaw tensed. He took in a deep breath and released it in what looked like relief. He took a step towards me, but waited for me to initiate any further contact. He dipped his chin to tilt his face slightly to gain better access to my line of sight.

"I'm fine." My voice cracked and I wrapped my arms around my bare chest.

"I know. I wasn't sure if you needed backup or possibly another drink?" He held up my glass that had been refilled.

I gratefully accepted it and swallowed half the liquor in one gulp. The burning in my throat and chest solidifying that I was safe in this reality and in my own home. I took a deep breath and drug the back of my hand over the tears still clinging to my eyelashes.

"Do you mind if I shower with you? I smell like a minivan and junk food." He gave me a hopeful smile.

My lips turned up at the offering tone in his voice and I nodded. Unable to choke words pasted the lump in my voice box that stung as I swallowed another gulp of whiskey.

I watched as he pulled his shirt over his head, his muscular chest and stomach riddled with half healed wounds. The deep complexion of his skin blotched with dark bruises. Even damaged and recovering from battle he was gorgeous. My gaze roamed over his black hair and heavy brows down to his misty grey eyes and full pillowy lips. A warmth in my chest bloomed as his sight caught and held mine. Shadowy vails draped over his irises, his lashes lowering as he dropped his lacks to the ground. Stepping out of them and closing our distance he looked down into me, inviting me closer with a hand to my bare hip. I took a deep breath as a tug behind my navel begged me closer.

He blinked and the small flame lit to life. The familiar beacon calling me into him. Inviting me to give into my every desire, give into him. The friendly blaze had become a tell— a warning call during training but then an offer for relief at more intimate times together. It's become something I've craved and looked for in him over the last couple weeks.

Weeks. We'd only known each other for a couple of weeks and yet I've committed so many of his features to memory. Drinking him in as often as I could since the wedding. Or maybe since he had offered to train me on how to resist Incubo's influence. The way the ends of his hair curled over his neck and ears when it became wet or mussed from training or love making. His scars along his arms and torso and a small crook in his nose; a body molded from training and defense.

His lips softly brushing over mine snapped me back to the moment. Hardened parts of him pressed against my belly, causing my heart to begin to race and a stronger gush of butter-flies erupting in my stomach. He caressed a hand up my spine, smooth at first but then a sharp pain shot through me. I jumped away from his hold and cursed.

"Are you ok?" He asked, concern clearing the shade from his eyes.

I turned my head towards the mirror behind me to get a better look at my back and saw what he'd touched. A walnut sized gash surrounded by a large bruise spread over the middle of my back. How I hadn't noticed was beyond the brain power I had in the moment. He took my shoulder and turned me to get a better perspective and pulled my hair to the opposite side.

"Don't touch it, I just need to shower and rest. I'll be fine tomorrow." I promised and stepped out of his grasp and into the shower.

I left the glass door open for him but he hesitated, "You're sure?"

"Amil, I'll be fine. Are you getting in or not?"

He didn't seem convinced but got into the shower anyway and closed the glass door behind him. The steam filled the space quickly and the hot water against my skin practically sizzled on the many cuts covering my body. Dried blood and dirt washed from my hair and trailed down my front. I moved out of the stream for Amil and began lathering my hair with shampoo. Grit and sebum loosening to my fingertips as I massaged my scalp. Amil stood facing me with his back to the shower head, he rolled his head back and let the spray seep through his hair and over his stubble covered face.

Water trailed down his chest and taut stomach then lower. Over the most sinfully beautiful parts of him. And as if he could sense me watching him he smiled and a deep haughty laugh came from his chest. He stepped out of the waters fall and playfully shook his head splashing me.

"You don't have to just look, you know." He smiled

I bit my lip to stop from smiling and nudged him out of the way so I could rinse the soap from my hair. I let the water flow over my face, bringing my hands up and covering my eyes for the moment, scrubbing the residual shampoo from my brows and lashes. I felt an arm wrap around my waist, gently pressing me between his slick frame and the cool tile behind me. Lips found mine. Water slipped between our bodies becoming a conductor to every spark shot from every nerve he brushed up against.

Arms moved from my waist to under my legs as he scooped

me up and nestled between them. I wrapped myself around the top of his hips and arms around his neck. The heat from between my thighs rivaled that of the steam filling up around us. Feverish kisses trailed from my lips to my neck to my chest then breasts. I could feel him begging for me to let him in the dark twisty crevasses of my mind. Into my body. He lifted my bottom a bit higher and slowly lowered me onto his thick shaft.

Every inch of him entered me slowly but that's what he wanted. He pulled me down but then stopped. Pulsating and lightly bouncing in place to entice me. Torture me. Bringing only him and his mischievous ways to the forefront of my brain. Taking every stress off my shoulders and crowning him with the burden of being laden with my worry. His teeth nipped at the peaks of my breast causing me to sharply take in a breath which quickly turned to a moan as he plunged deep inside of me.

He smiled up to me as our eyes met briefly, "Hold on tight." his words thick with desire.

I hardly took hold of him before he began thrusting rhythmically. The smooth tile heating at the small of my back from the friction. His fingers digging into the sides of my thighs. Holding me in place as his hips moved faster then pausing then harder still. Holding me on the edge. Building up my excitement to a sliver of the panicle but not allowing me to break over.

"Tell me what you want, Isa."

I cursed, fingers tangling through his hair. His chin tilted up and his lips pressed to my jaw. His motions stalled and my hips bucked, begging him to carry on.

"Say it." His luscious deep voice spoke around me. Through me as he held me still.

"Fuck, Amil. Please! I want you."

He smiled wickedly. Driving deep but stopping again.

"Tell me again. What do you want?" He was clearly enjoying himself and it was maddening.

I groaned in frustration, attempting to grind my hips against his but he pinned me harder to the wall deepening his position but not giving in to my plea of pressure.

"I need you. Please." I breathed, hardly louder than the water falling around us.

"Prove it." He gave me a dark smile and pulled away from me completely.

Setting me on my feet and dipping his chin to signal where he wanted me next. I took his length in my hand and got to my knees. The tiles warmed by the hot water against my bruised kneecaps. I rolled my eyes up to see a satisfied smile sat on his handsome face and he gave me an approving nod before I took him into my mouth. Deep into my throat. Cupping his testicles while dragging my tongue beneath his shaft to consume him fully.

He watched me all the while, the flickering glow enveloped in the deepest black of his eyes. The flame that greeted me and beckoned me to fall deeper into him. Gently pulling me under with the promise of euphoria. It felt like a lifetime since I'd seen the spark come to life within his coal orbs. Warmth and familiarity coursed through me and joined my own desire to pleasure him.

He held his lower lip between his teeth and let out a ragged moan as his hips sagged under his pleasure. He throbbed against the roof of my mouth. Every muscle in his torso flexing with every draw of breath. His chest stretched and relaxed with every rise and fall from his lungs. He was exquisite.

The fullness of him in my mouth mixed with the alcohol in my veins, both sensations reaching my brain and flooding me with want. Need. A hunger in my chest that would only be sated by rough and hot passion. He let out a heavy breath followed by a swear before taking my hands and pulling me to stand. He turned me around to face the wall. The chill of the tile bit at my breast as he pressed his chest to my back. He cupped my hip, pulling me back towards him and slipping inside me once more. His other hand brought my hands above my head and pinned them there. I could feel tendons and lean cords of muscles at his legs and hips priming themselves into position. He started out slow. Dragging himself in and out of me agonizingly slow. His breath against my neck and shoulder. Then teeth.

He held my neck between his lips, gave a small bite. Then suck. Then kiss. The sensitive skin danced for him, highly alert that he'd been there a moment before. He clamped down once more and I waited for his lips to slip over the spot again but he stayed and began thrusting deep inside me. I let out a gasp and moan as his pace quickened. Water slapping between our bodies with every impact. He squeezed my side, digging his fingertips into the soft landmark, controlling the motion. Bringing me to and fro as his hips chorused from behind me. Pleasure coursed through me. My entire pelvis gripped around him. Contracting and sending rushes of warm jolts to my fingers and toes. Waves of orgasm crashed over me.

My knees quaked and faltered. The wall caught the rest of my torso against it until he wrapped his arm around my waist and held me close. His release masked by my own euphoria as he slumped against my back. His chest rhythmically pressing and lifting from me as his breath sent chills over my spine.

He pulled away and I turned to face him, letting the water push my back to tile. I watched him run his face under the water as he scrubbed his hands over the dusting of facial hair that had grown substantially over the last few days. His typical shortly trimmed beard was long enough to trap beads of water and let them hang off his chin. I felt the urge to smooth my palms over his jaw and through his wet hair but my knees were still protesting.

When he saw that I was staring his lips parted in a crooked smile and he huffed an amused hum. His eyes back to their normal stormy grey hue. He came closer and placed his hand just above my ear, leaning against the wall. His other hand found the nape of my neck and fanned out his fingers up through my hair pulling me just a breath closer.

"If you keep looking at me like that, we are going to use up all the hot water."

His lips touched mine as my cheeks flushed.

"That wouldn't be kind of us." I said when he pulled away.

I nudged him out of the way of the water and rinsed myself before cutting the water off. I stepped out of the shower first and wrapped the towel around myself before tossing one to his chest. He tucked the towel in just below his hips, his lean torso tapering down into the fluffy linen. Even bruised and battered his body was a masterpiece cut from polished mahogany.

Amil redressed in the clothing he had been wearing and went out into the living room while I dried my hair and brushed my teeth. He poked his head into the still steamy bathroom a few moments later.

"Talos passed out on the couch. I'm going to head home so you and Althea can have your room. I need to pack and get ready for our trip tomorrow unless you'd like me to stay?" He looked me over, still wrapped in my towel and moisturizer dotted on my face.

"We'll be just fine." I rolled my eyes to him.

"I don't doubt you have enough weapons hidden in the walls to take on a small army, but I'll stay if you need company." He leaned against the doorframe and waited for my answer. His face didn't hold pity or concern, but comfort.

"I am positively exhausted. I will fall asleep satisfied and swiftly." I assured him.

He smiled and looked up to me through thick lashes. His cheeks dimpled and eyes began to shadow again. I padded over and lifted up onto the tips of my toes and kissed his pleased lips.

"I'll let Althea know the new arrangement. She's watching tv." He nudged a lock of damp hair from my face and traced the angle of my jaw, tipping my chin up. "You'll call me if you change your mind?"

"Yes. But I won't. We'll see you tomorrow at the train station."

Another kiss and he left me to finish tending to myself.

CHAPTER FOUR

After dressing in my room I was pulling the linens back when I heard a muffled rapping on the door. Before I could answer, Althea opened the door and stepped inside. She looked around at the modest room. I didn't care for much clutter around me. A dresser, full length mirror, and the bed with two side tables were the only pieces of furniture. A tv sat atop the dresser for late night lounging. I didn't keep art on the walls or knick knacks on other surfaces.

I gave Althea a welcoming smile as she rounded the corner of the queen sized bed. Her fingers slid over the duvet, and her eyes darted to the window when the sound of a car's backfire vibrated the pane. She took pause, clenching her fingers into a fist at her side. Color drained from her cheeks and inky clouds filled her eyes.

"Althea, are you alright?" I said softly, shaking her from her internal thoughts.

"Hmm?" She turned towards me but her eyes still far off as they cleared of dark smoke.

"Can I get you anything before we turn in?"

"No, I'm fine. But, can I ask you something?"

She pulled back the linens and sat down crossing her legs beneath her and pulling a pillow to her chest and held it tight. I nodded and waited for her to go on, but she hesitated a moment. With a deep inhale and sigh she finally spoke, "When we leave tomorrow... Will you really stay with me in Amples?"

"Althea, I—"

"You don't have to stay very long. A week, maybe two. My great uncle is... He isn't kind. He is more manipulative than my father is... more than my father was." Her voice quieted at her own reminder.

On my knees, I scooted to sit in front of her on the bed. I reached out my hands between us and waited. She put one of her hands in my palm, and I sandwiched it with my other. A single tear welled at the brim of her lashes, her arm around the pillow tightened bracing herself for my answer. Readying herself to be left alone in another strange place but this time without the prospect of marrying the man she loved.

"I have to find my brother. I have to be sure he is safe." My gut wrenched to have to disappoint her.

I owed her my life. The least I could do was stay with her to bring her some comfort.

"But once I find him and bring him home..." I couldn't make any promises. I didn't know what state Argo would be in when we found him.

"Amil and Talos will be with me. I will be protected. I just wanted a friend." She pulled her hand away and layed down.

She pulled the blanket up to her neck and closed her eyes. The tear coming loose and traveling over the bridge of her nose to fall onto the sheet below. Seeping into the cream threads. I turned the side table light off with a pull of the chain and laid down next to Althea. My vision adjusted quickly to the dimly lit room, the city lights blue hum leaked in through the window.

The shadow of Althea's mounds and ridges cast onto the canyon of blankets of our bodies. Her shallow breaths fill the space between us, an occasional sharp intake of air reminding me how strong she really was.

"Isa?" She whispered.

"Yes, Althea?"

"Neal is dead..." her voice pained and cracked against the words' surface.

I propped up against the pillows and pulled her closer to me. She willingly concave into my chest to let loose a heavy sob. I smoothed my hand over the crown of her head. With each exhale she shook with grief. Each inhale choked and thick as she fought through her own emotions.

I didn't have the right words. I didn't think there are any that exist to comfort someone who has lost everything that they thought held their future and their happiness. All the promises they had made to each other were gone. Every memory she held of him would haunt her dreams, good or bad. The life she had carved out from the hard stone she had been born into was shattered and bleeding into the earth.

"I'm so sorry, Althea."

She stilled for a moment, her body still quaking in my embrace, "We should be on our honeymoon in Hadera right now. Eating exotic fruits and drinking wine until our lips turned purple."

She didn't pull away as she spoke. Her voice muffled by my shirt and the blankets surrounding us, another sob escaped under her breath. She pulled her knees up and curled up against me.

"I miss him so much. I know that sounds ridiculous, of course I would miss him. But there are so many small things I dreamed of doing together that we won't ever experience in reality. At least when we were waiting to be together, those dreams were a promise. Now they're just dust. Burnt ash of the life we should have had."

The pain and anger in her voice could crack through the

thickest stone. I could see it as well. The love and future she and Cornelius had whispered about to each other in private finally coming to fruition on the morning of their wedding day only to watch him and so many others bleed out on the estate lawn.

"That doesn't sound ridiculous, Althea. What those assholes took from you is unforgivable and they deserved much worse than their quick deaths. I know of several torture tactics that they were worthy of."

She smiled against my belly and gave a huffed chuckle at that, "Thank you, Isa. For letting me stay with you tonight. I couldn't have gone back to my father's house or the brownstone. Not yet. His men would have been flies to an open wound."

Her eyes turned up to me, clearing of their storm clouds and revealing the light blue irises beneath the ash smoke. The pillowy creases of her lids pink and heavy from tears and lack of sleep.

"Tomorrow we'll head to Amples together. I'll make sure you're settled in before I go retrieve Argo."

She smiled sadly but graciously, and closed her eyes, her chin resting on my abdomen for a moment before she hummed in agreement choresed with a nod. I knew she needed me, but so did my brother. Neither my blood but both sibling-like nonetheless. When you've been in battle alongside someone— killed with them, you become bonded deeper than the sharing of a lineage.

"Isa?" She asked as I stroked her hair, "Do you love Amil?"

Shock and the absence of air bombarded my senses and must have been apparent on my face because Althea immediately started to laugh. Her infectious giddiness startled me at first. I covered my nose and mouth with my hands to hide the pink on my cheeks as I laughed along with her.

"Althea!" I choked out between gasps of breath.

I hadn't seen her smile in so many days. I hadn't laughed so deeply and shamefully since the last time I saw Zaida before I started working for Talos. She sprang up onto her knees at my side, "I'm serious! Do you love him?"

She still wore an amused smile as she settled in to hear my answer. I didn't know what to say. Or what I actually felt for Amil or Talos.

"I—I don't know. He's kind, and has saved my life a couple of times now. But I don't think I love him." I shrugged, pulling my knees to my chest and hugging them tightly.

"Do you love Talos?" She sounded more serious at this question.

"Talos is... Complicated. But also no. I don't think I love him either. Why do you ask?"

"Honestly? I wanted to know if their influence on you had pushed you to madness." She burst into laughter again and gave me a gentle nudge to the shoulder.

"So hilarious," I rolled my eyes, "I doubt either would be disappointed if I were deliriously infatuated with them. Both of their ego's would be bolstered by the idea of a Mortal pining for them."

"You joke, but you're not like other Mortals. Which is why they would consider it a conquest to have your full attention."

"It's complicated." I paused for a moment, "Actually, it's not. I've never been in love before. I don't really know what that would feel like, but I know the emotions I'm feeling when they're around isn't love. It's pleasant and exciting. They're both thrilling in their own ways. But Banner's don't find love. We never form romantic attachments out of our own ranks."

Her smile fell at this, possibly because it reminded her of the expectations that came with her title, and that would likely be thrust upon her again now that Cornelius had been killed.

"Hey." I laid a hand on hers, reassuring that I was not upset by my circumstances. "It's ok. I love my job and even more now that it has brought you into my life."

"I am too. Goodnight, Isa." She smiled warmly and laid down on her side to face me.

I rolled to the side and faced her. She held out her hand and took my fingers into hers. I could have counted her wakeful breaths before she fell into a deep sleep. Exhaustion had won out after the waves of grief were relieved. I hadn't had the right things to say to ease her pain and loss, but being able to see her smile and laugh made all the difference in the world for one night.

After only a couple hours of rest, Althea had been shaken awake from night terrors. Her brow and hair damp with sweat, her voice hoarse from the dry late summer air, and strain of crying. I was able to ease her back to sleep by holding her and humming a tune that Ms. Green used to sing to soothe me back to sleep as a child. Back when I would wake up screaming for my birth mother not to leave, terrified of the dark stillness of my room without street lights shining through car windows. No sound of police cars whizzing by with their sirens blaring at all hours of the night and morning.

Althea and I both slipped into fitful sleeps. Either one of us waking and reaching for the other in the dim light of the early morning. The train ride to Amples would be a blurry-eyed travel, but perhaps it would be uneventful and we'd make up for our lost sleep.

CHAPTER FIVE

In the morning, I got dressed and helped Althea pick out some clothing. She didn't want to go back to her father's home to retrieve anything to take with her. She had plenty of funds to buy new things now that her father's estate would be transferred to her once she reached the King and claimed the leftover wealth. As much as it pained her to claim his place in court and in the role he vacated, she had no other means of income.

Talos had left early in the morning to pack for the trip. Amil lived across town and would meet us at the train station. Talos was only gone for a couple hours, but in that time, he had showered, packed, and called several Incubo to let them know Althea was alive and well. He had to inform them that we were moving Althea, and arranged for the four of us to be collected from the train station in Amples.

Althea was sitting in the living room watching the news and was sipping a second cup of coffee. She had seen the report on the manor massacre, but there wasn't any new information from the article that Talos had shown me the day before. No identities had been released of the guests and the official count was still a vague 'upward of forty', which was hard to believe considering how efficiently Lawrence had placed his men throughout the high windows of the manor.

Talos honored my wishes and didn't bring any back up with him to my home when he returned. He made it back, and he came to find me in the closet. I had my open duffle bag, weapons case, and suitcase open on an upholstered bench sitting in the middle of the large space. Out of the corner of my eye, I watched as he fingered the fine fabrics of cocktail dresses and cashmere coats. He stopped and took a black dress off the rack, holding it out in front of him to admire it. His thumb rubbing over a small stain at the hem.

"I rather like this one." He said with a sly grin and rise of his brow.

"I bet you do."

I folded a pair of black slacks neatly and transferred them to my suitcase, then turned to pick out a blouse to match. He returned the dress to the rack and moved further down the row until he was standing next to me, rather closely.

"I reserved our travel arrangements. The tickets will be at the travel desk. We should leave here in about an hour. Will you be ready?" he looked at my bags that were half filled.

"I'm sure I will. I don't expect to need much."

I turned around to the wall of shoes and picked a couple pairs before opening the false wall and exposing my arsenal. Talos stood quietly as I strapped a belt to my thigh and waist, slipping knives into their sheaths. I took out the Alexandrite dagger he had given me and my blade cleaning kit. I hadn't had the chance to clean it properly after having to use it during our escape. Blood crusted the grooves and handle. I'd have to clean it then sharpen my throwing blades, but by the looks of the Alexandrite carved stone, it wouldn't need to be sharpened.

"Do you know why I gave you that dagger?" Talos' deep voice against the wall of clothing muted and thick.

"Do you mean besides protecting Althea from Incubo? No." I answered, absent of eye contact.

"My grandmother gave me this dagger. It killed her husband, my grandfather. She said that it was cursed to kill every man in my bloodline and that I should destroy it."

That caught my attention, my eyes roamed over his casual stance before speaking, "Why didn't you?"

"Because I knew how rare the blade was. How valuable it would be one day when I truly needed it. I would never want to murder one of my own, but the occasion has crossed my mind a couple of times over the years. Then, when murmurs of a threat against Althea reached my ears, I knew that whoever I hired to protect her..." his gaze intensified, "The last line of defense. They would need this blade. And if in saving her life, I lost mine, it would be worth succumbing to the curse."

Visions of the night before the wedding probed my thoughts. The blade ripping through Talos' clothing and piercing his skin, the look of utter shock on his face held new meaning. Guilt and something that felt close to regret roiled my stomach, a sour burn at the back of my throat.

"I trusted the right person." His words didn't chase the sensation away completely, but made it palatable.

"I hope you don't expect me to give it back. I've grown attached to it."

I ran my finger over the smooth surface of the blade, admiring the shift of colors as the light above us glinted off each polished angle. In the fluorescent light of my closet, the gem showed more of its sea green hues. Where as in direct sunlight, purples would catch the light. When I looked back to him, he smirked and shook his head in amusement.

"I would never dare attempt to take such a weapon away from someone so deadly. It would be an honor to die at your hand with that particular blade." He took a step closer and cupped my hip.

I stepped into him, allowing our torsos to meet, and laid the fine blade flat to his chest. "Promise?"

His chin dipped and eyes fell to the spot before slowly raising to mine, clouding in an instant as a wave of heat coursed through me. A snatching tug to my navel when he spoke again, "Only one way to find out, Isa."

I didn't have to think; I didn't have to breathe. His soft lips pressed to mind as his hand pressed to the base of my neck and brought the kiss deeper. I sank into his embrace, let him gather me up into his arms, and felt the tight bulge in his slacks. He didn't remove the blade from my hand; he didn't give one indication that he wanted to. Instead, he pushed me against the rack of clothing, ran his hands down my sides and thighs before hoisting me up to wrap myself around his hips.

He swiftly walked us out into my bedroom, he had closed the door when he came in. Unsurprising he had other motivations than our itinerary to find me in my room. He sat down on the bed and my knees folded around him. His tongue coaxed me, invited me, begged me for more. His fingers gingerly catching the hem of my blouse and pushing it upwards to expose my midriff. The familiar smell of his refreshed cologne, a lock of his his still damp hair falling between us. He pulled away and tossed his head back to clear his view of me. His eyes trailing down from my face to my chest, then to my hand still clutching the dagger at his chest. Once tip of his mouth tugged into a crooked smirk. A daring perk of his brows, questioning if I was going to make good on my threat.

I dropped my sight to the blade, then his neck now exposed to me. The vein plumply raised against his skin. His hands cupped my bottom and pulled me deeper into his lap, firm against his hips. The smile fading into hunger at my pause and the anticipation of my next move. Ebony hollows starring back at me, waiting. I slid my free hand up his chest, over his shoulder, and weaved my fingers through his hair. Palming a firm grip and opening my wrist to tilt his chin upward. I pressed the cool blade to his neck. The pulse of his artery quickening, his bottom lip caught in his teeth as he made a sharp inhale.

"Are you so confident that I wouldn't plunge this through your heart, Talos?" I whispered between his lips, not loosening my grasp on his hair.

"If I'm in danger, it's exactly where I want to be. Do what you wish, Isa." His arms wrapped around my waist, restraining me from backing away from the challenge.

I let the daggers edge ride along the sensitive skin of his neck. A small nip of blood was drawn and began an impossibly thin train downwards towards the neckline of his shirt. He didn't wince, not a movement of defense against me or the blade. If I didn't know any better, I could have sworn he wanted me to cut deeper. That this wasn't a game to him, he wanted the pain. Wanted me to hurt him. In a way it would only be fair considering the last time we had been in a heated moment together. But of course, Amil had been in the room with us and had ended up intervening resulting in Amil and I both being thrown across the room.

This moment was different. He wasn't testing my skills, he wasn't even attempting to use his influence to reel me in. Either he had moved past the need for it or he didn't want to upset me now that I knew how to sever that bond. He tried to pull his chin down to look at me fully but I only allowed him a small movement. He smirked with a throaty scoff.

"I must be sick in the head. At this moment I would do anything to have you slit my throat if I could only be buried deep inside of you."

"You wouldn't be the first."

I attempted to repress a mocking smile. He, on the other hand, found amusement and a rooted challenge. In one quick movement he spun me onto my back, driving his hips harder against my groin. Friction and heat rolled up into my gut and sent jolts of electricity to my fingers and toes. In the movement, the dagger had slipped out of my hand. When I realized it was gone, I pressed my forearm into his throat and wrapped my legs around his torso. Still holding onto the back of his neck but no longer having hold of his thick dark hair.

"I have no doubt there is a line across Chora of willing participants in a dangerous moment of passion at the tip of your blade. But, if you allowed me, I could show you new facets of that game. Or would you prefer Amil?" His comment wasn't laced with venom or jealousy. It still dripped of want and need but caught me off guard, maybe more so without the change of tone.

"What?" Was all I could choke out as I used my legs to push him off of me.

He pulled away and sat up on his knees with my legs still pulled around him. He rested his hands on my thighs, gliding downwards to the most sensitive region of me. My breath stalled as I watched his eyes start to change color, but not back to their typical smoke, but to a midnight sky covered in clouds.

"There's no need to be shy about your feelings for him. You are not the first he and I have had a shared interest in pursuing. I may be his employer, but he is as close as blood as far as I'm concerned. It may not seem like it, but my kind isn't threatened by competitors." He winked and brushed a thumb over my panties.

My stomach churned over, it wasn't some kind of secret but there was an awkwardness with how open and nonchalantly he was speaking of our three-way engagements. I wasn't ready to have this conversation with either of them. I didn't even understand my feelings for them, if I had any at all that were worth exploring longer than the next day that they were around for.

"Talos, I—"

I was interrupted by a knock on the door. It was Althea letting us know that the doorman had buzzed up that the town car was ready for us. Talos called back that we would be out in a moment before he glided off the bed and headed out the door. Leaving me feeling utterly confused, nauseous, and somehow more intrigued to know how often he and Amil had shared a common lover. Talos had once told me that he didn't like to share, but every action he had made said otherwise. He didn't hide his discontent that Amil and I had been intimate while he had been away to bring Pytr back to the Welp's manor. He had teased that he and Amil share me during our heated conversation the night before Althea's wedding. The thought of having them both equally thrilled and terrified me. Were their tastes so similar that this was an occurrence that happened often? Part of me didn't want to know the answer to that.

CHAPTER SIX

The town car Talos had arranged arrived to take us to the train station not long after he had left my room. He had instructed the driver to meet us several blocks away to not give away my home's location, which I was grateful for. Althea rode silently in the back seat with me. She had borrowed an outfit for the journey and would be requesting a curated wardrobe once we arrived in Amples. She had no bags or possessions to accompany her into her great uncle's home. A twinge of guilt clutched in my chest when I examined this thought too long. She was willing to leave every last bit of her life behind her twice since I had met her.

Cornielus had welcomed her into his home and his city to be his wife and Lady. She had taken a few bags with her to Arta, but had planned on building a home for them once their marriage was finalized. Her father's properties were not her home, she likely never felt the kindness of a place she called of her own and was now being whisked away to another relative's custodianship. The only items she brought with her was her grief, broken heart, and a friend who was eager to leave her as quickly as possible on their own duties.

We reached the train station a little while later, Althea sat fidgeting with her cuticles and tapping her fingernails against the seat. Talos and I hadn't spoken or glanced in the other's direction the entire drive. His statement about Amil still weighed heavily on my mind. My encounters with Talos had always been driven by his desires enchanting mine. Manipulating the attraction I had into a fire that I couldn't put out, and then left me feeling hollow, cold, and sick. Amil had used his interest in me to arm and train me against the influences of Incubo like Talos had been using. He had his own motives to offer his help, of course. I knew he had feelings for me that possibly he didn't fully understand just yet. He had taken his guard down and drew me in to experience the convoluted emotions that pressed in on him when we were together. As beautiful and tragic his affections were, I didn't know if I could return any of it.

Talos' driver dropped us off at the entrance and assisted in getting my and Talos' bags checked in which allowed us to find our platform quickly. The train cabin was larger than the one we had taken to Arta but was just as lavish. The walls of the sitting area were lined with blue velveteen couches bolted to the floor. One small table sat in a sectioned off area between the sitting room and the sleeping room. Across from the table was a kitchenette and the door to the lavatory.

Amil, who had met us at the platform, entered ahead of the rest of us and did a sweep to be sure there were no surprises waiting for us. After clearing, Althea sat on the couch near the window with her back against the barrier wall and gathered her knees to her chest. A single tear fell down her cheek as she watched the beings out the window. The dull roar of the crowd had died away once the door of the cabin had been closed. The thick windows blocking most of the sound of the busy train terminal. I remained on my feet in the middle of the sitting room and waited for Amil and Talos to finish putting their bags away and settle themselves. Amil came out of one of the sleeping rooms to join me. He had dressed more casually for our trip than he had while on duty at the manor. Dark jeans paired with a charcoal shirt and black leather racer jacket. He looked comfortable but just as deadly handsome in his usual suit and tie.

He laid his hand at my lower back as he moved past me to get to the cabin door, his chest brushing against mine. A sense of aching sprang to life at his touch, a wanting anticipation of what would come next. His eyes met mine when he turned back towards me after he closed the curtain of the window in the door and assured that it was locked properly. He shrugged his jacket off and laid it on the couch closest to the door and turned back to face me. No words were needed as he gave me a quick dip of his chin and walked back to the bedroom. I followed him, passing Talos at the kitchenette, pouring himself a drink and holding out a small bottle for me to take with me. I paused next to him and fingered the neck of the bottle, his eyes followed Amil's steps and nodded to him before he joined Althea in the sitting room.

The cramped sleeping quarters held two twin sized beds and a narrow walkway between them, not much else but the light fixtures on the walls and the window, which had been drawn shut. He leaned over the farthest bed and flicked on the side light, then sat on the side of the bed and waited. I peered around and saw that he had put my carry-on bag on the bed next to his.

"I thought we should talk strategy before we get down to Amples." He spoke, startling me in the abruptness of his deep voice into the silence.

"What do you mean?" I sat on the bed that was apparently mine for the journey.

"Your plan to get your brother back. I want to help, but I can't do that if you don't tell me what you need."

"Amil, you know I can't ask you or anyone for help. I can't tell you anything that involves the Banners."

He looked down to his hands clasped between his legs and shook his head, "You are allowing Talos to help you. Do you not trust me? After all we've been through, do you not trust that I wouldn't do anything that would compromise or put you in danger?"

"Right. Because we've slept together and survived a mass shooting, I should trust you with my family's secrets and the life of my brother who has been captured." I crossed my arms and rolled my eyes.

"You should trust me enough to at least try to help you. The Fata that attacked us are only a small part of the faction trying to take Incubo down." He crossed his arms over his chest, the bulging muscles stretching the fabric of his shirt across it. "This isn't just about your brother or your family keeping their mysterious inner workings to themselves. Talos and I have an obligation to the rest of the Incubos to track these rebels down and neutralize the threat to our kind."

"My family and I don't need to be a part of that." I replied coldly.

"This isn't just about you Isa. My kind is going to war with Fata rebels who would rather see us dead than keep the peace amongst Mortals. If you think this won't bleed into the lives of Mortals, you're not being realistic."

"Amil, I understand you're upset but it isn't my duty or assignment to protect all Incubo. Talos hired me to protect Althea, and I have done that. I haven't signed on to be the savior you're hoping that I would become for you or your kind. Right now, I only have a duty to protect my family and to keep the rest of the Black Banners neutral in whatever disagreements that Incubo and Fata are having."

"Neutral? You think you can continue to be neutral after what happened in Arta? Does Althea mean nothing to you?

Yamir, Cornelius, Talos. That all means nothing? I mean nothing?"

It stung. More than it should have. Of course, they meant something. Althea especially, but not above the Black Banners. Not above my family. As far as I knew, Argo was still being held captive and tortured until a proper trade could be made for him.

"Your silence says everything." The anger and hurt on his face was almost too much to bare as he walked out of the room.

My heart sank into my stomach, heavy with regret already. I didn't want to hurt Amil, he had been the closest thing to a partner that I've ever experienced. Talos was a great lay but when it came to emotions, he was scolding one moment then a frozen tundra the next. He treated me as if I were a pawn that he liked to take out and polish every so often. Not that he was terrible at doing so.

Althea was kind, sweet, and so strong. I hadn't only become close to her these past few weeks, but I've come to see her as a precious friend that I wanted to keep safe and assure had the life she deserved.

I stood from my bed, which would now be a more awkward sleeping situation, and headed back to the sitting room. Amil wasn't sitting with the other. I looked around and didn't see the jacket he had thrown to the couch.

"Amil needed some air." Talos' cool voice grabbed my attention, "Shall we talk about the exchange for your brother once we get to Arta?" he spoke over the paper he was reading.

I sat next to Althea on the couch across from Talos. He set the paper down beside him and laced his fingers together and set them on his knee. He had slipped into his diplomatic voice, he didn't want to let me go off on my own and lose track of me. He wanted to keep me in his employment, under his thumb.

"You and I will meet your brother's keepers at the drop site after we get Althea settled in tonight. First thing in the morning we will go retrieve him. When we are welcomed into the Kings home, we will be escorted to our quarters and deposited for the night. Evening meals will be waiting for us. Unlike the Welp's home, you will have your own suite and Althea will be in the family quarters which are in the west wing. Visitors are not permitted to enter those quarters without an escort, but of course, that could be arranged." He perked his brow.

"Is that where you will also be staying?" I asked but immediately wished I hadn't.

"You will know where my room is, Isa. I guarantee." He grinned wickedly.

I rolled my eyes and opened the small liqueur bottle he had given me earlier. Chugging it quickly, pushing past his suggestive statement to ask my next question.

"Have you already set up the drop site for my brother? I need the coordinates."

"Yes. We will be meeting the vagrants at the Claremont building. 7th floor out of 14 so you know they will have insurance placed on subsequent levels to be sure you aren't being naughty. I know you will likely want to invite your own members to the party but in this instance, it would be best to leave it to just you and I."

I considered him for a moment. He was right, of course. The beings holding Argo would fill the building with defense. I wanted to protest. Tell him that he had no reason to come with me to save Argo, but the fact of the matter was, I needed him. I needed to have him there as a disguise to free Argo without anyone getting killed. At least, no one I cared about.

"Fine. But I am in control of the operation. If they begin an assault, then you listen to me. My direction. I won't have your blood on my hands because you thought yourself clever."

"I would never dream of it, Isa. You being in full control of my whereabouts has been beneficial for me in the past."

"If the deal goes sideways, I won't be able to save you. I will need to get Argo out and safe."

His expression held admiration, but maybe a twinge of disappointment that I somehow wouldn't want to undyingly save him if these beings decided to make a mistake.

"Isa, what if it's a trap?" Althea spoke up from beside me.

I glanced to her, concern and warning in her gaze. She sat on the edge of the couch and hugged a cushion to her chest. I waited a moment longer for her to expand on her comment but she didn't.

"I'm prepared for anything. Don't worry." I assured her with a confident smile.

"Let's not forget, my dear Lady, our Isa is a born warrior. She will be able to handle herself and her situations with ease." He offered Althea a wink and shifted his attention back to me.

"You have my word that I will do everything in my power to see that your brother is transferred to your care alive and relatively unharmed."

I nodded in acknowledgment, thankful that he wasn't going to make this exchange difficult or hold it over my head just yet. But I would be foolish to expect him to not use his generosity as a way to hold me to him longer. That part of our agreement hadn't been fully discussed since the night before the wedding and I wasn't about to bring it up in the case that he wanted to solidify the arrangement he had proposed.

Amil came back to the cabin a few minutes later, nothing to report back to us. The train was about to leave the coastline and begin our route south west. There were many larger towns connected by freeways on the way to Amples but very few passenger-train stations. The largest there would be our only stop between Cinder and Amples. The layover would be about an hour, making our total travel time for the five hundred mile distance about eleven hours.

Amil sat in the chair across from me, next to Talos. They

spoke to each other about the arrangements at the King's mansion. Amil was to stay on the grounds in the same wing as me, but he would be Talos' first in command. Talos was comfortable with the Kings guard protecting the grounds and the wings during the night. He had trained most of them and had left many of his men there when he had been called to protect Althea on her journey to Arta. Amil glanced to me periodically, anger from our talk earlier still glooming his eyes.

"Isa has already expressed she doesn't want me to be involved in the exchange for her brother, but if you want me there, Talos—"

"That won't be necessary, Amil. I need you by Althea's side while I'm gone and by the look on Isa's face, I think your balls are safer elsewhere." He flashed me a sly smile.

I didn't chime into their discussion. They both knew my feelings on the matter and I was bored of the back and forth. I sat back and crossed a leg over the other, settling in for the journey. Althea looked between the two couches with worry brewing in her stormy eyes.

"What's going to happen to me when we get there? What does the King have in mind for his newly widowed great niece?" She spoke to Talos who shifted in his seat uncomfortably.

"Lady Althea, your uncle has the utmost respect and sympathy for your situation. He merely wants to house and protect you. He and I have spoken and he believes that this is the best arrangement for the time being. At least, until the Fata responsible for the coup can be identified and their leaders taken care of."

"He never does anything out of the kindness of his heart, Talos. You know that better than anyone. Every favor has a steep price when it comes to the King." She dipped her chin to the tops of her knees, hiding her lips after her statement.

I became aware that this conversation wasn't meant for me to hear. Amil shifted his weight from one hip to another, essentially turning his back to Talos on the couch. Talos adjusted his tie, his eyes began to cloud and he cleared his throat before he responded, "Yes, my dear. You're right. But for whatever price he demands, I would gladly pay to see that you are safe."

He flashed a dark glance to me, then rose from the couch and headed to the bedroom he and Althea would be sharing. He paused at the doorway but didn't look back to speak to the room, "I'm going to lie down for a bit. Wake me when we get to our first stop." And he was gone, the door closed behind him.

CHAPTER SEVEN

Amil had taken his leave to the bedroom moments after Talos had. He'd given me a cold look that gave me the impression I wasn't welcome to follow him. Althea and I kept eachother occupied while Talos and Amil rested. She told me about the last time she had taken the train down to Amples for the winter solstice ball that the King hosted each year. This was the event that my fellow Banner had lost her life at after attempting to kill Althea's father. I became very aware that I may be the next Banner to be in danger of the same fate at the King's Chateau.

Althea teared up as she spoke of her and Cornelius dancing together all night. They had been talking for months and it had been the first time they had been able to spend time together among their family. They had stolen away to a well hidden hallway for feverish kisses and admissions of love. It was then that Cornelius had proposed marriage to Althea. He hadn't spoken to her father, or anyone else for that matter. She said it must have been impulse and too much wine, but I knew he had to have planned out most of that proposal. The biggest gift he could have given her was freedom from her father along with the large ruby and diamond ring he had presented her.

"Did you know that Cornelius had employed a Black Banner to kill Pytr that night?" I asked, and her eyes fell to her lap.

"Not that night, no. I didn't find out until months later when Talos was looking for one to accompany me. He had been so impressed with how close she had gotten, but from what I understand, she had gotten too close." She pursed her lips.

"Like I've become too close?"

"No. Not this close." A tear fell from her lashes, "Talos had sensed her intentions immediately. He watched her and counted her mistakes. Watched her the whole evening until she was ready to strike. That was when he hauled her out to interrogate her."

"It's why he's allowed Amil to train me. He found her weaknesses while torturing her and once he realized I was able to defend myself against him and other Incubo men, he knew he'd stumbled on the perfect weapon."

She shook her head. Not wanting to further tarnish the image she held of Talos as her always valiant protector. "He cares for you, Isa. I know it doesn't seem that way all the time, but I have never seen him look at anyone else the way he looks at you."

"To be fair, I'm not sure that's a good thing." I smirked, and thought of Althea's mother. What Amil had confessed to me about the relationship between Talos' and Alessandra.

"Having anyone care for you is good." She spoke more to herself than to me, her heart still a gaping wound for her loss.

I reached out and held her hand tightly in mine, "You're right."

She offered me a weak smile and began telling me about her favorite places to visit in Amples. The restaurants, shopping, museums, and wineries. Amples was set within a hundred miles from the border of Meru. Our neighboring country to the south west. Rich in spices, textiles, agriculture, and steel mining. Many trade routes between our country, Chora, and Meru brought a mixing of cultures and many beings often held residence in both counties. Traveling freely between the two.

A couple hours later we had reached our layover stop on our journey. Talos had not emerged from the sleeping quarters and Althea hadn't been keen on being the one to wake him. Amil and I hadn't spoken either so I took it upon myself to wake Talos as he had requested. By the look of him, he hadn't slept much but had needed the time alone because his mood had improved slightly when he greeted Althea who was readying herself to take a walk about the station.

The train station in Fenton Falls was outfitted with several restaurants, a row of shops, and coffee shops. We had a little over an hour to walk about before the next leg of the journey and we all were itching to have a small bit of normality before being thrust into the new reality that would meet us in Amples.

Fellow passengers filed out of the train around us into the large open terminal leading to the busy stretch of shops. When we stepped out Althea hooked her arm to mine and strode me towards a small coffee shop next to a book shop. Talos stayed a few paces behind us with a watchful eye out for any suspicion. Amil headed to a shop on the other side of the street, saying he would be back after buying a few things to hold him over for our first night.

Althea ordered herself a chai latte before looking to me to order. It would be another several hours until we reached Amples but I had planned on sleeping once we got back on the train. I ordered a hot chocolate to hold and warm my hands. The train had been much warmer than the early autumn air outside.

Fenton Falls was known for its mild temperatures year round and hydrolyzed power resources. The entire province was encircled by two large rivers that brought trade from the north but also provided power to several other cities in *their country. There were farms but most were for winery and distillery purposes. Some of the best whiskeys in the world were produced here.

Althea pulled me into the book shop and only released me to run her fingers along the spines of the books along the closest wall. I watched her squint through the titles looking for one that struck her fancy. When she got to the end of the last row of books, I was sure she hadn't gotten lucky but instead she turned and called to Talos who had been eyeing the candy at the counter. As he walked towards her she began pulling one book after the other and began stacking them in his open palms. He wasn't at all surprised. As if this were a regular occurrence in their relationship.

I took a step back to watch them together. Forgotten of their previous bickerment, he smiled down to her as she took yet another book from the shelves and added it to the growing stack. With two more in hand, she turned to admire the assortment she had procured, she gave him a nod that looked like a *"yes, that will do"*, and they proceeded to the desk to be checked out.

If the shop clerk's eyes had widened at the stack of books, they had burst open at the clarifying sight of two Incubo in his shop. His pupils darted from one to the other, then to me. A mixture of awe and panic struck him for a moment at the development.

He began to ring up each book and turned to Althea, "Would you like a tote, Miss?"

"Yes, please." Althea offered the clerk a warm smile which eased his shoulders.

"You found quite the selection, Miss. Would you mind one last recommendation?" He waited a moment for her to consider her tall pile, then nodded to him eagerly.

He dashed around the counter to the rack of books, then

rushed back. Holding it out to her on the tips of his fingers, "This book here may seem bland, but it is a complete history of the spirits industry here in Fenton Falls dating back to its roots in the mountains. The founding families still live locally and contributed hundreds of historical pieces to be photographed and cataloged for this book. There is said to be a blessing on any who hike through the original distillery sites and leave an offering."

Althea smiled sadly but held the book in her hands. The front cover was a black and white photo of an old wooden shack surrounded by dark-barked trees. The title stretched across the top in deep green. *Hunters Whiskey: A Family First*

"That's my fiancés favorite whiskey." A small choke of her voice.

"Perhaps a nice gift for him?" The clerk chimed in, but she did not look up from the cover.

A tear escaped her eye and landed on the top of her blouse, the clerk looked from Althea, to Talos, then to me in a desperate attempt to understand how he had offended the young Incubo with a book. I grappled with the impulse to intrude in their conversation. To whisk Althea away and console her back on the train in our cabin, but then she smiled and looked up to the clerk who met her eyes.

"Thank you, I'll take it as well as the others. How much do we owe you?"

He finished ringing her order and gave her the hefty total. Talos paid the store clerk and we made our way out of the store. Talos carried the tote bag of books while Althea clutched the bibliography to her chest and sipped her drink. Amil was waiting out in the middle of the terminal with a coffee in one hand and a bag that clinked as he picked it up in the other. The tops of two very large whiskey bottles stuck up out of the black paper bag.

"I see Lady Althea found a book shop." He observed.

"Don't worry, I got one for you." Althea winked.

"She found something for everyone on the train by the feel of it." Talos, teased.

Althea nudged her elbow into his side and he smiled a crooked smile down to her. Our group tightened as we made our way back onto the train. Dinner would be served soon, then we would have time to rest before arriving in Amples some time later.

Talos set the tote of books down on the couch when we got back to the cabin and made himself a drink at the minibar. Althea sat down and began tearing into the canvas bag and stacking the books next to her. Examining each cover. She ran her fingertips along the spines and the raised lettering of each title. She raked her fingers through her hair and rustled it to the side. Golden locks falling down her shoulder, cascading down her cheek and curtaning her from the rest of us in the room.

Amil sat down on the opposite side of the cabin and sipped his coffee, his bag at his feet. Althea held out the book she had picked out just for him but did not bother to look at him. He had no choice but to take it from her hand and let her continue on busying herself in the tomes. He examined it, by the look of the cover it was a contemporary romance. Two young lovers caught in an embrace on the cover. The look of confusion on his face perked the edge of my lips up into my cheek.

Talos sat next to him on the couch. Talos had traded his coffee for a whiskey glass. Althea jutted a book in his direction and he took it. Setting the hardback book in his lap. The dusk jacket was black with red lettering, a shadowy figure staunch across the front. A thriller, possibly. He looked to Amil who was examining his book and gave him a mocking 'cheers'. I snickered but was then presented with my own gift. Althea had picked a excused myself and went to lie down.

Exhaustion had seeped into my bones, more specifically my shoulders. My stomach had been in knots since we left Cinder but with every mile closer to Amples, the more steady. I had always preferred action over waiting for an opportune moment. Creating my own outcome instead of leaving it up to chance, but this was different. Any misstep would cost Argo his life, and I'd never forgive myself. I've taken many lives in my time as a Black Banner, but I haven't lost one of my own. It was rare that Banners lost their lives in the line of duty, but not unheard of.

I kicked my shoes off and lied down on the small bed. The blankets were stiff but the fresh scent of lavender detergent wafted up towards me as I brought the linens under my chin. I expected to toss and turn, but what felt like moments later I was slipping into sleep.

CHAPTER EIGHT

I was woken up with a hand on my shoulder, a kind shaking and soothing voice gently waking me. The outline of Althea's face hovered over, "Isa, the dining cart is here."

The wafting of seared meat and vegetables from the cart followed her in through the door. I sat up with a yawn, I hardly felt rested and could have seamlessly fallen back asleep for several more hours, but my stomach rumbled at the smell of dinner. I didn't bother putting my shoes back on to follow her out into the sitting room. Amil and Talos were already sitting with their plates in their laps. The small table in the cabin was only large enough for two, but collectively we ignored it and ate together on the couches.

Amil and Talos exchanged anecdotes of the time they had spent in Amples over the years. Talos had hired Amil several years ago as a detail for the Queen, but quickly showed that he had skills beyond a typical body guard. He and Talos trained together for years. Amil and Yamir quickly became Talos' most trusted employees and friends.

Amil had left with Althea the night of the Winter Solstice

Ball. He spoke of the dancers, performers, and party-goers they had met in passing. The King and Queen had made a spectacle of their son's twenty-fifth birthday which landed on the same day.

"The Prince had been trying to escape for the first hour. That is until he noticed you, Talos." Amil wiggled his brow to Talos who looked to be suppressing a blush.

"He is much too young for me." He smiled.

"And Isa isn't?" Althea chuckled but the other two did not meet eyes.

She didn't let their awkward dodges deter her, "And at any rate, even if you and the Prince did have a fling, that's all it could be until he found someone to bear his children. You know the laws."

Her face fell at her own words. Something like realization had hit her that those laws would now pertain to her. And perhaps that she would be forced by law to have to bear the children of a stranger.

"Is that truely a law?" I asked to the room, not sure who would answer if any would at all.

"We have many different laws than the Fata or Mortals. It keeps the more power hungry of our kind in line so they don't consume more than they are entitled to."

"We are free to love whoever we want, even marry. But if it is our time to be called to help replenish the population, then we have to bear the children according to bloodlines. Match-making. Blend our families and our lives in order to further the future of our kind." Amil chimed in, not meeting my eye.

"But we all know that if it were up to the Queen, she would have us breeding on a schedule." Althea huffed and stood to return her plate to the meal cart.

"Incubo only reproduce when one of your kind passes. Isn't that right? Why would the Queen want that to change?" I had the suspicion I was starting to ask too many questions for Talos' liking. But I had several more that the brief conversation I had with Lawrence had inspired.

"She has only had the need to be impregnated twice, but she has stated that she wanted many children." Talos answered quickly and deadpan.

"And could she not be placed with a Fata-Incubo cross-breed?" My stomach tumbled as the words tipped off my lips.

Both Amil and Talos snapped their sight to me, then to each other. Althea looked between them, her eyes darting from one to the other waiting for an explanation as to what I had asked.

"Where did you happen to hear such a rumor?" Talos' cool voice slid back into his throat as he reclined in his seat.

"Is it a rumor?" I volleyed and watched him a moment.

The tips of his fingers rolled across his thumb as he contemplated how to answer. His eyes began to darkened. Roaming over me from my face to my feet.

"If you're suggesting that Fata and Incubo are compatible to reproduce, then you are suggesting that years of scientific research has been a lie."

I didn't answer. Irritation flushed his face. Althea shifted her weight towards the edge of the cushion next to me and looked from Talos to me.

"Isa, that's impossible. Our genes just don't mix. Incubo can only reproduce with other Incubo. Many hearts have been broken in that truth."

I offered her a sad smile and gentle nod.

"He was a liar and a conman, Isa." Talos spoke and drew my attention back to him across the room.

"Who?" Althea shot at him.

"Lawrence Codwell. That is where you've gotten this crazed notion, isn't it?" Talos' intense gaze did not leave mine as he spoke.

"The Fata that led the attack on my wedding?" Althea stood

and moved between us. "Talos, what did he say? Isa?" She looked between us, hysterics overcoming her.

"Who are you going to trust Isa? The Fata who ordered the kills of an entire wedding party? Or Me?" He smoldered.

Amil stood and placed his hands on Althea's shoulders, she shrugged him away and headed to the bedrooms with tears falling down her face.

"I think we both know the answer to that question after what happened in Arta." I quipped, a subtle reminder that he threw both Amil and I against the walls of his bedroom the night before the wedding.

"Then say it." Talos' challenge deadly.

A roll of my eyes was my only answer as hot acid filled my chest, rose up the back of my neck, and rested on my cheeks. I wanted more than anything to hurt him. To pierce his hard shell of security that he held up for anyone other than Althea. Let him feel the vulnerability he imposes on me.

"You've not given me a reason to trust your words over any other stranger. At least he made his intentions clear and didn't try to manipulate me without me knowing upon first meeting me." I spat.

The edge of his mouth turned up into a dark and menacing smile as his eyes turned inky black. A crushing silence began to press in on me, a shadow overtaking the cabin and pinning me in place, unable to move.

"Back to your old ticks then, Talos?" I narrowed my eyes to meet his gaze. "Are you too puissant that allowing anyone to get to you would threaten to topple the ivory podium you're perched on?"

Talos shifted in his seat, his posture resembled a viper ready to strike. Amil side stepped closer to me but didn't step between us. Each sharp angle of Talos' face cast a shadow over his dark features.

"My mouth only bothers you when it wounds your ego.

When was the last time you were held accountable for your predations?"

I closed my eyes against the blurred vision. My heart pounded in my chest and ears. Air thickening to constrict my lungs, and a pain radiated from my temple.

"Talos. Don't do this." Amil's muffled voice sounded around me in the shadow of prison that Talos had erected.

A hand encircled my throat, and lips pressed to my ear, "You have no idea what I have done to keep my kind safe, Isa. Do not think that your lovely utility is enough to keep you alive with these very flawed theories. "

His grip slid to my jaw, pulling my face up closer to him. His hard kiss a further message of dominance. When he moved away and released me, I gasped down fresh breath. The room came back into focus and light filled my view again. Talos had sat back and reclined, his ankle crossing over his knee as if he hadn't threaded to end my life seconds before. Amil clenched his jaw, his features tight and cross. His eyes filled with ashes smoke driving daggers into Talos who behaved as if he didn't see anyone but me in the cabin.

I slowed my heaving chest and calmed my nerves, I wouldn't give him the satisfaction of thinking that he had rattled me. I stood but didn't move, debating on whether to gut him for the display he'd just made. Or aim for Amil for standing by and doing nothing.

"You should rest, Isa. When we arrive in Amples, you'll need your strength." Talos picked up the book from Althea and began skimming through the pages, dismissing me.

I gave a stinging glance to Amil then turned to walk away from them both to the bedroom. I shut and locked the door behind me before lying down on the small bed. With no interest in sharing the sleeping area with Amil or having to be within the same country as either Incubo at that moment. I could hear

Amil's deep voice in the other room but couldn't make out his words. Talos only grunting in his responses. I hoped they both choked on the others arrogance.

CHAPTER NINE

Aknock on the door woke me some time later. By the calm and dark night sky out the window, I guessed I had slept through the rest of the trip and we were in Amples. I sat up and stretched my arms and back, stiff from the cramped bed. I pulled my carry-on bag out from the storage area under the bed and put it over my shoulder. Another knock at the door accompanied by a voice this time.

"Isa, please open the door." It was Amil, but only annoyance filled his voice.

I unlocked the door and pulled it open to find him leaning with his arm pressed to the door frame. His body blocking the cabin hallway and view of the sitting area.

"Althea and Talos are waiting for us out by baggage claim. But we should talk."

I pushed past him and dipped under his arm. "I don't have anything to say to you. We should go find them before someone else does."

"Isa, wait!" His deep voice boomed through the space between us in the cabin.

He'd not spoken to me that way before. Even during training

or the argument we had earlier. He had my full attention. I dropped my bag on the couch and crossed my arms, waiting for him to speak his urgency. He took two steps towards me but hesitated on the third.

"You're about to walk into the lions den and you're not at all prepared."

"And you've waited until the very last moment to tell me how to ready myself?" I huffed.

"You didn't give me much of a chance, did you?"

I shrugged. I shouldn't let pride get in the way of my own safety, but he and Talos were making the idea of being ambushed more appealing than talking to either of them.

"The King and Queen are wrapped up in their own world and likely will ignore you. But the Prince is less oblivious. He has ways of finding information on any and everyone. And he will use his abilities to get that information out of you one way or another." He took a few steps closer to me. "Do not let him corner you." He warned.

I felt for the small blade at my hip. He took one more step before I let my instincts take hold on my wrist and threw the knife. It missed his head by no more than an inch and buried itself in the wall at the rear of the cabin. He spun around as it passed him by, then returned his sights to me.

"I'll be fine." Feeling that my point was made, I brought my bag back up over my shoulder and walked out into the hallway and exited the train.

I found Talos and Althea standing nearby the terminal with all of our bags on a trolly ready to meet the town car. Amil reached us moments later. He looked down to me and silently offered me my blade between his fingers. Althea blinked at this but didn't question the exchange.

When we reached the parking lot, a large SUV and a familiar face were waiting for us. Yamir dipped his chin in greeting. Talos thrust his hand out to Yamir, who I had thought hadn't made it out of the attack on the manor. They embraced for a moment before Talos began loading the baggage into the rear of the vehicle. Amil wrapped his arms around Yamir for a long moment, then they cupped the back of the other's neck. Bringing their foreheads together in a show of brotherly admiration.

"It's good to see you in one piece, *akhi*." Amil said and took a step to the side.

Althea threw her arms around Yamir's neck and began to sob. Relief poured from her ash smoke eyes. Talos rounded the car and put his hands on Althea's shoulders, "My Lady, we should be on our way."

She released Yamir and beamed up to him before hopping into the back seat before Talos. Amil climbed into the passenger seat. Yamir gave me a nod and waited for the surprise to leave my expression to speak.

"It's good to see you too, *sadiq*." He spoke as if he hadn't survived certain death by a firing squad.

"Same." I blinked, surprise still lingering in my tone.

He gave me an amused, kind smile before he rounded the front of the vehicle and got into the driver's seat. I gave myself an internal shake and scooted into the back with Althea and Talos.

The drive to the chateau was another hour from the train station on the other side of the city. Amples was one of the largest metropolitan areas in the country with several hundred thousand residents within the city limits alone. The outer suburbs and surrounding towns held plenty of beings that commuted into the heart of the city for work. With several of the most powerful and advanced technology firms in the country, they employed and powered most of the country.

Hundreds of tall skyscrapers competed for the clouds above on each block. Parks and nature reserves many acres wide peppered across its map and for every street lined with trees and shrubs. Like Cinder, the city ordinances had mandated many parts of the city be covered in greenery to offset pollution and noise. This created a living concrete jungle. A wealth of fruit trees and planter boxes help contribute to the resident enrichment programs.

I'd visited Amples before for assignments but never on a whim or a rescue mission. The idea that Argo could be in any building we passed sent my insides tumbling. I wished so much that I could jump out of the car and go searching each building we passed.

As extravagant as the city itself was, the Incubo royal chateau was something out of a fairytale. Positioned on the south west end of the city, tucked away by private great lake and several acres of forest. A two story tall Curtain Wall made up the gated entrance that gave way to the purlieu. Manicured low shrubs lined and weaved about the white gravel drive and walkway up to the impressive estate. The cream colored stone four story lavish *building* was framed by a greenhouse half its height, and what looked to be a parking garage. The iron-green roof domed in on each end the middle. Rows of windows cut into the impossibly smooth surface.

No one would mistake this place for anything but what it was. The living quarters of a family of great wealth and power. Which was likely why I had never heard of this place or have any knowledge of anyone who would. They hadn't bothered to masquerade their royal family as an important figurehead at the top of a company, or well-to-do billionaire socialites. As far as the Mortals were concerned, this compound didn't exist and I wouldn't doubt they would do anything to keep it that way.

CHAPTER TEN

We were escorted into an open entryway that gave way to two elegant stairways and two long hallways to either side of the doors. A beautiful Incubo greeted us and snapped her long ebony fingers for two Incubo men to retrieve our bags. Neither seemed to be quadrilateral, going as far as to drop and break open on of Althea's larger trunks, spilling the contents on the steps leading just outside the door.

"*Unanitania!*" She shouted, her voice a mixture of annoyance and boredom.

"Please excuse them, we will have your things washed and returned to you promptly." She spoke to Althea then turned to Talos, "Talos, good to see you again in one piece."

"Anisa, you are looking as lovely as ever." He inclined his head briefly. "I'd like to introduce you to the Mortal that ensured we kept in one piece. This is Isa Nera."

He placed his hand at my shoulder and nudged me closer to Anisa. Her pale smoke filled eyes drew a line from my face to my feet then back again before she extended her hand.

"Isa," my name sliced through her teeth without savoring, "The Black Banner." she finished matter-of-factly.

My throat went dry and I shot an firy glance to Talos, who ignored me, "Yes, but she was much more useful than the last one our family had encountered."

Anisa hadn't taken her eyes off me. A wary chill held on her shoulders tense as she evaluated me. Amil stepped out behind Talos and stood at her side, facing away from the rest of us. He turned his head and dipped closer to her ear to whisper. She didn't break her gaze but her features softened and she gave a nod of acceptance.

I watched Amil take a few steps more into the foyer then pause. He looked up to the impossibly tall domed ceiling then down each hallway before turning back to the rest of us. Anisa spoke again, this time to Talos but still watched me for any sudden movements. Whatever Amil had said hadn't been enough for her to trust me yet.

"You and Althea will be in the east wing. Your men and guest will be in the west wing. The King and Queen will *fancy word for see* you in the morning for breakfast."

Althea gripped the back of my arm and pulled herself towards me, pressing into my shoulder. "I'd like Isa to be with me for the remainder of the night."

Anisa's long midnight lashes fluttered at this request, a smile much like one you'd give to a child who was scared of the dark crept onto her face. "Althea, my dear. There is nothing to worry about, and it's protocol for only members of the royal family to reside in the east wing."

"Then, I will stay with her in her room," she paused and glanced to me, "If that's okay with you, Isa?"

"Of course, I—"

"Lady Althea, I have to decline that request. It just isn't done." Anisa interrupted, her tone more firm.

"Anisa, I think that this request is best granted under the circumstances." Talos sternly countered.

Anisa looked between the three of us, then back to Amil for

support which he gave none. He hadn't as much as looked at me since we had our last discussion on the train and was carefully examining his wristwatch. She turned back to Talos and shook her head in defeat.

"Alright. We have higher security in the east wing so I will have Dorian and Sandros take both your things to your room... for the night."

With that Anisa turned and left us in the wake of her high heeled shoes clicking on the polished stone floor. Amil was already halfway up the staircase and veering to the left before I could draw my attention away from the most intimidating Incubo I have met to date.

The two other Incubo proceeded up the stairs with our baggage in hand. Amil had his own luggage and had disappeared around a corner when Althea, Talos, and I reached the first landing. Talos gave me a subtle nudge forward. The ornate iron railing winding and climbing alongside us on our accent. Each beige stone step glinted with silver and the edges etched with filigree. It seemed as though each step was designed and sculpted by an artist's hands. The first floor was lit by wall sconces and every several feet hung a crystal chandelier.

The first stop was at Talos' room, he took a look inside, dropped his bag then continued to follow to Althea's room two doors down. Dorian and Sandros deposited our bags then left without a word. The room had a sitting area near a carved stone fireplace positioned aside an oversized canopy bed. White velveteen drapes heavily hung from the golden support poles. It made the suite at the Welp's manor look minuscule and common.

Althea and Talos busied themselves with arranging her luggage in the spacious walk in closet. I sat my weapons bag down on a large white satin tufted wingback chair. I took the Alexandrite blade out of its sheath and held it in my fingers, debating whether or not to place it in my bag for safekeeping. I was clearly not welcomed by Anisa, and I had no knowledge of her role in the monarchy.

Talos appeared by my side, silent and rigid. "Be ready in the morning. We have to meet your brother's captors downtown at eleven o'clock."

"I'll be ready." I fingered the grooves of the blade and watching the glints of light catch in it's prisms.

"Anisa is not keen on strangers. Don't take it personally." He said then sat in the matching wingback chair adjacent.

"She seems to have a sour taste for my family." I place the blade back in it's sheath at my hip.

"Anisa has had a few encounters with the Banners. Long before the price on Pytr's head. Back when there was a price on the Queens head."

My eyes shot to his, he gave me an amused grin. He knew he would get this reaction and was savoring the shock on my face. He leaned back and placed his ankle across his knee, waiting for the pieces to fall into place.

"She and the Queen are close?" I asked. I took the bag of weapons off the chair and sat, waiting for his answer.

He signed regally and a playful grin stretched across his face, "They are sisters. Anisa is the Princess of Maisha. Next in line to rule life across the sea, as we so lovingly refer to it."

I watched him scruff the stubble across his chin with the heel of his palm, he hadn't willingly given me such *information* without wanting something in return. But this time it was different. I had nothing left to give.

"Why is she here if she has an entire country to reside over?"

"The same reason we are." The corner of his mouth twitched up into his cheek.

He stood and walked to the door of the room. Looking back to Althea before turning to me once more, "Until tomorrow." And he was gone.

CHAPTER ELEVEN

Althea and I shared a bed once again. The oversized pillows and mattress cocooned us in comfort, and I had slept deeper than I had in weeks. The heavy white linen curtains on the windows did little to shield the sun peering through as it broke dawn. I rolled over to see Althea still sleeping but trail stain of tear from the tips of her eyes to her temples. She hadn't wanted to talk much after Talos had left. She had sat in bed to read after bathing. Complaining that her hair still smelled like train exhaust even after she had shampooed it twice.

A soft knock at the door drew me from the duvet and down pillows. It was Talos, who gave me a brief time warning. He would be back to retrieve both Althea and I to be received by the King and Queen in an hour. Then he was gone. My stomach felt like it was doing somersaults as I washed up and dressed. I brushed my hair straight, the brown and bronze strands still damp from the shower.

I didn't bother to pretend I was anything other than who I was. There was no use in slipping back into my persona of Althea's long time friend and bridesmaid. Not here. Anisa knew exactly what I was and my place by Althea's side. Surely the

King and Queen would as well. And if by the off chance they weren't informed, they would find out quickly by my attire.

Black jeans that clung themselves over my curved hips and thighs. A black for fitting turtleneck shirt. Leather boots with three concealed knives in each, black leather *body belt* that held my blades close to my ribs and hips. Last, but my new favorite garment, the thigh sheath that held the Alexandrite dagger that Talos had given to me. It had become one of my most valuable weapons, especially with a new possible foe in my midst. A beautiful Princess whose gold dusted ebony brows only held suspicion for me and my position to Althea.

I looked to the bed to where Althea still slept. I hadn't woken her while I prepared for the day. I wished I didn't have to wake her. I doubted she would be jumping for joy to be embraced by more imposing relatives. I checked the time and had stalled long enough. She had about twenty minutes to ready herself.

Gently, I smoothed my hand up her back and rested on her shoulder, "Althea, it's almost time to meet with the King and Queen." I whispered.

She took in a deep breath as she rolled over towards me, her eyes blurrily fluttering open. Shadowed pupils retracting as the light washed over her consciousness. A hum of realization of where we were and a nod was her reply. I walked over to the sitting area to wait for her to get dressed in a simple white linen dress with a black waist belt. Her hair elegantly tossed into a bun atop her head. Reminding me that she was not only lovely, but she was effortlessly gorgeous. The curse of Incubo beauty.

Talos came to retrieve us several minutes later with Amil at his side. Yamir was nowhere in sight. Both Incubo entered the room and Amil stood at the door, locking it. Talos looked from Althea to me, evaluating out clothing. An amused smile bloomed on his face when his eyes landed on the gifted dagger. He tilted his head down towards me. Raising his hand and summoning me with two of his fingers.

"Is there reason to believe you will need to be dressed for battle over scones?" His voice hushed for only me to hear. "Not that I'm complaining."

My eyes perked to his, a wisp of storm clouds holed over his irises. The heat in his stare brushing my cheeks. I gave myself a subtle shake and took a step away, "I don't know what to expect after meeting Anisa. Better prepared than dead."

He raised his chin and gave me a perk of his brow, an acknowledgement of wit and respect. Talos looked to Althea and offered her a warm smile, which she returned.

"You look beautiful, my Lady."

"That's kind of you. I feel as if I look as exhausted as I feel." She placed her hands to her hips.

"Could have fooled me." He replied playfully.

Amil stepped away from the door and cleared his throat, his posture tense and cold. I cocked my head around Talos to get a full view of Amil. He was dressed in a suit: wine red with gold and black embroidered vines up his cuffs and hem. His white undershirt crisp against the contrast of dark vest, jacket, and black tie. He'd slick his black hair back, but let the top sweep off to one side giving it dimension. I hadn't seen him look this handsome since the wedding, which felt like a lifetime ago.

"Well, now that we've all had the once over of approval, we should go." Amil looked me over but spoke to all of us.

As a unit lead by Talos and Amil, we made our way to a dining room upstairs. At the stairway we were greeted by the two Incubo who had helped us with our luggage the night before. They silently took up the rear, sandwiching Althea and I until we reached a carved white door. They each took a handle and pulled. Revealing an immense open room lined with floor to ceiling windows. The sun dashed over the cream and white marbled floor, reaching the far wall where a long table sat. A fire lit in the fireplace behind a figure at the head of the table.

A figure to the left stood and was followed by two others.

The clicking of shoes hammered at each footfall as we made our way towards the elongated table surrounded by wing backed chairs.

"Welcome, dear Althea." A voice rang out as we approached.

"Thank you, Your Highness." Althea answered to a tall Incubo.

"And you must be Isa. I'm Prince Vassilis. But please, call me Vas."

My voice escaped me and I could only nod and flutter my lashes. Vassilis was painfully beautiful. His dark hair pulled into tight braids close to his scalp, each row adorned with gold bands and rings. His light blue suit jacket casually unbuttoned. He swept his arm out to introduce the other table mates. "It's my pleasure to introduce their majesties King Idris and Queen Malaika. Ruler of Amples and Oneira."

The royal family took me in and wore bright smiles in welcome. King Idris looked to only be slightly older than Talos, salt and pepper hair thick on his head and in his beard. His olive skin tone in contrast to his Queen. Her deep complexion had not been fully given to her son, but her radiant smile was clearly passed down to him. Her hair was wrapped in a colorful scarf and gold hung from her ears, neck, and wrists. Her floral dress casual and almost in unison to her husband's dark blue and red flowered suit.

"We have heard many things about you, Isa Nera. We owe you a great deal for saving our great nieces life." King Idris inclined his head in recognition.

"I suppose the gratitude should go to Talos for hiring me." I glanced to Talos who ignored my comment.

"Ah, yes. Well, Talos has made a sensible choices in looking for a Black Banner. That was a stroke of genius." He turned to Talos, "Hiring a contract killer to protect from other contracted killers. It's almost poetic."

Talos shifted from one foot to the other, either uncomfortable with the praise or there was more to this conversation than what was being said.

Amil pulled chairs for Althea and I but we remained standing. The Queen laid her hand on her husband's shoulder, "Althea, you have our deepest condolences. Cornelius would have been the perfect match for you. Your children would have been beautiful." Her hand absentmindedly fell to her belly, revealing the swell of pregnancy.

I looked to Althea. Shock and tears welled in her eyes but she never once let her smile slip. "It would seem that congratulations are overdue, your majesty."

The Queen smiled down to her womb, then to her son, "It is my greatest pleasure to be a mother again. I only wish it was under more favorable circumstances."

Her son gave a somber nod of his head, his eyes flitting from his mother's hand to Althea, then me, then landing on Talos. A wave of smoke and specks of silver passed over his sight. He returned his attention to the Queen, "Shall we save the remainder of our gabbing for when breakfast is served?"

He suggested she sit with a dip of his hand into her chair. Both the King and Queen took their seats followed by Talos, then the rest of the table. Prince Vassilis snapped his fingers and the doors opened. I slid a hand to a blade at my hip under the tablecloth, but through the doors came a dining cart wheeled in by Dorian. I wasn't expecting more Incubo to arrive, there were no other place settings at the table which meant that he would not be staying. He had been employed to serve the royal family in more than just protection. Aside from the royal family, I hadn't seen any other being on the grounds. Not a single Fata was present in the chateau. Not as guests or staff member.

Dorian placed plate after plate on the table starting with the King and Queen. The breakfast was much more simple than I imagined a royal meal would be. A small ramekin held an egg baked in spiced tomato hash, topped with goat cheese, and chives. Beside it was a crystal bowl of pineapple, grapes, and mellon. Toasted sourdough points for dipping finished off the arrangement.

Shakshuka was one of my favorite meals but it wasn't exotic or impressive. Any being with an oven with eggs, and canned tomatoes could make this dish. My thoughts wandered to their kitchens, where I didn't doubt held state of the art appliances and gadgets. The Fata kitchen manager and her assistant at the Welp's manor had sent up fresh handmade pastries every morning to our suite. They had planned out the meals with such detail, each more complex than the last. But here, it would seem, that was not the arrangement despite the importance of the residing residents.

Amil had sat to my right, he waited for the rest of us to start eating before starting on his own plate. He was tense and stoic, his face not giving away his thoughts. I gave him a light nudge with my elbow, "Are you alright?" I mouthed more than whispered.

His eyes jetted around the table, but not stopping on one individually for more than a second. He gave me a single nod of his head dismissing me, but not convincing me that he was fine. It wouldn't be the time to speak if there had been something bothering him, but Prince Vas glanced over to us several times, he clearly noticed Amil's mannerisms.

The royals spoke between themselves about their schedules for the day. Spoke of what they would have Althea do around the chateau to keep her occupied. Of gardens she could explore, or the stables for which she could take a horse out to the training ring for a nice ride. Talos suggested she peruse the library and observatory, and that Amil accompany her down to the orchards at the far end of the property. The fruit trees would be heavy and the grapes ready to harvest for the winery over the ridge.

Althea didn't chime in and only acknowledged them with a

smile when she was addressed directly. No one seemed to worry that she hadn't agreed to any of the activities they had laid at her feet. At the mention of his name, Amil stiffened next to me. He didn't rebuff Talos' suggestion but he glanced to me for a split second, catching the eye of one of our table mates.

Prince Vassilis glanced to Amil and then to me, curiosity dancing over his brows. As the meal went on, Prince Vas' gaze trailed from Talos, to me, then to Amil. His eyes lingering on Talos longer than Amil, and me. After a prolonged look to Talos, he shifted back to me, wrinkling his nose. The action quick and subtle, if I hadn't glanced up to him at that exact moment I would have missed it completely. This brought to mind a comment that Lawrence had said to me before he tried to strangle me. That he could smell Talos and Amil on me. Sense that I had slept with both of them. I wondered if that was a Fata trait or Incubo. I didn't have shame but from the side eyed smirk I was getting from the Prince, I was hoping he was more concerned for the blades strapped to my body and not which scent was strongest on me at the moment.

CHAPTER TWELVE

After breakfast the King and Queen excused themselves. They explained they had a doctors appointment to attend. The Queen was still in her first trimester, and was likely expecting twins by the size she had said she grew almost overnight. Althea clenched my had under the table linens at the mention.

The Prince on the other hand stayed after his parents had departed. He reclined casually in his lush dining chair. Dorian had taken the plates away and had left the Prince alone to contend with the four of us.

"Talos, what's this I hear of an outing with Isa later this morning?" He spoke over his delicate coffee cup.

"I have made Isa a promise to help resolve an issue." Talos explained.

The Prince hummed an approval. Talos checked his wrist-watch for the time then signaled to me that it was time to leave. I dabbed my lips with my napkin and turned to my left to speak to Althea. "I'll be back as soon as I can."

Her grip on my hand tightened but she let go a moment later. Talos and I stood, and so did Amil. He followed us to the door of the dining room and opened the door for us to step out into the hall. "Isa, I would feel better if you let me come with you. Please."

"I believe Isa is capable of completing this task without our help, Amil. I am only going as a catalyst." Talos spoke for me.

"Stay with Althea. She needs you while we're gone."

"When should we expect you back?" Amil spoke to me but again was answered by Talos.

"Isa will ensure her brother is safely deposited within their own ranks, then she will join us back here to retrieve her things. From there she will decide whether she will be staying on with us, or leaving back to Cinder with her family."

Talos wasn't as cheerful about this plan as he sounded. Amil's jaw feathered as he looked from Talos back to me. He took a step towards me and dipped his head to meet mine, a hand to my shoulder. "If you need anything, I will come. All you have to do is call."

"We'll be fine." I assured him, but the truth of the matter was that it was possibly a lie. Talos had kept information on Argo's whereabouts close to the cuff*breast*turn of phrase that means secret*.

Amil brushed his lips over mine. A brief flare of heat coaxed behind my navel. Our eyes met and the warm guiding flame ignited in his clouded eyes. My heart swelled, close to bursting knowing he has in agony to watch me leave and possibly not come back. But as heart filled as the idea was, I couldn't let his infatuation cloud my own priorities. I bounced up on the balls of my feet and landed a kiss on his cheek and pulled away from him. Talos and I headed down the hall to the staircase and neither of us spoke or looked back.

A car was waiting for us out front the chateau. Talos rounded the front of the black sports car and got into the drivers seat. I pulled my phone out and sent a text to Zaida:

We're approaching now. Wait for my signal.

-Isa

A dull buzz was the only reply I needed to know she was ready with the others. I didn't trust Talos enough to not have a back up plan in place. Not when it came to my family.

I slid into the passenger seat and closed the door in time for him to begin tearing down the drive. Gravel and dust in our wake through corners and weaving through the bush lined front garden. At the chateau gates, Talos slowed his pace and made his way to the city.

"Did you know the Queen was pregnant?" I hadn't seen his face earlier when it was revealed.

"I didn't but I am happy for her in this joyous time." His response sounded rehearsed.

"And the Prince. He is very interested in you?" This was more of an observation than a question but he had almost reveled in the attention.

"Prince Vas and I have had a complicated entanglement in the past. He is young and brooding. Both things are attractive but now is not the time for him to have eyes for anyone other than someone who can bear him offspring."

"That doesn't bother you?" I knew the answer, Talos hadn't shown true heartfelt interest for anyone or anything but Althea.

"Are you jealous, Isa?" He passed me a sly smile.

I blinked and sat back in my seat, "No. I'm just curious."

"I have no need for a companion. The Prince is fine company on occasion but he is well aware of his stature in the court and his importance to our kinds survival. Frivolous love affairs with the lower class is only acceptable for so long."

"Do you have a title? Does Amil?"

Because Incubo were small in their numbers, many would have long extended families. Though Talos was the head of Althea's family security, he was likely distantly related to her family. I was guessing her father who had been a Duke of Cinder.

"I am a Lord on my mother's side but I renounced my title and passed the duties to my younger brother. Amil's father is a Lord over seas in Medina but has not passed titles down to his son and daughter. They will likely be called upon to help repopulate their numbers if any other attacks occurs. Like many others."

The weight of his statement sank into my chest. An image of Amil holding a small child of his own threatened to overtake me. His duty to his kind, what that meant in its entirety hadn't crossed my mind.

"Would that include you as well?" I clipped back.

"Are you offering your services?" The edge of his lips wrinkled his cheek at his own wit.

"Is that not impossible? You were very clear on the train that those sorts of ideas were blasphemy."

He didn't have a quick witted response for me, instead he shook his head and wet his lips; dragging his teeth over the bottom and softly biting one corner.

"Where was Yamir this morning?" I gifted him with a subject change.

"He is on a different assignment for me. He will be back later this evening."

The thought that Yamir had escaped and made it to Amples unscathed baffled me. Lawrence had spoke of a body count. That his band of rebellion had counted off each of the dead, specifically checking for Talos and his men. How was it that Yamir had not only dodged Lawrence attack but wasn't on Lawrence's list to search for death confirmation?

Several other questions stemmed from this train of thought. Many of which, Talos wasn't likely to answer. He owed me no explanation when it came to his command of anyone other than myself. Which he didn't have at the moment. He had fulfilled my contract, payment had been transferred with a bonus. I didn't question this one. He was grateful for breathing but lucky he hadn't been slain by my own hand after the mental attacks he had put me through.

The city skyline came into view not long into our mostly quiet car ride. Talos had not given away the location yet but it didn't matter. He could keep it a secret up until we were in the exchange room. Zaida and the others were tracking my every mile. They would know my location within feet of the building.

The city was dotted with houses that were so old they were falling apart. For every tower of glass there were crumbling bits of the cities history, silently falling to dust. Several stories of broken windows and boarded arched doorways. The mix of architecture old and new blending together for the sake of charm. Plaques planted in front of each dilapidated home that read "The *Greek last name* House" or "The *Aribic last name* Manor". Often we would pas one of these buildings and half of the home would be covered with scaffolding for renovations. Restorations to these landmarks were likely attempts to facelift older parts of Amples to draw tourism.

Talos pulled into a underground parking structure and drove us down deep into the lower levels. When he satisfied with the emptiness of the level he parked and got out of the car, waiting for me to follow. I sent a quick text to Zaida that we had arrived. The signal was dead but once we made out way up to the higher levels of the building above, it would surely reach her.

It took my eyes a moment to adjust to the dim light of the parking garage around us. The smell of motor oil and damp earth mixed together with the city life outside. A sticky and unclean feel to the entire place. Cinder had its fair share of city sights and smells but with many city programs, the was one of the cleanest cities in the country.

Talos pointed towards and elevator at the end of the parking isle and only the sound of the soles of his shoes told me that it was our next destination. I trailed behind him, the echo of our footsteps bouncing off the stone pillars and walls. Each additional drip or scurry of rodents in dark corners had every one of my nerves on edge. A dull chime of the elevator gave me a slight panic for what would be waiting for us upon our accent but a breath of release that for a few moments longer, I wouldn't have to fight for my life.

Talos illuminated the 47th floor button and the doors to the lift closed. He leaned against the back wall and crossed one ankle over the other, his hands in his pockets. He exuded cool and calm.

"Does this give you deja vu?" He looked to me with a cocky smile on his face.

I rolled my eyes, "You mean, am I once again feeling as if I may lose my life after being in an elevator with you?"

"Oh it hasn't been that terrible, has it? You've grown so much in skill since meeting me." He gave himself a lot of credit for a skill I shouldn't have ever needed to learn. I didn't answer him. He didn't need one by the expression of annoyance on my face.

The lights of each floor ticked by as we raised farther and farther into the building. I took a blade in each hand and readied myself for a battle. Balancing on the balls of my feet, coiling the muscles of my calves and thighs ready to burst through gunfire or any other opponent waiting for us. Talos only stood silent, cooly leaning against the handrail of the lift. His fingertips rhythmically cascading in boredom. The only sound filling the space between us was the hum of the lift and the dull thudding of flesh to metal.

Each floor came and passed with the increase of the sound of my heart throbbing in my ear. Anger and fear swallowed me whole. Not fear for my own life. No.

Fear that it was too late. That Argo has been brutally murdered and I hadn't gotten here fast enough. Fear that Zaida, Derek, Markus, and Talia are too far behind and could get caught in the inevitable crossfire. I couldn't imagine a scenario where I walk out of this building with Argo peacefully as Talos was expecting. I'd dealt with the sleazy city underbelly type before. They often didn't walk away from those encounters.

The final floors passed and our lift slowed. The dull chime of the door reaching its destination. Then the metallic glide of the doors opening into a dark room. We were met with silence. Not even the muffled sound of breathing echoed around the room.

Talos stepped out first and I stepped out behind him checking left and right to nothing but darkness. Talos reached out around a corner and with a click turned the lights on. The buzz of fluorescent tubes sizzled above and lit each corner to reveal no one. Not a single soul haunted the abandoned floor. What would typically have been office cubicles sat stack of forgotten conference chairs, an overturned table on the far wall.

I spun around, searching every corner for anything. For anyone. But it was only Talos and me. An overwhelming rush of heat hit my head as I turned to Talos, his face empty of any surprise.

"Where are they! Where is Argo!" My voice echoed off the bare walls.

"Your guess is as good as mine, Isa." He reached into his pocket and pulled his cell phone out.

He turned away from me while he dialed and waited for someone to answer the other line. There were no other doors to this large room. No other offices sectioned off for the sake of bureaucracy. The only door was the emergency exit to the stairwell.

"This is Talos Amargo..." he paused to listen to the other end, "Don't waste my time. I'm here at the drop location and my parcel is nowhere to be found."

A fresh flush of rage swelled inside of me at the casualty of his voice. The calm he held as he spoke to my brother's captors, and likely his murderers. An urge crept up my throat, tightening at each passing silent moment. I paced and waited for his next exchange.

"I see. That sounds quite unfortunate for you." With that he hung up and turned around to meet my eyes.

"Where are they, Talos?" I seethed.

"They were tipped off of our arrangement. I don't know how but I will find out and we will find him, Isa."

"Fuck!"

My stomach roiled, my jaw clenched as a burst of frustration ripped from somewhere deep and angry. I bolted to the door and bounded down the stairs, only a piercing high pitched siren met me as I tore open every door on my way down the emergency staircase. Door after door held nothing but empty rooms. Flashing red lights filled the stairwell. Argo's name echoed off the cavernous concrete structure.

I had reached several flights, tears burning my throat when a force grabbed the strap of my body belt at my shoulder and hauled me to a stop at the top of a landing. My back slammed to the wall and my feet lifted from the floor. Talos' eyes met mine, deep and as dark as I felt. I kicked out towards him but he only pressed his body into mine to hold me still. He pinned my arms and waited for me to regain calm, or at least some form of it.

"They've killed him! It's my fault! I should have come sooner! I should have been here!" I wailed, and cursed. Pain and pressure all sinking in on me.

Talos didn't speak, but there was a thickening in the air around him, darkness encased us, the blaring lights and sirens silencing as a pull bloomed in my belly. The air in my lungs honey thick bringing me not to panic but to slow my breathing. A pain in my temple bringing me out of the rage and helplessness.

"I can feel the pain you're in, Isa but you have to be the cold hearted killer you know you are. Do not let these degenerates break you." He spoke through his teeth, the strain of holding me back and using his influence challenging him.

I fought back against him. Mind and body. The handle of a blade heavy in my palm, warm from my grip, the awareness of still being armed pushed me to plant my feet to the wall and push out against him, plunging the dagger into his bicep. He released me with a cry of pain, dropping me to the floor and air filling my lungs once again. He pulled the blade out and held it in his fingers a moment longer, likely weighing his options before dropping it on the floor in front of where I was crouched.

"That's my girl." He practically purred. "Now, when you've composed yourself, we will go back to the chateau and I will send every man I have out to find your brother. No one will sleep until I have delivered your brother to you along with those who have taken him and toyed with my time."

He gave an elegant extension of his hand to help me stand. A clutched apprehension held me on the floor as my mind struggled to catch up. In a flash of moments, I had been seconds away from witnessing Argo breathing, safe. To squatting on a cold tile floor surrounded by emergency lights and the remnants of an anger fueled rampage. A blush of shame washed over me but I took Talos' hand and stood with my chin high.

"My other siblings should be waiting outside. I need to speak with them before I agree to go back to the Chateau with you."

He nodded and gave a 'shall we' gesture to the nearest door. We had made it all the way to the thirty second floor by the time he had caught up to me. My legs burned as adrenaline slowed and released my muscles and a dull pain in my shoulder crept into place where I had thrown it into each door I had come across. We took the elevator down to the lobby and I stepped out to find not a trace of Zaida and the others. I checked and saw I had texts from her:

Zaida: My Sorella, they aren't here. Not a trace but you and that Incubo brute you brought with you. Call me.

I looked to Talos then dropped my eyes back to my cell-phone. I dialed Zaida's secure line, and it only rang once. "We do not shy away from the dark." She spoke into the other line.

"For we are the shadows… Z." I faltered.

"I know. We'll find him. Where are you?"

"I'm in the lobby. I need to speak with you all." I looked around but saw no sign of them.

"Four down, three north. Five." And her line went dead.

I pocketed my phone and turned to Talos. "I have to meet my family."

He considered me a moment before he spoke then tossed something in the air. I caught a bundle of metal, clinking in my cupped hands. The keys to his car.

"For when you're done." He thumbed his phone then put it in his pocket.

I didn't thank him. Perhaps I should have, but instead I left the building and set off down the street four blocks, up three, to the door of the fifth building, a hotel.

CHAPTER THIRTEEN

The quaint white-brick faced luxury hotel stood between a cafe, and a handmade home goods store. All three businesses washed in white and black. The front desk faced a sitting area of white loveseats and a low table, absent of any guests. A slender blonde Fata stood waiting, watching as I approached with a smile on her face.

"Welcome to Marvro Spiti, do you have a reservation?" She beamed.

"It's under Black."

She clacked at her keyboard, a smile still plastered to her face. "Here we are! Just for the night?"

"Mhmm." I nodded, peeking out the window for any sign that I had been followed.

"Here is your key, you're in room 403 and your friends have already checked in. Is there anything else I can do to make your stay with us more enjoyable?"

"Could you send up a bottle of tequila?"

"Of course! I'll have it sent up right away."

"Thanks."

She began to dial her phone and fill my request. I didn't wait around to find out how quickly she could get someone to find and deliver a bottle of liquor and headed to the elevator. Once inside I took in a deep breath and readied myself for the onslaught of questions my family would surely have for me.

When I got to the door of the room, I paused. Silence met me from the other side. Not a sound from the adjacent rooms or hallway. I knocked twice, waited, then knocked three more times before slipping the key into the lock and opening the door. The hotel room opened up into a short hallway, the bathroom to the left and a sitting room further in. That's where I found Zaida and Talia sitting in the two armchairs in front of a window. An empty loveseat sat across from them.

To the left of them was the bedroom which was separated by a wood planked wall, it's large door open to the rest of the room. Two queen sized beds dressed in cream and black linens, my brothers Markus and Derek sat at the foot of each bed. None spoke but their grim thoughts were plain as their eyes on their faces. It took a moment to look into Mortal eyes, without the clouded smoke filters that Incubo had. They were all dressed in tactical gear, armed to the nines with their preferred weapons.

Derek stood and walked to the doorframe, leaning against it with his shoulder and crossing his arms. He was tall and broad, his thick dark hair hung over his dark brows. His bronze skin and dark eyes gave him dangerous essences. He didn't ever look like he'd been in a fight he didn't win. He preferred guns to knives but was a deadly aim with both.

Derek's deep voice broke the silence, "Isa, where's Argo?"

"There is so much I have to tell all of you—" A knock at the door interrupted me.

Talia stood and answered the door, only out of sight for a moment and came back in with the bottle of tequila I had ordered and a tray of shot glasses. She set the tray down on the table between the two armchairs and twisted open the cork of the bottle. She poured us each a shot then handed them out.

Talia's bronze skin mirrored my own but her eyes were a clear blue to my caramel brown. She had always been my sparring partner growing up. Her skills in hand to hand combat had been far beyond my own, and she could anticipate an opponent's next move down to the breath.

Zaida held out her glass to us, "To family. Thicker than blood. Stronger than iron." And we drank.

"Isa." Markus turned towards me, his kind face drawing me out.

I looked to each of them, none judging or blaming me but waiting for their sister to point them in the next direction. My heart cracked open as I told them everything I knew of the Incubo, my assignment, and the attack on Althea's wedding. I told them about the Incubo royalty, and Lawrence's plot to overturn our society. I told them that Lawrence claimed to be a halfbreed of Incubo and Fata. That it should have been impossible but that he wanted to use me to coerce the rest of the Black Banners to dismantle the Incubo hold.

They took in my words. Talia poured herself another drink, then held the bottle up to the room to offer a second round. Markus scrubbed his hand down his stubble face and let out an exasperated sigh. He walked over to the loveseat in front of my sisters and paced a moment before finally sitting down. He rested his elbows on his knees and held his face in his hands.

I cared for Markus dearly. He could take down a firewall as easily as a body. He was slender, more docile in appearance than Derek. But his high cheekbones and sharp jaw made everyone swoon. He often passed for an IT analysis or accountant on assignments but for what he lacked in intimidation, he made up for agility. He'd crafted his own weapons to be accustomed to his own style. A baton that extended into a pointed escrima, and blades longer than my own.

"So do you trust them?" Markus spoke through his hands.

"I don't know. For Argo's sake, I think I have to." I questioned myself as I spoke but felt like I had come to a crossroads.

"Sorella, I don't think this is the right strategy. We can find Argo without Talos or the other Incubo. If Lawrence was telling the truth, there is a war coming and we cannot be a part of it. It's not what we do. We don't fight wars. We don't pick sides." Zaida stood addressed us all, even if the reminder was directed towards me.

"Z, I don't see another way. Argo's life is worth the risk."

She turned away from me, peering out the window and crossing her arms. I didn't fully trust myself at the moment. I wanted to believe that what I was suggesting was true, but had no proof that Talos would be able to track down Argo's captors. I also didn't have any reason to believe he wouldn't set miles of fires to show he was a being of his word just to have something to hold over my head for when he needed a favor.

My heart clenched in my chest at the thought of Argo still out of reach. Still being held and likely in pain. The urge to retreat back to the chateau and agree to anything Talos wanted hit me like a brick wall. Perhaps I did trust Talos.

"We'll stay here until he's found. Check in and give us any leads they find." Talia instructed with a firm voice.

"Are we really talking about this? The Banner council would have our head for this!" Derek chimed in to the room at large.

"The council won't know. If it were up to them, Argo would be left to die." Talia replied.

"And your point is? We've done our duty. Argo broke protocol. We shouldn't risk our entire careers to save his ass. The pillars say that a rescue mission gets one attempt. One. That is only if capture isn't apparent. Who knows what Argo has told them." Derek began pacing the floor, frustration filling his voice.

"You're not suggesting that we leave him to die?" Zaida turned back to him, her brows furrowed.

"He's as good as dead already." Derek snapped back.

"You can leave if you want, but I'm staying. I promised him that I would find him and I'm not leaving. Dead or alive." I said, attempting to steady my anger and surprise that Derek would abandon our brother.

"We stay and wait for word. Derek, do I have to remind you that you owe Argo after your last trip to Cardonia? If it hadn't been for him, you would have been sent home in a bag." Markus looked up to Derek, his words dripped of acid.

Derek huffed and retreated back to the bed he had been sitting on earlier. Talia ran her fingers through her hair, a worried expression hung on her beautiful face. She worried her lip a moment then turned to me, "What about this Amil. Do you trust him?"

The question pierced me, Amil wanted more than anything for me to trust him. To confide in him and turn to him instead of Talos. The flash of Amil's face crowded the forefront of my mind. The curve of his cheek, the smoke that filled his eye. The small flame that called to something deep and old inside of me. Something that I had a difficult time resisting.

"I trust Amil." I answered truthfully. The muscles in my throat tightened at the admission.

She nodded in understanding before speaking, "Zaida, it's your call."

Zaida considered me, then looked to our siblings. She shook her head and pressed two fingers to her temple, "If you trust them, then so will we. We'll check in when we move. You do the same." She closed the distance between us and reached out her hand. I took it in mine, "Isa. Stay alive. Otherwise, I will find every last bit of Alexandrite I can and choke Talos and Amil with it."

She pulled me in for a long embrace. I took in the smell of her hair, the pressure of her arms around my shoulders. "We do not have fear." I spoke into the crook of her arm.

She pulled away to answer, meeting my eye, her voice brimming with determination and love, "For we are terror."

CHAPTER FOURTEEN

On the walk back to Talos' car in the garage of the empty building, my chest and head felt heavy with too many emotions to process at once. Anger and anxiety both heated and cooled my insides when I thought of Argo still missing and not safely with my siblings. Annoyance and betrayal that my brother Derek would rather us leave Argo to die than try another attempt to save him. Longing to stay with them at the hotel and not return to The Chateau to face Amil and his empathy. Anguish over every step I took to get to this point and being one step closer only to fall several steps behind. A stalemate of wits and ammo.

I unlocked the door and got into the driver's seat, but took a moment before putting the key in the ignition. My siblings were putting more faith in me than they had before and in turn, I was running back to the Incubo for help. Going to Talos once again to what felt like begging for relief of all this pain and confusion and heartbreak. At that moment I would do anything to see Argo alive again. To wrap my arms around his neck and just hold him close like we did as children after one of us would wake up from a nightmare.

One of my strongest memories was when we were a little older than ten, Argo had resigned to sleeping on the floor in my and Zaida's room. He had been bunking with Markus and they got along fine but Markus had never had a nightmare about losing his first family like Argo had. Both orphans but for very different reasons. Argo's first family had abused him until he was school aged and teachers began to take notice, then his father would take his frustrations out on his mother. Eventually killing her in a night of pure rage in front of Argo. His father had gone for him next but to Argo's luck, he'd tripped and cracked his head open on the dining table and broke his neck. Argo was alone in the house with both his first parents dead for over twelve hours before he shook his shock enough to wander to his neighbors house to call the police.

Mr. Green retrieved Argo from the police station several hours later after a former Banner had gotten word that an eight-year old boy had been left orphaned. He never had to sleep alone after that night. When either of us would have a night terror about the bad nights from our past, we would comfort the other. Late night snacks in the kitchen and cuddling up together to read under the same blanket. Zaida would join us often if we woke her, but there were so many times it had just been Argo and I at two in the morning, eating marshmallows and reading tales of warriors and kings.

Not one of those Kings from our storybooks were like King Idris. King Idris was more handsome and dressed in the finest suits I had ever seen even to merely grace guests for morning breakfast. I wondered what Argo would think of this King, if I'd ever see him again to share this story.

Sitting in Talos' parked car wasn't going to answer that question for me. I needed to move and the only course of action I had was to go back to The Chateau and wait for Talos to come up with a plan. He owed me this debt. I saved his life and Althea's, he owed me my brother still breathing.

I ignited the engine and pulled out of the parking garage, headed back to the King's estate on the outer most cusp of the city. It was remarkably not hard to remember the way there or to find the towering home. More time had passed than I realized, when I pulled the drive, the sun was hanging low to the east. I'd been lost in my own thoughts for so long that it was the bitter evening when the Incubo Dorian opened the door and retrieved the keys from me.

I surveyed him before dropping the keys in his open palm. He'd been everywhere since we arrived. Done every miniscule task that anyone had asked of him. But he'd fumble on several occasions, grimaced at tasks that seemed beneath his usual status among his kind. Not a single Fata trimmed the hedges or served the food.

I perked an eyebrow to him when he promptly said, "Thank you madam, have a lovely evening." Then drove the car off to park.

I strained my eyes up the front ivy covered wall of The Chateau. Windows had began to be lit up and the large front doors gave off a warm amber glow as the chandeliers inside the entryway welcomed visitors inside. I took a deep breath and climbed the stairs, I reached for the doorbell but one of the doors opened up to the sight of Talos. Had he been waiting for me this whole time? Worried I might pilfer his vehicle and track Argo down myself? Should I have done that?

I certainly would have much rather had done that than return here and wait but it was too late for that now. It was far too late because Talos was standing in front of me with a concerned look on his sultry face. A small voice in the back of my brain screamed *slap that pitiful look off his face.* I didn't want or need his pity. I needed him to fulfill his end of the agreement.

"Are you going to let me in, or just lurk in the doorway?" I crossed my arms and waited.

A small smile broke the tension of his brow and jaw muscles.

He stepped to the side and waited for me to pass him before closing the door.

"Dinner will be served in the main dining room. That way," he pointed down the corridor to my right, "I'll show you to the room you'll be staying in for the remainder of your time here at the Chateau."

He made to turn to climb the double staircase off to the right, where Amil had disappeared the night previously.

"Is that what Althea wants?" I asked, surprised that this choice would be hers organically.

"Lady Althea has requested that you stay with her in her room, but I spent all day *fancy word for talked her into/manipulating* her into allowing you space of your own to breath and sleep comfortably. You've had a rough time here in Amples and you'll need your rest to ready yourself for tomorrow." He took several steps up the staircase without waiting to see if I would follow.

"You already have a location on Argo?" I took two steps closer, but didn't mount the stairs just yet.

"No. Tomorrow you begin your training with me. Or have you forgotten our deal in Arta?" He spoke in his treacherous tempting tone but didn't turn to meet my eye.

Heat rose up the back of my neck and my stomach churned. I hadn't forgotten about the arrangement we had made but that was before the wedding massacre. Before having to run for our lives and almost being strangled by Lawrence. Something like a stone sank into my gut. I didn't have any reason to argue, as much as my gut told me to refuse and reject his training plans. Not after almost dying at the hands of a Fata-Incubo halfling with a taste for vengeance.

I followed him up to the second floor guest quarters, and by the looks of them, each had been maintained to impress anyone who came to call. My room was several doors down from the stairway and more lavished than I imagined. The whtie and gold sleigh-bed was made so tightly that several coins would have bounced in unison if attempted or needed to do so. A low fire was lit in an *nice word for big/enormous* carved marble fireplace. Framed with rows and rows of books on white shelves. White leather loveseat and wingback chair sat cozy in front of the fire, inviting the inhabitants to lounge.

French doors out to a balcony that held a low table and two patio chairs that looked out onto the back garden of the Chateau. An intricate garden shrub maze was in full view. Talos opened the doors and peered out onto the grounds, still silent but all concern gone from his mannerisms. I came to stand beside him and was met with the sight of an early fall spectrum of color. Deep greens shifting to yellows and orange, a mix of fruit heavy apple trees and late blooming flowers cascaded the perfectly pruned flowerbeds.

The air carried the crisp scent of freshly cut grass and citrus trees up to the balcony. It was likely one of the last warm evenings of the year. Amples climate changed much more rapidly than Cinder. Beings of Amples often had snow weeks before any made it far north to us.

Talos turned to me at last, absent of pity in his expression or voice, "I let you down today and for that I am morbidly sorry. I am still a man of my word, and I will track down those bastards who are holding your brother and making a fool of me. What you do with them after I've had my moment is up to you, but might I suggest that it be slow and agonizing."

He raised a hand up towards my shoulder but stopped himself, pulling back, slipping his hands into his pockets. I could have given him a weak smile. I could have at least acknowledged his gesture but I had been drained of energy and empathy. But I let a nod be my answer to his suggestion. Those who were holding Argo would pay their pound of flesh*check that this isn't racist* for what they've done to him. They would feel our wrath, but they would also have to answer to the Banner council who would pass down their official death decree. Argo would have first rights to deliver those actions.

I walked back into the bedroom and sat on the bed, immediately sinking down into the lush mattress. Talos turned to face me, "I'll have a plate sent up. I will let Lady Althea know that you are resting and I will come to call for you at seven o'clock tomorrow morning. We'll train before breakfast. In three days time the King and Queen will be holding the funeral."

My eyes shot to his, "What funeral?"

"Fallen Incubo are all honored at the Chateau after death and their bodies emblazoned on the premises."

"Cornelius—," I began but a pang in my chest for Althea choked me.

"Yes, every Incubo that had fallen at the wedding will be mourned here. Althea will have to hold space for her father and late husband. Which is why I believe it's best for everyone to rest comfortably and prepare for that day's events. There will not be many attendees due to the danger of circumstance, but the King and Queen will be residing over the ceremony."

I had no words. Somewhere on the grounds there was a place to not only hold a funeral, but to dispose of the bodies. He didn't wait for me to form thoughts that were tangible enough to put into sentences. He left and shut the bedroom door behind him.

A cool breeze trailed in from the open balcony doors, feeling like an invitation. I went to shower with the plan to eat dinner looking out over the grounds, a small resemblance of what I loved to do on my own balcony at home in Cinder. The posh bathroom was wall to wall cream and gold. The claw foot bathtub large enough for two beings to lie down in. Detached was the large steam shower with a wide rain-shower head which accompanied two additional heads in different angles. I made note to get a similar setup installed in my own bathroom.

I stepped in to the hot water and rinsed the sweat and regret from my hair. Fumbling around for the exotic shampoo placed there by the Chateau house cleaning staff. Scents of pomegranate and honey filled the air.

The last memory of my shower at home was that of Amil and I together. The visions of water cascading down his muscular farm sent a wave of warmth low in my belly. I gliding my hand down my stomach and the trail of excitement. My fingers followed it down between my thigh, guided by my imagination. I wanted his hands all over me, craved his lips on my most sensitive places. His arms wrapped around me to hold me in place as he pounded and filled every nook of me. Tension mounted as I pulsed the pads of my fingers in circles and massaged my needy nerves until I spilled over the edge at the thought of the waves of his pleasure thrumming deep within me as he shattered. I could clearly feel his hot breath against my neck as his fingertips dimpled my hips at his climax.

Endorphins flooded each muscle, soothing aches I hadn't realized were there. Whether from stress, anger, or slamming my body against every door on my way down the building that should have held my brother. Exhaustion would take hold after the slacked afterglow of release had faded away. The oversized bed in the other room was calling to me louder than the promise of dinner on the evening balcony. I hadn't felt hungry or much of any physical sensation in a long while.

I wrapped my hair in a towel, then another towel around my body. When I opened the door, steam followed me out. The sun had gone down and a cool breeze had cleared the last bit of summer warmed air from my room. A chill crept up my damp legs as I walked over to the bed, my night clothes laid out waiting for me. I pulled on the silk camisole and shorts and pulled the linens back.

With each movement towards the middle of the bed, my knees sunk into the mattress. I pulled the blankets up under my chin and closed my eyes. A low buzz of crickets and the high pitched croak of frogs outside lulled me deep into sleep. The down pillows cradled my neck and head perfectly, it felt as if I were sleeping on a cloud.

CHAPTER FIFTEEN

I woke up to the sound of Talos' heavy knock on the door. Rays of hazy blue light peeked through drawn gauzy curtains that I didn't recall closing. I stumbled to the door and flung it open only to turn around and retreat back under the bedcovers. He broke the threshold and took several steps inside the chilly room before he cleared his throat.

"Not that I'm not fond of you in bed, Isa, but we had an agreement and our training time is fleeting. Guests will be arriving for the service this afternoon."

I gave a frustrated huff as my answer to his expeditions. Throwing the linens back and tearing away from the opulence to grab clothing to train in and headed to the bathroom to change. Talos sat on the arm of a chair next to the fireplace and waited for me to quickly dress and throw my hair up into a ponytail.

"Do you have any news on Argo?" I shouted from the bathroom.

"I have several of my most trusted men tracking him down as we speak. But until he's safely located, you will have to busy your mind with training with me." He called back.

I didn't like this answer, but didn't have much of a second option. My siblings were looking, Talos' men were out looking. To keep that many bodies out there looking for Argo, I had to keep my end of the bargain. Train with Talos for any future assignments, and keep watch over Althea who would be surrounded by vultures wishing to rip what remained of her apart after such a substantial loss. I took a long, deep breath and checked myself in the mirror. Gaunt after the disappointment of yesterday's mission, but I had to push through.

When I emerged from the bathroom he gave me a once over glance and nodded. He waved his arm out towards the door and proceeded to follow me out into the hallway. The rest of the chateau hadn't risen it seemed. Every door to the visitors quarters was closed and every window was still drawn closed. Talos lead me down the hall to the staircase which we climbed two flights to what looked to be a grand entertaining area. Vast and open with very little furniture. Oak paneled walls stretched the length of the gathering room, a crimson rug with what looked like a coat of arms stretched from one end to the other. I wondered if this was the room that my fellow Banner had been caught trying to assassinate Pytr under Cornelius' instructions. If she had been tortured somewhere close by, or even in the room I was currently sleeping in.

My stomach dropped at that intrusive thought but Talos pulled me back out. He had reached the middle of the rug, his feet firmly planted on a shield pierced with a purple sword. His irises already clouded in storm clouds. He slipped his hands in his pockets and raised his chin at a slight angle. The shadow of the morning hung at his cheekbones, darkening the stubble on his jaw. He took one step towards me but no more. He was setting the tone for the session. I would have to engage and try to anticipate his full attack. Not just rely on my defensive skills.

His eyes cast to a spot on the carpet near my feet and flicked his sight to mine, a heavy hummed sigh gave my skin a skittering jolt. Even several yards away, it was as if my skin was rising to meet the lingering expulsion of his breath. Hair at the back of my neck dancing as if his lips were only inches from the crook of my neck. A flickering pull dwelled behind my navel at the thought.

I closed my eyes to the room, feeling his essence press in all around me. The air thickened down my throat and into my lungs. I waited for the familiar darkening of the room around us before focusing on breaking the tie he was holding me with. A shadow behind my eyelids engrossed me but it wasn't his power.

"Ready or not," he whispered.

Talos had swiftly and silently moved to stand in front of me. I kept my eyes shut as he glided the back of one of his fingers down my arm. Each and every hair stood straight up in his digits wake. The sweet scent of peach blossoms filled the space around us. A warm and pleasant comfort bloomed at my chest as he rested his hand there. The sensation seeped into me and spread down to my fingers and toes. My shoulders slacked at the slip of his palm to the back of my neck to cup the base of my head. He pulled me in close and pressed his lips to mine. In a burst of light behind my eyelids, pleasure dipped from my belly, between my thighs and clutched my senses. Every nerve exploding in a symphony through a climax, then followed by another so intense my knees buckled.

He wrapped an arm around my waist as another wave of ecstasy rolled through me. I held my breath and bit my lip to hold in the solatous moan of his name caught behind my tongue. My fingernails dug into his shoulder, failing to assist in holding me up off the floor.

"I warned you, Isa. I could have you screaming in pleasure," he paused to allow yet another orgasm ebb, "and in anguish."

Searing, screaming, scorching pain split my skull from temple to temple. My cries of pleasure turned to shrieks of pain in only seconds. My eyes bolted open to see his lips forming a crooked and pleased grin. He dropped me to the floor and I writhed in the bone splitting agony. I yelled out to him to stop. Threatening to rip his manhood off with rusty knives.

"Break the tie, Isa, and you can do whatever you'd like with my manhood." He hummed a dark chuckle.

The gleam of the face of his watch caught my attention and I focused on the gem encrusted rim. The rubies inlaid at each number, and the rose gold of the wrist cuff. With each tick of the second hand, the grip of burning pressure released my head. The crushing of my bones lightened, and the air cleared of it's sour thickness. I pulled myself up to my hands and knees and waited for the weight of my torso to become familiar again to my limbs.

Talos extended his hand down to me, his elegant fingers gave a subtle encouraging twitch. I stood on my own. Swaying for a moment and taking a couple steps back from him. Anger and a flush of embarrassment brushed my cheeks while I watched him slip his hands into his pockets. He took a relaxed stance and waited for me to gather my emotions and thoughts.

"We are not that different, are we?" His voice echoing in my slumping consciousness. "We both have our ways of weaponizing pleasure for our own gain."

"The abilities you have are much different than my own." I said through labored breaths.

"Power can be taken. Skill can be learned. But to inveigle your opponent into giving over to their deepest sinful appetites," He prowled around me, dark brows shadowing his eyes, "that is a true gift."

"Is that how you justify your malevolent actions? You are solely gifted in torture so why waste it?"

"If this type of brutality causes you to hate me, then I will be preparing you to the fullest prowess." He watched me closely, waiting for me to work his intentions out.

I wanted to rip his throat out but knew that he felt this degree of severity was necessary after the attack on Althea's wedding day. However, something about these continued lessons was still bothering me now that we had moved Althea to the most secure Incubo residence in the country. His eyes had cleared of all clouds and he held an amused smile and devious glint on his brow. I readied myself for his next advance, palming a blade and rolling my shoulders to loosen the last remaining knots that his attack had caused.

"Why did you decided to continue training me? Althea is safe here and won't need me. Lawrence and his crew didn't walk out of that manor as far as we know."

He nodded knowingly and returned to his predatory circling around me.

"Fata militias are becoming restless after the attack in Arta. Small factions are gaining momentum and threatening the Incubo way of life. We are a sleepy giant but if poked too long, we will have to retaliate and that would mean we would need hired help to fill out our numbers. I'd trust you by my side in that war."

"And if the Banners refuse to be involved in such an altercation? We don't choose sides. Our skills go to the highest bidder." I quipped and mirrored his slow footsteps around the rug.

"Your organization will find that we have plenty of funds to acquire your services. No sides will have to be taken. Just fairly paid for in full. If you'd like your family to have an advantage, these lessons will give them that. It would have helped your dearly departed Banner."

My stomach churned at the thought of the Banner he had tortured in similar ways he had just done to me. Had he played with her in the same way? Had he thought to use her in the same way or had the thought to use Banners as personal guard dogs not come to him whilst taking her life?

Acid squelched the back of my throat and I shook the image

from my mind. He watched me, his wolf-like expression following each foot fall. "What did she tell you before you put a bullet through her skull?"

"That, my dear, is between her and I. A secret that has only been heard by me. I promised her that courtesy before I took her life."

My feet planted to the rug and my sight caught his. A fresh heat of anger flooded through me. I wanted to fulfill his family curse and plunge the alexandrite dagger into his heart. I wanted to twist and rip through his flesh until he bled the secrets he'd taken from my fellow Banner.

"The taste of your disdain for me is almost as enticing as your lust. Would you like to taste it? I could show you." He gave a cocky grin.

He took a step closer, his irises sinking into a pool of ink. "Ready for round two, Isa?"

He'd hardly gotten the last inflection of his question to pass his lips before the air in my lungs had begun to choke me. I gripped the dagger tighter, letting the ridges of the handle bite into my palm. I glanced down to the light reflecting off the jewel blade and the colors changing with each small tilt. I caught my own shadowed reflection in it and could almost feel a vibration of eagerness in my wrist.

I didn't wait for him to strike first this time, I leaped towards him and rolled when he moved out of the way, like I knew he would. I stretched my arm out and caught his calf with the tip of the blade. He stumbled with a limp out of the way and hissed in pain. He cursed and turned away which was his second mistake, I dove to his ankle and cut upwards catching the back of his thigh. Blood dampened his dark trousers and began to pool at the heel of his leather loafers.

"Enough!" Anger shot out towards me coupled with a sharp pain to my temple and chest.

My body writhed on the floor, my mind gridlocked in his

wake. I dropped the dagger and pressed my palms to my skull in the hopes that counterpressure would aid me. A scream broke through my clenched jaw and he released me. I laid heaving and waited for the blurred vision to clear. I may not have wounded him for long but I made my vivid point. I wasn't going to allow him to torture me in the name of training without striking back. The blurred figure of Talos sitting in a chair several feet away began to sharpen. His rage had subsided and he was pulling his pant leg up to examine the damage.

"I supposed I should have known you wouldn't be ready so quickly." He spoke out to the room, a bead of sweat trailing down the side of his face.

"Or perhaps you aren't the right instructor." I got to my hands and knees, slowly gaining strength to stand again.

He sat back and his shoulders shook with a spiteful amusement then wet his lips. "But I am enjoying it far more than Amil would. Watching your face shift from euphoria to anguish in a matter of a moment gives me such satisfaction."

"You're a sadistic asshole." I spat and sat back on my heels.

In an imperceptible swoop, he'd appeared kneeling in front of me, my face framed in his large hand. Onyx pools bore down to me, his expression not full of hate but a blend of malicious power and dangerous temptation.

"Is that what I am, Isa? Was I a sadistic asshole when you were begging me to fuck you?" His hot breath washed over my cheek with his vitriol comeback.

The stagnant air of the room became his vignette. I felt for the blade tucked into my boot holster, I slipped that think knife from its sheath and into my fingers but a wave of warm butterflies let loose down in the cradle of my hips overtook me.

"Am I still your villain when I can bring out this reaction from you?" A fox like grin crept over his face.

My lungs and thighs clenched, I was moments away from crashing over the edge again. He pulled my chin up and to the side, lightly caressing his pillowy lips down my neck to the nape. I gasped when he parted his lips and nibbled the tender skin, swirling his tongue on the spot then pulling away to lightly blow cool air. A chill shot through me and I crashed into ecstasy. I moaned loudly and he smiled darkly, relishing his effect on my body.

He released me. My muscles laxed in the ebbing release. I was lightheaded but tracked his movements around me. His predatory circling started once again, priming himself for another attack. Not giving away if it would be more pleasure, or pain. My breathing hadn't fully returned to normal before he began again, this time my skin scorched. Sweat seemed to be boiling as it prickled up on every surface of my body. I jumped to my feet and let loose the blade I had tucked into my palm. He pulled his shoulder back, twisting at the torso so the blade would miss completely. It stuck out from the wood panel wall behind him.

I'd broken his concentration and attack. I rushed towards him to hook around his waist; knocking the wind from him and taking him to the ground. I sat on his chest and pinned his neck with one knee. The other dug into the nerve of his shoulder to cause him sharp pain if he chose to move. I detached a blade from my hip and pressed the edge to his cheek right below his eye.

His chest heaved under my weight, raising me slightly with each labored inhale. My own ragged breathing falling into his cadence.

Another sly grin broke over his features, *"Meravigliosa,"* he was satisfied with the progress of our last spar.

CHAPTER SIXTEEN

Talos was called away to oversee a meeting of the staff that would be hired to protect the Incubo who would be arriving for the funeral leaving me to wander back to my room on my own. When I got there a cart with a coffee carafe and breakfast was waiting for me. I wheeled it in and showered. Talos' scent still pungently clinging to my skin and hair. He had told me that he would had the ability to cause me great pain and had shown me before, but his hinting at being able to create pure pleasure without touching me felt like a bluff. That was until he showed me. Shame and embarrassment seeped into my core. Pleasure shouldn't be a vulnerability faced in a fight for my life.

The way he had such ease slipping into the role of punishing teacher didn't feel foreign to other personas I had seen him take on. The dutiful protector. The cunning killer. The diplomat. The lover. Each a different facet of his being that shifted at his will seamlessly. Blending together at times to create a new monster ready to strike in an instant. In a way I respected the way he could move through his repertoire of personalities to suit his need. It made him unpredictable to everyone, not just me. He was a powerful being without it, but it made him into a dark and twisty cruelty for anyone he saw fit to unleash himself on. A molten kernel of excitement nagged at my middle at the thought.

A knock on my door shook the thoughts of Talos from my eyes, and I thankfully hopped up to answer it. Althea stood in the hall. Her eyes stormy and raw. She looked as if she had been sobbing for hours. I stood aside and let her into the room. She was unescorted to my surprise.

I followed her over to the seating area but she didn't sit. Instead she paced the floor in front of the fireplace. Her high heeled shoes deadened by the rug.

"Althea, are you alright?" I knew the answer, but willed her to explain.

"They're terrible. Horrid. Vile snakes." She hissed, bringing herself to a stop and looking down to where I sat.

"Who are?"

"My great aunt and uncle. They went on and on about how they had heard the wedding was lovely up until the shots were being fired." She huffed.

I blinked, unable to grasp why anyone would say these things to her.

"They blamed Neil for not being prepared or able to protect everyone there. Said that if he were a more fit liege, he would have had armed guards in every corner."

"It is much easier to talk ill of the mistakes made in hind-sight. No one could have dreamed that the wedding would have been the target for an attack. Talos himself didn't expect it." I forced an assuring tone, trying to calm her mind.

"Talos should have known." Tears welled and her voice strained against the words.

"He knew something was going on but he hadn't fully shared what he knew with me. When he hired me, it seemed that he thought another Incubo was behind the threat. Obviously, that wasn't the case."

I had suspicions that this wasn't the full truth. Their union was vocally opposed by their own kind and Talos had equipped me with a weapon to fend off Incubo. I had the feeling that plans had been made by Incubo to stop Althea's wedding but Lawrence and his Fata rebels engaged first.

I walked to the forgotten breakfast cart and poured myself a cup of coffee and one for Althea. I offered it to her and she took it in both hands but didn't bring the lip up to her mouth. She looked down into the dark liquid mirroring the shade over her eyes.

"Will you teach me how to fight?"

I practically spit out my coffee at her question. "You want me to teach you? Wouldn't another Incubo be better equipped for that? With your abilities, I wouldn't even know where to start."

"Start with the very basics." She sat down and scooted to the edge of her chair, "I don't want to be vulnerable like I was at the wedd— at the manor."

Her face fell at the haunting memory.

"Okay. But we are going to need help." My voice penetrated the gloom surrounding her and brought her back from the hell she was reliving.

"From who?" She asked, her tone shallow.

"Another Incubo will know how best to help you and Amil as been a good teacher to me in the past."

She sat with the idea silently for a moment. Turning it over in her mind to examine all its parts and what that scenario would look like. Amil and Yamir had been employed by Talos for years and she had known them for just as long. She had known each of them familiarly enough to warn me of Amil's past with other Mortals but held no ill will towards him for his past discrepancies.

"I'm sure he would be happy to help." I assured her and the

corner of her mouth pulled up, unsure but willing to try. "In the meantime. I'm going to show you how to hold a blade."

I went to my bedside table and took out a small dagger that I often concealed in my boot. It would fit in her palm well enough to get familiar with the weight of it on her wrist. I unsheathed it and passed it to her gently. She held it in her delicate hand and turned it over to examine the sharp edges. Her hazy eyes meeting mine when she was ready for the first instruction.

"Alright, before we start I am going to warn you that no matter how long and hard you train, when the moment comes that you feel like you need to defend yourself, you will forget everything I am going to say." I reached for the Alexandrite dagger and held it out, showing her how I held the hilt.

"You will rely on your instincts. Your blade will become an extension of your body. Lethal and determined." I rotated my wrist, my fingers finding their home on the handle.

She mimicked my hand motions and watched intently.

"When you want to wound but not kill, there are plenty of areas to aim for." I pointed to my largest muscles groups first, then moved to sensitive areas that would slow someone down from surprise and pain. Upper thighs, upper arms, hips and chest.

I held my arm out and made exaggerated slow slashing movements. Then indicated to her to follow the lead. She caught on quickly and held the knife firmly, repeating the movements.

"Great, now I'm going to show you how to disarm someone."

I positioned her hands up, blade planted in her fist.

"Okay. Come at me."

She gave me a look that asked if I was sure, I nodded and she took a few short steps into my reach. I gripped her wrist and twisted up and around, guiding her to the ground on her back. Even with gently pressure she whimpered in pain and surprise.

"I need to know how to do that." She smiled and stood up ready for the next part of the lesson.

I sheathed my dagger and held in a offensive stance. I talked her through the grip and twist, allowing her to maneuver my body and become familiar with how her muscles reacted to the attack.

"That was good. Now lets try again but faster and harder." I got back into position for her.

She nodded, determination hard on her face. When she grabbed my wrist, she didn't hesitate to twist and pull me to the ground. Whether it was anger or pain fueling her motives, she was learning quickly. After several more times practicing, I began to resist her a little more with each new try. She was strong. Not as strong as Talos or Amil, but she was still Incubo and that natural strength they held was evident with each courageous strike.

After about an hour, we sat and rested. The dagger I had lent her sat in her lap as we caught our breath and sipped our water.

"You'll be able to defend yourself easily in no time. You're a natural."

She blushed at my compliment and set down her glass. "Well, I do have the advantage of learning from a Black Banner."

"True." I giggled.

She looked down to the blade and held her hand above it. Focus and shadows veiled her as the knife trembled in her lap. It lifted slowly, hovering just above her legs and rotated counterclockwise. It shook and her jaw clenched. A bead of sweat trailing down the side of her face. She let out a grunt and the blade flew across the room and impaled into the door of the bathroom.

Her mouth gapped open and her eyes cleared. An proud smile broke over her face and she looked to me.

"That was incredible!" I got up and retrieved the knife, passing it back to her. "Can you do it again?"

"I can try."

She held the knife out in her palm out in front of her. Focusing on it intently, but it did not rise from where it sat. My shoulders fell slightly and I reached out to her knee but before I could make contact, she pulled her hand down and the dagger was frozen in place. Suspended out in front of us. It didn't quake or move as it had before. She let out a concentrated breath and the blade went flying again, making another hole only a few inches from where it had before.

She bounced up and down in her seat, giddy with her accomplishment. "I can't believe I did that! It's taken me years to simply move a tea cup."

It was as if the sun had chased away a storm when she smiled like that. Pride filling her up to the brim. As much as it was a moment of strength and skill, it was a sign that she was much more strong willed than she had known. She had survived the attack in one piece but it had broken a part of her soul that would likely never fuse back together. Perhaps that crack to the pristine interior liberated a vehemence to more than just survive. She would no longer be reliant on others for protection.

"I should go clean up. I have to meet with the Queen and go over funeral plans." She said, passing the blade back to me.

I held my hand up, "Keep it." I stood and found the sheath and handed it to her.

She smiled and held the concealed weapon to her chest. "Thank you, Isa."

AFTER ALTHEA LEFT, I TOOK IT UPON MYSELF TO BECOME familiar with the Chateau. There were four stories above ground, and what I assumed to be a basement. I started at the staircase of the guest wing and climbed my way up to the top floor. This was where the several galleries lined with priceless art and antiques. Glass domes over extravagant gemstone necklaces, and earrings. In one gallery, the walls were lined with over a dozen monuments dedicated to past royal family members. Stones the size of figs placed at the center of tiaras and crowns sat on satin pillows. The past owners' portraits hung on the walls behind each one.

I walked along them noting how the styles had changed over the centuries. Some were simpler than others, only crowns of golden leaves woven intricately with ruby or diamond in the shape of flowers or olives. One of the oldest was crudely made, the gold was unpolished and thick and absent of precision stones. The imagines of the previous owners were also diminished and tarnished. The age worn edges yellowed and pain peeled away, but they shared one thing that every other subject did. Their eyes pitch-black.

When I had my fill of the galleries on the top floor, I went down to the second floor. In the east wing, a grand ballroom took up most of the floor. The west wing was taken up by parlors and offices. It seemed that many of the offices were in use but the inhabitants were busy with other matters. I passed by several offices before I reached one that wasn't empty.

Amil sat behind a large solid wood desk, his chestnut waves falling down his brow as he leaned over a stack of papers in a manila folder. He fiddled an inkwell pen back and forth in one hand and rested his chin on the other. The strain of focus created lines on his handsome face as he poured over the pages. If I called his name, he would break the surface of his thoughts and come back to the present, but something about the way he had engrossed himself in his work fascinated me. This was a side of him I hadn't experienced before. There were many parts of Amil I hadn't seen and possibly never would see after Argo was returned to me.

The bitter taste of that thought dried my mouth and dipped

into my stomach. I could reach out to him and chase away that discomfort. Run my fingers through his locks and kiss his lips. He would make promises that neither of us knew if he could keep. We would embrace long enough to block the rest of the world out. With one touch he could ease my worries and pains. It would have been a selfish reprieve that he would graciously offer.

I was lost in those thoughts when the sound of Talos clearing his voice came from behind me. He pulled open Amil's office door completely and waved the way for me to enter into the office before him. Amil's eyes shot up to the both of us in wonderment.

"Good, you're both here." Talos said, laying a brief case onto Amil's desk.

Amil wordlessly stood and rounded the desk to Talos' side. I stood on the other side of Talos and watched him open the case and pull out a gun, a bag of used rounds, and a full clip. Setting each item on the table then waited for us to take in the sight.

"Yamir brought these back from the Welp manor." He explained as he thumbed out a round from the magazine into our palms, then held one out in front of himself.

A dazzling gem sat at the tip of the shell. The ammunition was both beautiful and deadly. I had never liked the feel and cold distance of guns. The weight of them cumbersome on missions, and hard to conceal in scant clothing. I had to admire the craftsmanship of these bullets, they could have been mistaken for jewelry.

"Where did Lawrence get this technology?" I asked, still admiring the lethal gem in my hand.

Amil held up the bullet between his thumb and forefinger, sun passing through and casting purple and green light across the table.

"I have an inkling but no confirmation yet. One thing is for sure, whoever is responsible had privileged information and this conflict has now elevated to a lever in which we may not escape without many more casualties than we have already seen." He replied.

"Someone went to great lengths to start this war and equipped Lawrence with what he needed to cause panic and great deaths." I added. "He knows more than what he offered to me."

"He would have told you more if you would have agreed to join his ranks." Talos said, picking up a spent casing.

"Next time, I'll be sure to comply so that I can gather more intel." I quipped back.

Amil grinned to himself, staying out of my and Talos' squabble. Probably the safest place for him to be.

"The sniper rounds were more proficient than their hand funds. Yamir found several discarded guns that had jammed when the alexandrite broke to pieces in the chambers. As brilliant as the concept is, I believe the wedding was part of their prototype process in mass manufacturing." Talos continued, ignoring my comment.

Amil rolled a bullet between his fingers then stopped to read a marking on the underside of the casing. "This is from Hadera, look here," he pointed our focus to the symbol on our own bullets, "that is the seal of a mid level precious stone mining company just outside my fathers province."

"That would explain how they were able to get their hands on so much Alexandrite to process the rounds. It's been difficult to track the supply chain. They are minding the stones then smuggling them out of Hadera to be processed elsewhere. They are likely taking them to Meru before bringing them through Chora." Talos spoke as if he would figure out the chain of supply before our eyes. He was likely not far off from the bullet's origin, but there would still need to be verification to be able to stop the influx of ammunition on the criminal market.

"What will you do next?" I asked, adding a couple more

bullets to my palm to inspect next to one another.

"The mines will have to be locked down to raise the value of precious metals and stones high enough to entice Fata and Mortals to sell their inventory to Incubo who will pay a high price to get it in our hands. This will limit the amount of Alexandrite in circulation long enough to find the munitions manufacturer and see to it that they forget how to produce this particular ammo." He finished, lost in his own thoughts.

"I should go in person." Amil's voice brought Talos out of himself.

My eyes shot to Amil but he avoided my cold gaze. We may have not spoken since the train, but I didn't want him to leave. I shifted my weight from one foot to the other, words clamoring through my thoughts but falling short behind my lips. I looked between him and Talos, who was still calculating the way his actions would put a stop to the killings.

"I need you here," he finally looked to Amil, "I have a much more important mission for you and Yamir when the time comes."

The worry on Amil's brow was not lifted by this response, "You're sure?"

Talos turns his full attention to Amil before his tone sank into one of admiration and beseechment, "*Émpistos aderfós*, you and Yamir are the only men I can trust with this critical task and until the time comes, I ask that you stay close and prepared to leave at a moment's notice."

Amil pursed his lips and nodded in begrudging agreement. These would be the matters Amil would have to parse if he were to take his fathers place in their lordship in their country. He had the responsibility to his family and lands to find the Fata who were buy the minded deadly gems for mass murder, but he had pledged his loyalty to Talos and the King and Queen of Chora. He'd taken his position without the threat of rebels overturning hundreds of years of, what looked to be, peace.

CHAPTER SEVENTEEN

Several hours after Talos and I finished training I had cleaned myself up and started getting ready for the funeral processions that were being held at the Chateau. I didn't doubt that I would be sore and bruised from going several rounds with Talos but his minor wounds would be healed before he finished bathing and dressing. I was envious of that particular Incubo blessing. Among the ability to strum Mortal emotions and play them like a harp to a tune that suited an Incubo's every wish, their strength and agility were also useful defenses. Althea had told me that some gifts were sparsely distributed, like her ability to move items with her mind. Or

Dinner had been delivered to my room but I was only slightly hungry. Eating the roasted tomato soup, rich with spices and cream with a side of fresh roasted garlic sourdough rolls. It was a slight comfort from my sore muscles and pounding headache.

Many of my bruises and cuts had healed over the course of the last few days, but my deeper lacerations were still tender. The marks on my body from battle and escaping mingling with new torn ligaments and sprained tendons from charging through the empty building looking for Argo. I went to my luggage and chose the most mournful clothing, which turned out to be a black and grey turtleneck cord knit sweater and black tapered jeans. I would likely be the most underdressed being in the Chateau but I would be rather invisible. Being the only Mortal amongst the invited would have me standing out well enough.

I finished getting ready and attached several throwing blades inconspicuously to my hip and made to meet Althea down in the receiving room. When I opened the door Amil was standing on the other side, his arm raised as if he was about to knock.

He was dressed in an all black suit and undershirt, maroon filigree embroidered at his cuffs and lapels. A matching handkerchief tucked into his breast pocket. Every bit of him primped and primed. Not a hair out of place on his head, and his five o'clock shadow closer to a short cropped beard.

His eyes roamed over me then behind me. "When are you leaving?"

He must not have heard that we didn't find Argo. I realize he must have been looking for signs that I was packing my things to travel back to Cinder.

"Not for a while. Argo is still being held captive. Talos is going to track the bastards down, but until then I'll be staying close by and training."

He absorbed the update, a somber look dawned his strong features. His jaw tightened a moment before he spoke again, "Can we talk a moment before, what I'm sure to be, a very draining event starts downstairs?"

I stepped aside to let him in the room. He walked to the center between the two sitting chairs in front of the fireplace and the four poster-bed. I shut the door and took a few steps closer but kept the distance between us broad.

"What is it?" I crossed my arms and waited.

"I wanted to apologize for the way I behaved on the train. It was selfish of me to ask so much of you in your vulnerable position. Talos spoke lightheartedly about it, but I know your anger towards me is valid. But you have to understand that I can't allow anything to happen to you."

"What does that mean, Amil?" I rolled my eyes, already annoyed with where this conversation seemed to be going.

"Isa, I can't explain it fully. Not in a way you would understand, but I need to take care of you. I need to be by your side in this fight."

"More cryptic Incubo deep rooted emotions that I wouldn't possibly understand? My fragil Mortal brain could not comprehend the amount of feelings you possess." Annoyance was flushing my face.

"You say that as if you don't have first hand knowledge of what I feel for you. This is complicated but being here has amplified this… instinct to protect you. This unbearable shredding of my soul knowing that I can't be the one who grants you with what you need so you can leave this place. Fuck, Isa, it's killing me!" He turned away from me, tussling his hair.

"My brother is likely being tortured for information, starved and beaten for any scrap they can pry out of him and you are expecting me to fall to my knees and put all my trust in you to find him and the sons of bitches holding him because *you* feel awful? No, Amil. I can't grant you that relief. I don't owe you anything. I don't owe you any forgiveness for the bullheadedness you've shown me in the last few days."

He didn't turn around, he hung his head as I spoke but didn't turn to face me. I knew I had hurt him. He'd shown me a glimpse of how deeply Incubo felt when they felt a connection with another being. He'd try to help me understand. But treating me as an incompetent child was not sitting right and an itch in my palm was begging for a throwning knife to remind him how deadly I was on my own.

"I can feel disdain brewing in you, Isa. Don't you think I know how absurd I sound in trying to convince a Black Banner to allow me to become a line of protection for them? The insanity I'm experiencing is galling but I can't walk away, the fear of losing you is all consuming ."

"What do you want from me, Amil? I don't need you or your help. I don't need your pity or affection. Our training sessions were just that. Training."

"Don't push me away. I can feel your anger but know you don't mean that." He finally turned around, a stony look in his eyes.

Anger was bubbling to the surface, I may not have fully meant the words I was saying but I also couldn't give him what he wanted or needed.

"You are forcing my hand. I don't need a watchdog or a babysitter."

"Did you expect me to fade into the night after our assignment was over? Did you think I would walk away in silence?" He eased the space between us, the clouds of his eyes turning dark. I waited for the familiar spark to flicker to life but it was nowhere to be seen. A heartbreaking mix of anger and desperation hung on his face.

"I didn't think about it." I lied, I had thought about it. Or at least I had tried not to think about how much I would miss him.

"Well, I did. Every second we were together, I agonized over the moment I would lose you. And when I walked into the suite, and Lawrence had his hands around your throat. The look of death on your face—" Rage spilled into his tone, "I wanted to rip my own beating heart out of my chest to allow you to live long enough for me to meet you on the other side of all of this."

He let out a heavy sigh, sagging his shoulders in a reminder of relief, "From the moment you took a free breath, I knew I could never lose you again. I can't allow anything to happen to you. I would not survive losing you."

He reached out and held my hand in his palm, brushing his thumb over the top of my fingers. Tears welled in my eyes and my throat tightened at the visualization of what he had seen when he, Talos, and Althea had burst into the room to find my body lifeless beneath Lawrence. The guilt he was holding on to that I had been so close to death and he hadn't been there to save me. That I had leaped out of a window rather than stay in the safety of the library with the three of them. The mess of emotions he had felt flowed from his hand into mine, up my arm and created a pit in my chest. The gapping exposed nerves that were my own complicated feelings became my exchange.

I knew that at some point I would have to come to terms with these feelings I held for Amil and Talos. But in this moment, the only thing I could comprehend was that Amil was standing in front of me offering me his whole self and I didn't know how I would be able to accept anything. A twitch of the muscles at his throat bobbed the angular notch as he swallowed down the taste of my confusion and something like gratitude that he would not only kill for me, but die just to be laid by my side.

He pulled me into an embrace, wrapping his arms around the tops of my shoulders, lips grazing my temple and top of my ear. He inhaled me deeply and relaxed his muscles that had been full of tension. I slid my hands up his back and took handfuls of his jacked, burying my face in the crease of his chest and strong arm. Breathing him in, appreciating the sweet persimmon and bergamot.

"*Hayaat hayaati.*" He pulled away to look me in the eye, the warm flicker finally peeking through his dark eyes. "I've never been more certain than I am right now, Isa. You're what I have been looking for each day that I have been breathing. A part of myself that has been missing."

I had no words to exchange but slid my hands up and fanned my fingers to the back of his neck. Weaving my fingers through his soft waves, a merciful nudge to bring his lips to mine. I opened up completely to him. Let every convoluted emotion burst open and flow to him. A palm to my lower back bringing our hips together, another to the nape of my neck as the kiss deepened. A tangible push of force from him in response, warmth and safety melting away the anxiety and desolation from the last couple days freeing from my body. A rush of butterflies to my stomach. A new ache low in my belly called out to him unashamed.

If there was one thing I was most sure of, it was that with Amil, I didn't have to be abashed for having needs for him. However raw and unexamined these thoughts and feelings were, he wanted them all. He wanted me. The simplicity of it terrified me more than being thrown into a fight without a weapon. I was more naked and bare when my guard was down around him than in any stranger's bed.

The heat between us grew as lips and tongues caressed over and over. Hands and harms pulling at the other, willing clothing to fall away. He backed me to the foot of the bed and sat me down and looked down to me, his chest heaving in anticipation. I drug my eyes up from his face, down his well tailored suit and the front of his slacks tight against him. I knew the look on his face well at this point. That type of familiarity was rare for me, but I couldn't mistake it for anything but lust. Hunger. Need.

Our eyes met again and we each waited. Watching the other for the first move to the hem of a shirt, a button to slacks or jeans but instead we heard the chime of the clock near the door. It was time for the ceremony to start, mourners would be filing in from outside and heading to the gallery. None would pass this corordoor but we were both expected to be in our places already.

He looked to the clock and took a deep breath. He pitched the bridge of his nose and shut his eyes tight, crinkling their edges. I sighed and he leaned down and kissed my brow. Taking my chin between his thumb and forefinger, lifting it to meet him, "We'll finish this later."

My stomach gave a leap and I wished desperately for the next several hours to end quickly. He ran his hands through his hair and straightened his fine suit and then offered me his hand.

We walked together down the cool marble staircase to the first landing where Althea was standing alone. She was gazing out over the railing to the surf of incoming Incubo, although she seemed to be looking through them and not at anyone in particular.

"Althea?" I pulled her away from within herself.

"Hmm?"

"Amil and I are going to walk down with you, is that alright?"

She nodded but her eyes still seemed to be void of what was happening around her. I could only imagine she was feeling numb and put on display for all to gawk at during what would surely be one of her most painful days.

Amil and I stayed one step behind her on our descent. At the foot of the stairs, Talos swooped in and offered his arm to Althea. He acknowledged Amil with a dip of his chin, then slid a dry glance to me. My jaw tightened, and I straightened my spine. I was sore from our training but my ego was more bruised than any other part of me. He'd caught me off guard, tore my to pieces, and left me questioning everything. The image of him standing over me, my own throwing blade cutting into my ribs rushed to the forefront of my mind.

"Isa." He greeted, "I hope you're well rested after our games earlier. You'll need your strength for this event."

I didn't answer but quickly looked around the open foyer. I hadn't thought about the amount of Incubo that would be gathering at the Chateau. I was under the impression that like most other events, I would be tucked into the background. Merely an ornament for Althea's comfort and protection. But several Incubo passed by and each of their smoke filled eyes traveled over me, pausing at my face. Likely noticing that I was the only Mortal present. A realization I was just coming to myself.

"I believe after the workout you gave me earlier, I'm well prepared for anything anyone here would throw at me." I lifted my chin and pulled my shoulders back. I was ready but I was also armed and wouldn't hesitate to draw blood if I needed. I had had enough Incubo torture for one day.

His brows lifted and he tipped his head to me, "It was a pleasure to assist you in that."

I narrowed my eyes to him.

"If only looks could kill." He chuckled then moved Althea into the crowd, weaving through the throngs towards the large archway at the end of the corridor. Amil laid his hand to the small of my back and gave an encouraging nudge. He walked closer than he normally would, unworried that these visitors would get the wrong impression of me being tucked into his side. Grey, charcoal, and ash glances followed us at every step. If he was at all miffed by the attention, he didn't show it. Amil's strong frame shadowed me, daring anyone to question my reason for being there.

We approached the archway where Talos and Althea had entered to find the Prince Vassilis greeting every guest. He was dressed in a light grey suit with a deep purple dress shirt and pocket square, a complement to his golden brown skin. His cheeks dusted with gold highlighting which drew out the sandy smoke of his eyes. He exuded a regal presence, each Incubo that passed bowed their heads to him and graciously accepted his words. Hanging on his every word until he relinquished them.

Not one bit of him could be mistaken for anything other than royalty. When we came upon me his face lit up in merry surprise.

"Isa! We are greatly honored to have you with us still. I was worried we wouldn't see you after your outing yesterday. I would like it very much if you would join me for a nightcap after the ceremony." His eyes moved to Amil, "That is, if Amil doesn't mind sharing you?" His gold adorned ears perked at the sound of Amil's deep voice.

"My Prince, Isa is more than capable of making that discussion on her own." Amil volleyed back.

"I wager she is." He gave a telling grin and brought focus back to me and waited for my reply with a rise of his brow.

"That would be lovely." I mustered a kind smile.

"Excellent, I will send for you tonight. Eight o'clock?" He said, his voice slick with delight that didn't match the tone of the rest of the room.

I nodded and Amil and I moved on for the Prince to continue his duties. Amil led me towards the back of the room, veering away from the center of the great hall. The impressive space was empty of furniture, not a table or chair obstructed the floor. Incubo dressed in black and white floated around with trays of wine and glass bottles of water. It was unlike any funeral I had attended. The guests all dressed in a range of casual to ball gowns and three-piece suits. There didn't seem to be a fashion expectation for this soirée.

There was a raised platform at the back of the hall where the King and Queen were being presented to guests. The graciously inclined their heads to each Incubo who approached them. They were both dressed in midnight blue. The Queen's dress hugged her curves and the moon of her swollen belly. The floor length gown brushed the top of her matte black high heeled shoes. The King's suit mirrored his wife's attire by way of black matte dress shirt, pocket square, and shoes. As if you would look upon them and not realize they were vastly more important than anyone else in the room, they each wore a crown of gold and sapphire.

The crowns themselves weren't gaudy, the subtle haloes looked in their proper places. The Queens crown sat nestled in her tight black curls, peaks of oval sapphires were separated by diamond encrusted crocheted arches. The King's crown didn't hold any gem but the sapphires. A band of gold sat atop the tips of his peaks creating a more dramatic effect.

Behind them stood several rows of podiums. Wooden boxes sat on top of each one with a photo propped up against them. There were dozens and dozens of wooden graves memorializing each fallen Incubo. I was expecting the remains to be cared for after the ceremony and the sight of so many faces of the dead staring out over the crown became unsettling. I had to squint to distinguish where one row ended and another started. They were so densely layered.

Amil stepped into my line of sight, his hand to my chin to get my full attention. "I have to circulate. Don't stab anyone while I'm gone." He offered me a crooked smile.

"I'll do my best." I teased back.

He leaned down and feathered a kiss. *"Nour 'yooni."* whisper against my lips and he was gone, leaving me with butterflies.

A scanned the crowd and caught sight of Talos standing with a group of Incubo, a remorseful expression drawn on his face. Althea stood glued to his side, her arm at the crook of his arm. Her misty eyes filled with tears and sorrow as another guest expressed their condolences. This would be her role for the rest of the day, the grieving widow. The remaining member of her bloodline.

"My heart is breaking for her." Came a sultry voice from behind me.

Anisa loomed at my side, I hadn't heard her approach. Her gold strapped heels hadn't made a sound on the marble floor.

She was wearing a feminine pantsuit, the black wide-legged pants stopped mid-calf. Her white silk blouse open in a plunging V, a large canary diamond dangling from small silver links.

"She's stronger than she knows." I assured her. Althea was heartbroken, and in great pain. But she was much more than she appeared.

"I hope you're right. Much is expected of her now that her father is gone and the Welp's estate and title will be passed to her. She will have to be loud enough to speak over anyone who intends to oppose her authority." She took a long sip of a glass of red wine.

I didn't reply, I knew nothing of their hierarchy. From what I understood thus far, the Incubo royal family poses as land and business owners who tend to control how many other businesses in their chain operate. They held great wealth and power in their communities which influenced Fata and Mortal lives. The rest of us were unaware of their titles or customs.

"I hope you understand that your time here, the events you are about to witness are sacred. No other Mortal has seen these practices done in over a hundred years. It would be wise to keep it that way." Her tone was casual but I caught her subtle venomous threat.

"I'm grateful to be able to be here for my friend and offer her comfort. Your rituals are as safe as if I weren't here."

She gave me a sideways glance and a sceptical look, "Enjoy the show, Banner."

She didn't wait for me to reply. Her figure weaved through the crowd up to the platform with her sister and the King. When she faced the onslaught of beings, the room grew silent. The King stepped forward and his voice projected out to every corner and every ear.

"*Oikogéneia*. It is my deepest regret to be standing here and to behold so many of our loved ones missing. Each and every one of us has faced great loss but we must stand united through any threat. We will not allow fear and misguided actions banish us into darkness." He surveyed the room, a somber look hung on his brow.

He gestured towards Althea, holding out his hand to invite her up onto the stage with him. "Our dearest Lady Althea of Cinder now faces great responsibility and action. I expect that she is met with kindness and good nature." He turned slightly and addressed Althea but did not lower his volume, "Lady Althea, you have the entire court's heart. You will not wish for anything in your time of grief and cohesion. Your resilience will be the cornerstone to building your fortress* of strength. Allow Queen *name and myself to be your pillars of strength, and your people be your pride and inspiration/motivation."

The King gave Althea a bow of his head, and she mimicked. He held her hand up and the room and the words were spoken in subdued unison, "May we only separated by ash and gold."

Anisa turned to the first podium and retrieved the wooden box, presenting it to Althea with muted words. Althea lowered her eyes and the Queen stepped forward between her sister and Althea, opening the lid to the capsule and retrieved a tiara. She held it out and spoke loudly to those observing.

"With this last gift, your fallen will be with you until you join them. In ash and gold. I present you the remains of your father, Lord Pytr *last name* of Cinder. Guardian of Chora. In his last will and testament, he designated that his bones be presented to you in a gift befit a princess. He wished these words be his last message to you:

I kóri mou, my dearest treasure. My only wish for you is to fulfill your hearts desire and to carry me with you always. The ash of my bones melded into an adornment that is only enhanced by your beauty. A ruby for each year I was blessed to be your father. For your, my child, a figure of my undying love and admiration."

The Queen placed the tiara on Althea's head and waited for

her to meet eyes before continuing, "May you find comfort in his lasting presence." She offered Althea a warm smile, one a mother would give their child to bring them strength and comfort.

A tear fell from Althea's watery eye, she did not speak but turned to her audience. Her head held high and shoulders awaiting to bare the weight of all that was expected of her. My friend's face held sadness but also ferocity. She had lost her everything and she would not allow that loss to be presented as weakness. Not to a crowd who would be looking to her for assurance in the coming future of their kinds place in this world.

Anisa returned Pytr's box to his podium and retrieved another from the second podium. She opened the lip and addressed Althea herself. Her voice sweet and kind like the night we had arrived, "This last gift is being presented on behalf of Lord Cornelius Welp of Arta. He had not had an up to date of last wishes but as his lawful wife and predecessor to his estate, it was our duty to present his remains to you."

Althea peered into the box and took a deep breath before reaching inside. Another river of tears streamed down her cheeks and fell to the ground. She pulled a necklace. A gold chain and a pink stone pendant. The gem was easily half the size of her palm, surrounded by white diamonds in the shape of a heart. A sweet momento of her lost love. She turned to the Queen who held her hands out to accept the trinket and assist her in putting it around her neck. Again, she faced the crowd and pulled her chin up with grace, allowing the Queen to pull her hair to the side and laying the large stone to her chest. When the necklace was clasped, the Queen placed her hands on Althea's shoulders a moment then stepped back.

The guests clapped and whispers crept through the room. I did not clap, I only watched as mist, and ash eyes passed looks of suspicion or pity to one another. Talos approached the foot of the stage and bowed deeply before the King and Queen. He inclined his head to Anisa, then offered Althea his hand. The both of them moved to the far edge of the stage and the King began calling Incubo from the awaiting hoard to be presented gifts from falling loved ones.

Broaches, bracelets, necklaces, wristwatches, rings, and even an inkwell pen were all among the items passed from the King and Queen to next of kin. Some, like Pytr, had last will and testament statements. But many did not. These deaths were not anticipated, the planning that had gone into these gifts must have been done quickly after the bodies had been retrieved from the manor.

Amil appeared back at my side sometime into the lengthy ceremony. We stood in solemn silence as box after box was emptied and the remains were presented. A numbing sensation had taken me over, a shell of myself stood in my shoes as hours passed. When the final boxes had been opened and the gilded remains had been distributed to their next of kin, the hall began to buzz with low conversations.

The gawking of items was exchanged before moving on to a new cluster of admirers. Amil pressed his hand to the base of my spine and leaned down to my ear, "I can't wait to be done with this plodding ceremony so that I can take you to bed and devour every part of you." He slipped his hand down my back to my rear and gave a playful squeeze.

I spun around, pressing my hip to his, and looping my arm up his bicep. Our eyes met and no words had to be exchanged. A shock of warmth passed over me, a wash of contentment. The tumult around us dulled, leaving only a muddled ocean of voices beyond his blaring gaze.

"Eh-hem", a voice broke our heated enthrallment. It was Talos.

"Isa, could I have a word before you turn in for the evening?" He continued, dismissing Amil with a nod.

I turned to face him, my eyes immediately connected with his concern expression. "What's wrong?"

I looked around for Althea, and spied her chatting with Anisa near a refreshment table. Talos had followed my line of sight before continuing with his statement, "She has asked for you to stay longer but I have more pressing matters to discuss with you. Prince Vasilis says he is keen to meet with you later this evening. It would do well to find an excuse to resend that invitation."

"What reason would I have to insult the Prince of the Chora Incubo? For your comfort? Worried I might let something slip?" I was egging him on, but after the mornings training session I felt like I owed him a bit of ultion.

"Now isn't the time to give me your cheek. Prince Vasilis has ways of digging for information he could use to keep you in his pocket."

"I'd be interested in the type of dirt he has found on me or the Banners." I said smugness marked on my face.

I wasn't concerned about what Prince Vasilis thought he had on the Black Banners. He wouldn't be able to find our organization's strongholds to confirm anything. It would be more beneficial to me to hear what the Prince may have gotten out of whoever he had in his pocket.

"Obviously, our session earlier is clouding your judgement. I am not your enemy, Isa. I only want to arm you to the teeth with a skill you need to wield against Incubo like the Prince. Do not let his friendly demeanor draw you into a false sense of comfort. His game is much more advanced than you give him credit for."

"I'm not the one who tends to underestimate others, Talos."

He seemed to be wounded by that shot to his character. He straightened his jacket and looked me over. The smoke of his eyes shifting from storm grey to a hazy ocean grey, "Rest well, Isa. Tomorrow's training will be just as rigorous as this morning and I will not give you any leeway for overconsumption."

With that he walked back into the assemblage. I took my leave before being cornered by anyone else. I followed behind a group of guests out into the corridor, and headed out towards the large staircase but was stopped by an Incubo I had hoped I would see again soon.

CHAPTER EIGHTEEN

Yamir approached me from the shadows of the marble pillar, I was sure he had been dead when we left the manor. I don't know how he got out of there alive and likewise how he ended up here at the Incubo Kings palace.

"Hello again old friend," he said in an unexpectedly kind voice.

"How—"

"You underestimate my skills," he gave me a playful wink, "I'm insulted."

He smiled and clasped his hands behind his back. The gold flecks in his clouded eyes danced, amused by my surprise. Footsteps down the hall of the bustling funeral guests shuffled from the banquet hall to the lounge. I eased the space between us and we lessened the volume of our conversation. Those in mourning didn't need to hear how another Incubo escaped the wedding attack but their loved one didn't.

"I waited until the four of you had gone into the manor, then cut down anyone in my path. I waited on the first floor until night had fallen and I heard the breaking of a window from a few floors up. I moved to the second floor and took out as many

137

that crossed my path as I could, moving any other survivors to the stables to wait until you, Talos, and Amil had cleared the rest." His spoke as if we had been working together the entire time.

"After the four of you escaped, I was able to organize the survivors and caravans to safety. I took my leave here to Amples after I'd heard from Amil the next day. I told the Kings guard the events and waited for the call from Talos on when to expect Althea to arrive. I was pleasantly surprised to hear that you would be joining her here."

"I had to come." I answered, unaware of what he knew from Talos. "I won't be staying long."

We both watched as a group of mourners shuffled down the hall. The ceremony had been short and Althea had stood with such grace as many Incubo offered her their condolences. She would be fulfilling the duty of grieving daughter, widow, and family member for at least another hour before it would be seen as decent for her to retire to her room.

Yamir gripped my elbow and pulled me closer behind a nearby pillar, shadowed from passersby. His heathered eyes scanned around us before severity pushed into his timbre, "Isa, I know why you're still here, but there is more that I have to warn you about. Talos doesn't wish for this information to reach you but I would be putting you at a disadvantage if I didn't step in."

I hadn't known this aspect of Yamir. His etched features sharpened to show the hunger of his potential to kill. The eyes of a warrior pierced down to me, a look I had grown to feel comforted. My brothers all had the same lethal presence when the time came. The veil of his carefree attitude had dropped and I could see why he was part of Talos' closest garrison.

I nodded and waited for him to go on.

"Lawrence was not among the dead. I did a sweep before the police came and his body was nowhere to be found."

The muscle of my jaw clenched and my stomach hollowed. A

flash of blood pouring from above me, and his hands around my throat. I took a deep breath and blinked the image away, but my mouth had gone dry and it was hard to find words. I'd never come that close to dying. Not on any previous assignment or training. I was sure Lawrence's blood soaked white-blond hair would be the last thing I ever saw.

"But Talos—"

"I can't explain where he had gone. Dead or alive. His body was not present."

My brain was both reeling with explanation and static. Yamir placed his hand to my shoulder when I didn't reply. Unblinking, he held my sight. Whether he knew it or not, his gaze centered me, stabilizing that I was alive and standing in this hallway with him. Gold flecks wisped across his hazy irises. He dipped his chin down towards me, deepening his voice, "He will not finish what he started. I put my life on that."

"I need to know how to kill a halfling. The alexandrite blade didn't slow him down, it didn't seem to slow him while strangling me." I hadn't realized I was breathing so heavily, but my words shook with anger and, admittedly, fear.

I'd never encountered a foe I couldn't kill. There was never a question if a mark had been left to live another day. Each and every being that had been put in my crosshairs had tasted my metal and steel before taking their last breath. Not only had I slit Lawrence's throat, but Talos had beat him to a bloody pulp after Althea and I escaped. Amil had been sure he was dead before coming to find us.

"What do you mean halfling?" He furrowed his brow and looked around once more.

He urged me closer, pressing my back against the cool marble column and turning his back to the hallway framing me into place. The spice of his cologne wafted around me, we hadn't been this close to each other before and the contrast to his mannerisms to that of Amil's or Talos' gave me comfort, oddly enough. I knew he wouldn't attempt to ensnare me or seduce me. He had no attraction to me the way the other two did, he'd told me as much back at the Welp's manor, but there was a familiarity that I couldn't quite put my finger on.

His face rounded back to me, the coast clear behind him. I wasn't sure what to tell him, Talos had been visually irritated at the insinuation that the Fata and Incubo cross could even be a rumor. Would Yamir believe me? Or would he also attempt to gaslight me into disbelieving my would-be murderer? I supposed I would have to find out, he wasn't going to let me back out now.

"Lawrence was Fata, but he was also part Incubo. He showed me his Incubo abilities. His eyes shifted like yours," as if on cue, Yamir's eyes changed from grey to impending storms, the gold flecks raging over his vanishing pupils. "He was able to cast the same hooks into me as Amil and Talos do. I slit his throat with the Alexandrite dagger and he was still able to wrap his hands around my neck without slowing."

Yamir scrubbed a hand across his chin and cheeks, pursing his full lips in the accusation I'd just presented him. He looked to my throat as if to see if he could see any remaining markings. His fingers gently pulled at the neck of my sweater down, and I turned my head for him to get a better look. He wasn't doubting my word, there was no disbelief on his face. The dingy bruises dotted across my neck and chest still, dark purple hues against my soft brown complexion still haunted me at every pass in front of a mirror. The quick glimpse of what Lawrence's hands had done had him shifting his weight from one foot to the other and anger clouded his stormy eyes. The flecks of gold spinning furiously. He didn't speak, whatever he was feeling he wasn't sharing with words.

"How do I kill him, Yamir?" I repeated the question, snapping him out of his anger.

"I don't know," he paused and seemed to be remembering his

place and removing his hand from my neckline, "but I'll find out."

I nodded in gratitude and solidarity.

"He will pay for that." He gestured to my neck with a dip of his head.

"Yes. He will." I said, emphasizing that it wouldn't be him to do the punishing. I had no need for anyone to inflict payback on my account, I was more than adequate in that respect.

He nodded, then did something I hadn't expected. He took my cheek in his palm and kissed my forehead. His lips feather-light against my brow. When he pulled away his eyes met mine again, cleared from his previous brush of anger "*Sadiqa mukhlis.*"

Devoted friend.

CHAPTER NINETEEN

Amil was stationed at the Chateau's entryway to escort
Incubo out from the ceremony. Talos had also been
employed by the Queen to debrief a collection of Incubo who
had volunteered to stay at the Chateau to increase protection.
Anisa's Incubo guards had came to my bedroom door, sent by
Prince Vasilis to bring me to the third floor terrace.

Vasilis had changed out of his dashing suit from the earlier
and now wore a pair of dark blue jeans and a black t-shirt. The
casualty of his clothing caught me off guard. He was more
muscular than his suits showed, his shoulders and chest
stretched the lush cotton fabric. The short sleeves cuffed tightly
against his biceps. I hadn't changed from the ceremony and was
feeling slightly overdressed in my long pants and turtleneck
sweater.

When I stepped out onto the terrace Prince Vas welcomed
me with a smile. He swept his arm out over to the cozy lounge
and table set for tea. The seating area was surrounded by large
antique gas lamps, and tea lights set along the ledge. The crisp
white caged chairs large enough for two beings to lounge in.

"Isa, thank you for joining me. I don't drink alcohol but

could I offer you tea?" He gestured to a tea cup set in front of a chair I assumed was meant for me.

"Tea would be nice, thanks." I replied and sat at the seat indicated to be for me.

Prince Vasilis waited for me to be seated before leaning down over the table. He poured tea in two bone china tea cups, each painted with purple flowers and green vines. The scent of jasmine and ginger rose up from the delicate vessel. Steam dampened the tip of my nose as I took my first sip of the sweet and calming tea. A bitter aftertaste quickly dissipated and remedied by a spoonful of sugar.

Prince Vas watched me over the rim of his cup, setting his down only after I had done so first. He sat back in his cushioned chair, crossed a leg over the other, and cleared his throat.

"Amil is rather taken with you. I've never seen him fawn over a Mortal before." His brilliant smile didn't reach his eyes, but a mix of jealousy and amusement danced in its place.

"Talos also seems to be caught up in your orbit. What is it about you that has them both so smitten?"

"Your guess is as good as mine, your highness." This wasn't a total lie. I didn't fully understand why Amil and Talos were so drawn to me. If I had to guess what Talos had seen at first was out of amusement, but I wasn't so sure that was the case any longer.

He chuckled and his tone deepened, "Call me Vas. Your Highness is much too formal. There's no need for such rituals among friends."

There was something uncomfortable about the way he was so easily stripped away from his title. His clothing and ease around someone he knew to be a contracted killer. A way to disarm me, let me be fooled by his attempt to give the illusion of a common acquaintance.

"That is kind of you, but out of respect, I feel more comfortable addressing you by your title at the very least. I think Talos would prefer I at least conduct myself as such." I waited and watched the way his body shifted under my mention of Talos, but he wasn't going to give any discontentment away.

"That's an interesting thought for a Mortal. You have adapted to the Incubo society very easily. But I suppose being a Black Banner has given you quite the advantage to any other Mortal who would have been thrown into your position."

"I suppose." I took up my cup for another sip of tea, and he mirrored the action.

"The Black Banners are a fascinating institution." He lowered his voice for dramatic flair, something I was beginning to see he relished in, "Very hush-hush, of course."

His eyes roamed over me, lingering at my hip for a moment before continuing, "But I have found a few tid-bits of information over the years and minor encounters. No other Mortal faction is as hard to infiltrate as yours."

He viewed us as a challenge whether he would gain anything from possessing the knowledge or not. I knew he wanted a reaction from me. He wanted me to ask what he knew, and how, but he would be disappointed but his expression didn't change as he moved on.

"Would you be surprised to hear that you are not the first Banner I have had the pleasure of entertaining? The last one was a wonderful dancer. Do you like to dance, Isa?" He took a long drink from his cup, watching me over the rim.

"I don't know if I am as well rehearsed as she may have been, but I haven't had any past dance partners complain."

"As beautiful as you are, I'd wager they were just happy to be close enough to have their arms around you." He tilted his head and ran his bottom lip through his teeth.

"As kind as it is of you to assume that Prince Vas, I'm afraid most of my dance partners aren't around to ask about their experience."

"You are delightful." A wide smile crept across his face. His eyes darkened slightly going from sandy ash to a stormy beach. "Have you ever been to Meru? Your dark sense of humor reminds me of my mother and aunts quick wit."

Meru, Chora's south western neighboring country, was vast, but had very few large cities besides the Capital. Travel between our countries was encouraged on both sides due to trade, employment, and exploration but Meru was a dryer climate and crops grew poorly most months out of the year. Meru was rich in livestock, wool, spices, and grain crops. Much of our textiles were a collaboration between Meru and Hadera to the north west. Yamir and Amil were both Haderi.

"I have been once. It's beautiful. Do you have the opportunity to visit often?" I attempted to adjust the conversation back to muted small talk.

"Yes, my mother and I travel to her family home often to visit my aunt Anisa. She is unwed and will soon have to find someone to procreate with. The courtship traditions dictate that the mate be evaluated by the surrounding family members. Your dear friend Amil is on that list of suitors. If chosen, I'm told he will have to take his place at the head of his family in Hadera to unify the lands. I'd imagine that would be rather painful to watch for you?"

"If those are his duties, then that is what he will have to do. I'm not Incubo, I couldn't bear him children and have the feeling that any such relationship would be forbade." I responded, my stomach threatening to reject the tea at the thought of Amil leaving. I took a composed breath, determined to not show anything but poise and grace.

"That's rather noble of you. To deny your true feelings for him to permit him to fulfill his duties." His cunning tone accompanied a crooked grin.

"I don't believe I have a choice and by the sound of it, neither does he. Your aunt is lovely, I suppose they would be happy together if that is the result."

Another amused look at my response. He picked up his cup and took a noisy sip. Not once dropping his gaze. "Would you like a choice, Isa?" The inflection on my name perked.

I stayed silent. No answer would lead the conversation away from my personal life. He must have grown bored of waiting to drag me through deeper feelings because he adjusted in his seat, readying himself. "I could help you, if you let me."

"I am flattered that you find my feelings so concerning, but Amil will have to make that journey on his own. I won't stand in the way of customs I know very little about."

"Because you believe you can't provide him an heir?" He suggested.

"I've been assured that the Incubo can only reproduce with your own kind, Prince Vas."

This is the conversation I was hoping we would have. I wanted confirmation or contradiction of the claims Lawrence had made. The Prince looked me over for a moment before he looked to the guard at the door. A wordless dismissal and we were alone.

"Offspring between Mortals and Incubo are a complicated subject. Many would preach it is impossible to achieve, but something tells me that you have suspicions that it may not be the case?"

"And what of Fata-Incubo crosses? How complicated would that be?"

His eyes darkened again but somehow lit up at my question, "That is less of an impossibility. But it is highly frowned upon."

"Why is that?" I wasn't sure I was breathing, I strained my ears to hear every word he would say next.

"The treaty says Incubo must only reproduce with our own kind and only when our numbers have decreased to a certain percentage of the overall population. But the probability of an unplanned pregnancy to crop up between that time is lessened when Incubo takes companionship with Fata or Mortals. Those little accidents are an unwelcome stain upon the Incubo's bloodline. At least that is what we are told by the Incubo elders. The keepers of the peace." He paused for effect and a sip of his tea. "Unless the child can pass for a full blooded Incubo or Fata, they are given to be raised by the appropriate family. Blended into their societies under the guise of a miscalculation of the census."

I didn't doubt that if the children of Fata and Incubo were given to be raised by Fata, they wouldn't have to worry about regulations of the treaty being kept. Fata and Mortals didn't have rules set by their ancestors on their procreation or population. This portion of the treaty would make it more challenging for a new Incubo child to be seamlessly integrated. But Lawrence had said that it was such a rarity that quite possibly, there hadn't been a Fata-Incubo offspring that resembled their Incubo family in many years.

"If any blended abilities are apparent, the child would be disposed of along with the Fata who created it. For population control. You understand?" He continued.

I didn't. Not at all. Abortion by choice was free, legal, and accessible. There was no need to murder a child because it presented the mix of abilities given by its parents. One solid rule the Banner's held dearest was to never accept a job in which the mark was a child. Not that the occasion was presented often, but Senators and CEO's had come to a Banner after they had impregnated their mistress and didn't want to lose face or their money to their partners. In fact, it would be the quickest way for a potential employer to become a target themselves.

"And what becomes of the children raised by Incubo when they grow and don't process Incubo talents? Are they tossed back to the Fata community?" I asked, dancing around my encounter with Lawrence.

"They are cherished in our community until they die of

147

natural causes. Likely never knowing they were not full blooded Incubo." He said simply as if it were the natural order of things.

This was the moment I had to choose between giving away what Lawrence had told me, or holding it close to the vest until I could feel the Prince out more. Whether he was more interested in pulling strings than stopping the war that was brewing between Fata and Incubo. I had to take the chance, in a split second I had decided that this might be my only chance to get the truth.

"What about Fata children who grow to possess Incubo abilities. If they can blend into Fata society but in a moment of emotions, their eyes shift and they can cast out their influence to others? What would happen to them?"

He looked to be practically salivating at this question. He wanted dearly to tell me this, possibly from the moment he heard I had been involved in the massacre. I wasn't sure how he would have heard who was responsible or why they had called for the attack, but by the eagerness in his posture, I knew he at least had his own suspicions. I watched as he leaned over his lap, resting his forearms on his knees and laced his fingers together. A quick glance to the doorway before he began speaking again.

"In the case of children, or grown Fata-Incubo crosses that live within the Fata world but are bestowed the gifts of their Incubo bloodlines, they are kept quiet. Blending as well as they can or else face bringing down the consequences on themselves and their families. Retribution would be taken out on the child's parents on both sides of the affair and death would follow swiftly for all those involved. An accident staged to cover up the nasty business of betrayal."

Lawrence had laid in wait until the moment had been right to expose himself as a halfling. He had thought he was going to walk out of that manor without anyone knowing what he had told me, showed me. But I knew. And whether Talos truly believed me or if he were still trying to cover up this truth, I had told him everything. Lawrence's secret was out to at least five people now that Yamir knew and was helping me find a way to kill him. Did the Prince know how to kill a being like Lawrence? Did I dare ask and give away further information?

"I can feel your anticipation, Banner. Why are you biting your tongue? We are friends now, you can speak freely here." He leaned back in his chair, his teacup in his hand then taking a long sip.

"Are the Fata-Incubo crosses harder to… dispose of?" I hesitated but was able to choke out after an apprehensive pause.

"Oh yes," he grinned morbidly, "very."

My head was swimming. I needed to know how to take down Lawrence if he came after Althea or tried to stage a larger coup here at the Chateau. The Alexandrite blade had done little, Talos had gone in on him at his full strength and yet he possibly had escaped. His body was missing from the count from the manor grounds. A thickening of my throat cutting into my oxygen, another flash of blood splashing into my eyes. I shut my lids tightly but was having a hard time prying them back open.

A crash came from across the table, my slit of vision seeing the blurred figure of the Prince holding himself up against the table, his cup in pieces and scattered about. He was grabbing at his throat and his face red, falling out of my line of sight. But not because of his own movements. No. I was slumping in my chair, every muscle in my body weak. Every blink of my eyes, the longer it took for them to open even slightly.

I tried to push words out of my mouth, but my lips felt like lead. My tongue swollen twice its normal size and thickened by the second. Another crash and a crack of pain to the side of my head. My blood hammering upon my eardrums and drawing the sound of the Prince's labored wails of fear and terror. We'd been drugged, by something strong by the small amount of tea I had drank.

Moments were slipping away, images of Amil's face, then Talos. Darkness. The clamor of voices and outrage clanging around me. My stomach rebelled against the toxin and pushed bile up my esophagus but it was halted. I choked and coughed but was losing consciousness for longer periods of time.

A hauling of my body up off the floor and onto a hard shoulder shook me awake for a moment before I slipped under again.

Cool water to my face and neck roused me again. Hands and a cloth wiped away the sick from my skin and hair. I tried to open my eyes but it was no use. I was boneless, nothing for any sort of muscle strength to cling to. I blacked out once more, this time I slept. I knew I was sleeping because I had dreamed of Amil and Talos both in my bed. Holding me. Kissing my forehead and smoothing my hair from my face. Cooing to me and making wildly interesting promises if I woke up again.

A beam of light shook me from the tantalizing slumber. It must have been hours later, the windows of the room pitch black. The only light was a pen light being shown in my crusted eyes.

"We thought we may have lost you there for a moment." Came the baritone voice of Amil. "Don't try to move too quickly."

I couldn't if I tried. I was being held by Althea on my other side. The sweet vanilla and eucalyptus of her shampoo at my shoulder. I turned my face into a pillow of her hair, she was asleep.

"She hasn't left your side since we found you and Prince Vas." He explained and put the penlight away. His face hardly visible by the dim light coming from the bathroom.

"Prince Vasilis?" I croaked.

"He was taken to the hospital and the royal family's doctor alerted to meet them there after evaluating you here. It would be quite the sight for a group of Incubo to bring a drugged

Mortal into the emergency room. But the doctor administered ipecac and an antitoxin. He'll be back soon to check in. Prince Vas is going to stay overnight for observation."

My head was pounding. I reached up to a thick layer of bandages on my forehead. I hissed in pain, but was able to bite back a curse to not wake Althea who I realized was laying on my arm.

"Here," he lifted Althea's head and freed me.

I sat up slightly but was still weak. Amil held up a glass of water with a straw, offering me a drink. The cool liquid filled my sore mouth and drenched my dry throat. The sour-acid taste of bile diluted with each mouthful. I drank deeply until it felt as though my stomach would purge itself again. I laid back down on the pillow and took in every edge and crease of Amil's face. He gave a relieved sigh and set the glass of water on the side table.

"Try to get some more sleep. I'll be right here if you need anything." He had pulled over one of the wingback chairs from the sitting area in front of the fireplace.

I watched him get comfortable, wedging his back into the crease of the chair and propping his feet up on the foot of the bed. He watched my heavy lids close and I fell back to a deep sleep.

CHAPTER TWENTY

Morning came too soon and the heavy knock on the door was far too loud after the long and painful night. I looked around to see Amil but he had gone and the chair had been put back. Althea was still sleeping next to me soundly holding onto my arm.

Talos didn't wait for me to answer, he knocked a third time before entering the room. He looked to be ready for a fight, his eyes dark and brooding. "I heard you had an interesting chat with Prince Vasilis last night?"

His eyes traveled over Althea before he slipped his hands into his pockets and watched me for my answer. I didn't bother to try to explain or sit up. My head wouldn't allow it. He warned me against the meeting with the Prince and I hadn't listened. I needed the information the Prince had divulged to me before the spiked tea rushed to my head. Briefly, I wondered what came of the Prince. If he was also waking to a thundering headache and if an investigation had been ordered to find who had tried to poison him and, additionally, me.

My stomach growled and roiled at the slightest movement.

Talos took a step closer but then hesitated, "Can I get you anything?"

I wasn't sure what could calm the storm in my gut or the chaos ringing through my ears but I managed to say, "Water, and aspirin."

Went to the side table and popped open a bottle of pills I hadn't seen before that was set next to a full fresh glass of water. He shimmied out a couple of the small white pills into his palm and offered them to me. I placed them on my tongue and took the glass of water from his other hand. Swallowing irritating a bulge in my throat, likely from vomiting while unconscious.

Next to me, Althea stirred awake, catching sight of Talos beneath misty morning eyes. She sat up and looked to me, sadness and remorse on her face as she scanned over the bandage wrapped around my head.

"She will be in good hands, Lady Althea. The King and Queen will be waiting for you in the sunroom for breakfast." Talos assured her with a permissive tone.

"Isa, I don't need to go." She spoke to me in a hushed tone.

I mustered a smile, and glanced to Talos before answering, "I'll be ok. Let's have lunch on the terrace later. Okay?"

She nodded but was still apprehensive as she slid off the bed and padded out of the room. Talos turned and watched her leave, pride and sadness weighing on his shoulders. When he turned back, however, his guilt and aggravation was back and clouding his pupils.

"I hope whatever you and the Prince discussed was worth the concussion, and stitches to your scalp." He raised his chin pointedly to the top of my head.

"He had plenty to talk about before the sour tea silenced him. Have you found who tried to poison us?"

"Perhaps. We've rounded up all the Chateau staff for questioning. We'll have the being who's responsible by the end of the day."

"Why would you lie to me? You knew what Lawrence had said about there being Fata-Incubo halflings was true."

"What you have to understand, Isa, is that his existence and the public debate would put all Incubo at risk. His every breath would go against the Treaty of Eiríni." His shoulders slumped and his head hung heavy with his confession.

He sat on the side of my bed, crossing his ankle at his knee and supporting his head with his fingers and thumb.

"What is the Treaty of Eiríni?" The Prince had eluded to a treaty but hadn't had time to explain. "Why would one Fata with Incubo abilities threaten all Incubo?"

"To understand the treaty you have to know the true history of the balance to our society." He looked up, finding a spot on the floor and focusing on it before he continued. "Not long enough ago Mortals and Fata were ruled by Incubo. The rulers were cruel, and uncaring for any beings other than their own. The wealth of power, land, and resources all laid at the feet of Incubo who used their gifts to overpower who they though were lesser beings than themselves."

"Fata and Mortals staged an uprising and a great war broke out. Fata and Mortals were losing hundreds of beings daily to Incubo. They couldn't sustain themselves or their troops for much longer. They were facing defeat and subsequent imprisonments for treason. That is until a small group of Fata discovered Alexandrite was our weakness. The one true way to kill an Incubo."

"How could they have possibly found that out?" I huffed in disbelief.

"A traitor, Aricci Bengalli, was tortured for days until he cracked. Giving into the Mortals demands and becoming a traitor to his own kind."

He paused and looked up from the floor, a ghostly look crossed his face and I wondered what haunted him.

"We were on the brink of extinction. The most powerful

among us banded together to formulate an attack that would bring the Mortals and Fata forces to their knees. The plans were leaked by sympathisers to the enemy, but they accomplished their goal. The Fata and Mortals wanted to call a truce. No more bloodshed."

I watched him carefully. Pain and regret riddled his face.

"The Treaty of Eiríni was formed to keep the power of each being in check. Mortals and Fata would essentially forget our weakness to Alexandrite and we would keep our numbers low and seclude ourselves to lessen our power. We retained our holds on the lands of our families. At least those of us left."

"And the halfling's? How do they fit into all of this?" I asked, but he didn't look at me to answer.

"Halflings were seen as a loophole in the treaty. A way to weaponize the mixture of blood to take hold of power that we were no longer permitted. We were to be tamped down, kept in our cage of mystery and elision. If new generations of Mortals and Fata feared us, we could remain hidden in plain sight without the fear of another war being waged."

" Wouldn't mingling the bloodlines mend the relationships between Fata and Incubo?" I asked only one of the hundreds of questions I had buzzing through my mind, fighting to get out first.

"That restriction was imposed by the Incubo elders who contributed to the treaty. They thought that to keep the illusion that Incubo were too powerful for any other beings and that we preferred the company of our own kind. We have buried the truth and have passed it off as preference and out of respect for our fallen. For our kind to keep our remnants of our power and wealth we had to agree to only breed to refresh the bloodlines by way of semi-arranged marriages. Keep our lands and resources to our own kind. Many of our oldest leaders believe that only the purest of Incubo blood is worth the weight of gold we create from our ashes."

"Are you saying those items that were given to Incubo at the ceremony were made from the ashes of their loved ones?"

"Our bones are pure gold. Our blood and organs when burned becomes golden dust. It is tradition to have our remains made into items for our remaining loved ones. To be passed down from generation to generation. Another means to keep wealth and prosperity to the Incubo."

I had heard of Mortals and Fata losing loved ones and having their ashes mixed with metals or resin to create trinkets. The concept was only mildly awkward to hear during the ceremony. But this was unfathomable. I drank in every ounce of Talos that I could see, trying to see a sparkle or glint of gold on his skin or in his pores. If I looked long enough, surely, I would be able to see a shard of gold protruding from him.

"Why isn't the treaty common knowledge? I'd never once heard a whisper of this agreement?" I moved on to bring us back to more of what I needed to know.

"If every being knew of the treaty, then we could not uphold it. How would it look to you if you knew of the history of our treaty and stumbled upon me in that elevator?"

I thought about that for a moment, tried to put myself in my own shoes now that I had all this new information on the tortured past of our species. Would I have tried to kill him on the spot if I had known how? Probably.

I decided to move onto my next question, an answer to his in itself. "Tell me about the Incubo-Fata halflings."

"There are those who have taken Fata or Mortal lovers and offspring have occurred. In those cases—"

"You kill the children..." I finished for him, repeating what Prince Vas had said.

"Only if they can't be passed off for one or the other species." He confirmed.

"Likely, Lawrence passed for a Fata well enough that he was

permitted to live." He continued. "That has been proven to be a mistake on our heads." He finished.

I rolled my eyes, shooting a pain from the bridge of my nose to the corners of my eyes. It hadn't been a mistake to let him live. That would be absurd. Killing someone because of what their parents were.

"The mistake was letting the treatment of his kind go as it has been for this long that it has gotten to this point. He has every right to be angry and hurt. He has been treated as an outlier his entire life. Seen how his Fata family has been treated by his Incubo family. Do you not see the ramifications of this treaty for beings like him? For children like him!" My head was pounding with anger, the volume of my voice raising as the pressure of my blood through my veins with fury.

Talos' stoic eyes watched me, an icy exterior meeting my fire, his hushed voice practically a whisper, "His kind isn't meant to exist. They are a threat to our way of life. To the only thing keeping every one of our species from ripping each other a part. The Incubo who sired him should be locked up for putting our entire society in danger of being exposed. He is a symbol of betrayal. An act of war seen by the Mortals and Fata who agreed to keep the peace as long as we stayed in our own world."

He stood up and walked to the middle of the room, I sat up further, expecting him to leave in his anger. "I was not lying when I said I had done many things to keep my kind safe. I would do them all over again if it meant stopping a war that would wipe out what is left of us."

The pain and weight of it all hung over him. He didn't choose to be part of the enforcement of these rules, but he wholeheartedly believed that he had to uphold the treaty for the survival of all Incubo.

"Talos. Lawrence's body wasn't accounted for at the Manor."

He turned back to face me and walked back to the foot of the bed. Storm clouds had become darker with each step closer. He sat down and the plush mattress sunk under his weight, bringing me down closer to him.

Placing a hand on my thigh, he sounded apologetic, "I know, Isa."

"I need to know how to kill him. If he knows we're here—."

"I would never allow him to touch you. Not again." He promised, softly stroking his thumb along my cool skin exposed from the mess of blankets.

A wave of warmth and sickly sweet calm pulsed up from his touch. Whoever had undressed me had left me in my panties and a tank top. Likely looking for any other injuries at the time but left me feeling exposed in that moment.

"I don't need your words. I need your help."

"I'm sorry, I can't help you because I don't know how. I've never had to step into that situation. Those secrets are kept even high above myself. I have been sent to round up and dispatch the traitors but their offspring are given to an elite group of Incubo who are sworn to secrecy. They test the children extensively until there is no doubt that they can not be permitted to live. The means of disposal are my kinds darkest secret. All I can offer you is my apology and my word that for as long as you are here, I can protect you." His tone was calm but his intention was glaringly obvious.

He still wanted me to stay on with him, to protect Althea and anyone else he saw fit. I was after all a Black Banner under the mercy of his cooperation in finding my brother.

"Expressing your guilt is a sorry excuse for an apology" I said, a hiss of annoyance still coursing through me, "until Argo is found, you owe me safety."

"As soon as I hear of the whereabouts of your brother, you will know. But I hope you change your mind and stay on after. For your life and Althea's. You and I both know that if Lawrence is still alive, he will be coming for you first. You exposed yourself to him that night as a weapon and a weakness to one of the most powerful Incubo alive."

"Does Althea's position in the court truly make her that powerful?" My brows knitted together at his comment.

"Not Althea." He looked to me then, obsidian eyes penetrating me, "Me."

My heart slammed against my ribs and my muscles went rigid at the weight of his words. I didn't have anything to say to his confession.

"Then he will go after Althea in the hopes of slitting her throat before she can take her place over Arta and Cinder." He continued, sparing me from my failing attempt to form a thought or words. "I know what I am asking. I understand that the Black Banners will not approve, but your life and my kind is in danger. I need you to stay with us. Stay with me."

He had made this request before, but it held more meaning this time. Further wedging me into a position between him and Amil that I wasn't sure I belonged or wanted to be in. But I knew he was also right about Althea. I knew Althea's life was in more danger now than it had been before. As the last heir of her bloodline and the widow of the lords of Arta, she would now carry both titles and care over all land and wealth of both cities. In one failed attempt, Lawrence had done what he had set out to end. He placed one Incubo in power over the dozens he had murdered. She was now his biggest threat and I was still alive to protect her.

CHAPTER TWENTY-ONE

After Talos left, I willed myself back to sleep if only to relieve the pounding in my head and the worry in my chest. The walls felt much closer than they looked, less thick and more permeable than they had the night before. Frustration had found its way into my dreams. Images of running down long corridors of locked rooms and pitch black windows. Bulletproof glass, and lights above that flickered when I tried to read placards on doorways. Voices calling out to me from behind hardwood barriers. Althea. Zaida. Argo. Amil. Markus. Relentless tears obstructing my vision as I tried to call out to them but the words being caught in my throat. Gunshots sounded followed by screams of pain. My fists pounding against the floor until they bled and broke.

Finally the hallway faded to black as I woke to the familiar smell of bergamot and persimmons, raising my senses from the lucid sleep and into the hazy gaze of Amil sitting on the side of my bed, leaning down to me. My shirt clung to my sweat damp body. A brush of soft full lips and the cushioned facial hair to my forehead, just below my bandage. My breathing steadying at the sight of him safe in front of me.

"How's your head?" He whispered, bookending his words with another kiss to my temple.

"It only hurts when I'm awake." I offered with a smile when he pulled away. "Nothing some aspirin and another nap won't cure."

He huffed a laugh, "Well, then I suppose you'll be back on your feet by the time I get back." He sat up and moved a lock of hair from my face.

"Back from where?" I shifted to see him better, a pounding to my head as fresh blood surged with the movement.

"Talos is sending Yamir and me out on assignment. We should be back in a couple days." His expression changed then, a gloom shadowed his eyes.

"Where is he sending you? Did you get any information from the staff on who poisoned the Prince?" More questions whirled in my head that my mouth couldn't keep up with.

"We might know who it was and another man is on it. This is much more important but I have been sworn to secrecy on the very few details I have been given."

"Amil—"

"Isa, I can't protect Althea if I get fired for opening my mouth when I was instructed not to. We both know that Talos can easily get the truth out of you and I'd rather not think about his will or hands around you while I'm gone." He furrowed his brow.

"I suppose I'll see you when you get back then. Keep each other alive. Yamir already escaped death once this month."

He chuckled at that, "I promise to watch over him carefully."

"When do you leave?" I said, pulling his hand to come closer to me.

"Yamir is waiting for me downstairs. I wanted to check on you before I left and remind you to be careful here. Anisa is furious over the poisoning of her nephew and is on a rampage to find the culprit."

"I'll stay clear of her and the other royals unless needed. Althea will be back up later for lunch and training. I'm sure she'll have news to share." I said with another tug of his arm.

He relented and leaned down to me, allowing me to wrap my arms around his neck and kiss him. A hand smoothed up from my hip and scooped under my shoulder, bringing me in closer and deepening our kiss. A warm relief washed through me, then a pulse of want as he pulled away. His eyes black, the friendly flame alight in their depths.

"*Te 'ebsheeni.*" His lips fluttered against mine before one last kiss.

"Be safe." My tone begged more than warned. I had the sinking feeling that he wouldn't be returning in one piece but there was nothing I could do. He had to go and I had to stay.

"When I get back, perhaps I'll fulfill some of those promises I made you."

"What promises?" I asked, a vague memory of his and Talos' voice in the darkness mixed with the poisoned tea.

He gave me a wicked smile, looking me over. His teeth gave his lip a tug and he was gone. I could only hope that whatever they had promised was worth not dying for.

Althea came for lunch a few minutes after noon. Sandros closely behind her pushing a wheeled cart with a tea service, tea sandwiches, and tarts. I had called back to sleep after Talos left, but the doctor had stopped in and checked my stitches, all ten of them, and evaluated my other wounds. I had hit my head pretty hard on the balcony floor but the poison would take time and plenty of water to flush out of my system completely. He would be due in to check on me again tomorrow morning but gave me his approval to get back to normal activity but warned against falling off any more chairs.

I made him no promises.

Althea watched the other Incubo lock the cart then nodded her dismissal. At the foot of my bed she looked me over and smiled sadly to me. "Do you need help standing?" She held out her hand and moved to the side of the bed.

"I'm fine. My headache has subsided and my stomach has calmed down. I'm actually hungry. That has to be a good sign, right?" I stood and we moved towards the seating area next to the fireplace.

"Absolutely!" Hope flushed her face at the sight of me walking on my own.

I hadn't thought about how it would have effected her to see me in such a state. She had seen me almost die, after all. But I supposed she had felt we were safe here at the Chateau.

"How is Prince Vasilis?" I asked as I sat down and she offered me a cup of tea. I hadn't heard if he was back from the hospital yet.

"I went to visit him earlier today. He is still in a medically induced coma. The poison you both ingested was very potent to Incubo. Rare and very hard to grow here in Chora. The treatment will be prolonged but he should be awake tomorrow."

"Any word on who could have access to the kitchens? Has someone been held responsible?"

"Talos has Amil holding interrogations of all the staff and anyone involved in the grocery delivery. But no word yet if he's found any suspicion."

That explained why I hadn't seen Amil in so long, he and Talos would be working tirelessly to track the being responsible for the Princes condition. I hoped Amil gave me a moment alone with whoever it was. I'd like to repay them for the new scar on my hairline.

"Can I ask you something?" I asked over the top of my teacup, the sight of which churned my stomach at the thought of the last tea party I had attended.

Althea nodded and I set the tea cup down. Trading it for a cucumber and dill cream cheese sandwich. "Why aren't there any Fata on the grounds? The Welps had many Fata employed, but I haven't seen one since we arrived." This had been bothering me.

"The King and Queen said it was for the best. I didn't feel it was my place to question their judgment. Not after losing much of their long time friends in court and family."

"Of course. And with the Queen carrying life again. I imagine they want to take every precaution. How far along is the Queen in her pregnancy?"

Althea looked into the tea cup set in her lap and worried her lip. My friend was uncomfortable and didn't know how much to tell me. "Althea? You don't have to tell me if it puts you at risk."

"No, it just... Isa, you can't tell anyone and you have to trust that it was likely an accident."

I perked my brow, "My only loyalty here is to you." I assured her, reaching out my hand and offering her my good faith.

"She is in her sixth month." She said, her voice low.

"Did you know the Incubo who passed?" I asked but knowing there hadn't been one. It would have been in the news like all Incubo deaths were. It happened so rarely, it was practically like a celebrity passing.

"I'm not aware of who had fallen. I assume she would have been next after the attack at the Manor anyway." She squirmed in her chair.

"Hmm, I suppose it wouldn't matter now. Would it?" I eased and she gratefully sighed.

We sat and ate our meal in silence. She didn't look up from her fig and goat cheese tart for a long while and pushed olive and plump cherry tomatoes around her plate from edge to edge. I couldn't say that would cut her discomfort. The Incubo we were residing with had broken the treaty, their own laws but had been saved by a loophole and the death of many of their own kind. I had some suspicions of my own but hadn't any proof to formulate any end.

I finished my fourth helping of tea cake when Althea found her voice again, "Are you feeling well enough for a lesson?"

"As long as you take it easy on me." I answered with a wink.

"Even with a concussion, I wouldn't be able to best you."

Althea took the thin blade I had given her out of her pocket. She had wrapped it in a ripped piece of silk pillowcase. She unsheathed it and held it out flat in her palm. On the end of my bed I propped up several pillows to be our target. I wouldn't be able to assist her in combat training, but we could run throwing drills. I would send her to Amil after to spar with when he wasn't busy and she was done with her daily meetings with the royals.

I stood next to her and we took in a breath together. Taking in air deeply from our noses then letting it out our mouths. She looked to me for the

"Do you feel well enough for a tour of the Chateau? The gardens are gorgeous this time of year." She straightened her spine and changed the subject.

"I thought you'd never ask. I need to get out of this room." I teased with an exasperated sigh and she laughed, her eyes lightening to a cool mist.

I wasn't sure Althea was going to allow me to dress myself for our walk, but I had been sleeping for so long that my body was overpowering the pain in my head. I didn't dress to be nearly presentable to the royals dwelling around me, but I was comfortable. A pair of black leggings, a silk sage green tunic blouse. A black belt to conceal a thin blade, and matching boots with blades tucked to my ankles. I left the Alexandrite dagger safely closed in my bedside table.

A Black Banner in the King's Chateau would feel more than a bit threatening, I didn't need to parade the cursed gift from Talos in the case it would have made me less welcome.

Althea had us start out on the grounds. The vast gardens and water fixtures further gave the illusion that the Chateau was a hidden wonderland. As we walked through the hedge lined rose garden, Althea remaninsed about the first time she'd come to the Chateau as a child. She had hid in this garden while playing hide and seek with her cousins. They took so long in their search that she had fallen asleep under a rose bush. Her Fata nanny had to find her after she'd been missing until after nightfall.

We moved from garden to garden until we made it to the back door of the Chateau. Our first stop inside was the observatory. The glass domed ceiling towered above us, wispy white clouds hovered overhead as the sun warmed the room. Set in the middle was an oak desk and telescope. Maps of the sky riddled the top of the studious surface.

The next room was the library. Rows and rows of books filled the spacious chamber, lit by skylights and wall sconces. We stepped inside, our footsteps muffed by the tomes despite the dark marble floors. Althea lead me towards the middle of the shelves where a long table dissected the library, leather and green velveteen chairs lining it.

"Every Incubo family history is housed here." She explained, dragging her fingers along the polished table.

"For all of *Continent name*?" I awed at the enormity of it.

"No, just for Chora. Meru, and Hadera have their own Capital Libraries where they keep their bloodline records. When a family does cross the border, for marriage or immigration, a copy of each family is sent to the capital from the original country. So that both Capital's have the same information of its citizens."

"That sounds like a lot of work."

I peered around at the massive volumes seeing names like *Torrini, Harris, Loch, and Amargo.* I pointed to the spine of that particular book and looked to Althea. She gave a confirming nod and made to take the book off it's shelf.

"His lineage goes back for centuries. One of the founding

families of Chora. Back when all of *Blank continents name* was being divided up."

I gawked at the aged pages as I flipped through images and family tree drawings. I reached more than three quarters through the book and came upon a photo of an Incubo who looked like Talos but older, with a child wrapped around his leg. I looked to Althea who had been watching me.

"Is this Talos?" An amused smile sprawled across my face.

"It is, and this is his grandfather, Erebos Amargo." She pointed to the taller Incubo that Talos was clinging to.

Above young Talos' head was the glint of a pommel of a familiar dagger. I couldn't be sure, but it looked to be the same dagger Talos had given to me. The dagger that he had said killed his grandfather. The weight of that sank me into a plush leather armchair. I turned the page to see a fully grown Talos standing with two Incubo women, both about much shorter than he was.

"That is his mother." Althea pointed to the Incubo to his left, "And that is my mother." The Incubo to his right.

I gazed upon the face of Althea's mother. Remarkably, she didn't look much like Althea. She had dark hair and curved features. Her hips less narrow than her daughters and clearly shorter in height. They had similar facial features, like their lips and cheekbone structure, but Althea clearly inherited more of her father's genes. I wondered if that was painful for Talos, or a hidden blessing that Althea didn't resemble a lost love.

"They were inseparable until my mother was betrothed to my father. He used to tell me stories about her when I was growing up. Until he was promoted and sent here. I hadn't seen him in years. Not until about a week before he hired you."

I looked up from the page we had been sharing, her grey glassy eyes still pinned to the photo.

A realization hit me, one I hadn't questioned when I first met Talos. The title on his business card read "Head of Royal Security". She had not been in Talos' care her entire life. He'd only been recalled to take her to Welp manor. The child of the woman he'd loved to be married to the man she had allowed to choose herself when her mother hadn't been given the luxury. The complication of feelings that must have brought on didn't elude me and explained the severity of his protection over Althea.

"He must have missed you terribly."

She smiled softly, "The feeling was mutual. Other than Cornelius, Talos was the only being who would look at me and see me as I am and not what my title holds. Until I met you."

Her misty eyes held mine in admiration. More than ever I felt our hearts call to each other. I was also only seen for what I was employed to do. My siblings and I would never be seen outside of our profession as anything other than deadly. Our work and our titles were much different, but we both had to go out of our own society to find beings that truly cared about us and saw us as who we were and not what advantage we were to others.

CHAPTER TWENTY-TWO

W e moved on from the library after a few more peruse shelves and volumes. Althea had shown me her family's history. A three volume set that started alongside Talos'. Althea and I walked about the subsequent floors of the Chateau and made it back to the East wing, where the royal family resided. We passed by an open door on our way to Althea's room and a voice called out to her, "Althea? Cousin, is that you?"

She froze and turned around into the the doorway, "Princess where have you been hiding?" Her voice gleeful and courteous.

Althea waved to me to follower her into the room. This room was large, spacious, and painfully clean. Pearl white with gold accents on every surface including the furniture. The phantom voice came from a young Incubo woman who was sitting at a desk near one of the many floor to ceiling windows. She twisted at the waist as we walked in, shuffling papers before turning around to greet us.

Her bright sand dust veiled eyes reminded me immediately of the Prince. Her umber skin aglow in the shining sunlight from the gauzy white curtains. She placed her hand on her very pregnant belly beneath the white and gold summer dress she was wearing. A doll matching her surroundings.

The look of surprise must have been plain on my face, Althea nudged me gently before embracing her cousin. When we arrived at the Chateau I was aware of the Prince, King, and Queen. I'd known the Queen had only had the opportunity by treaty to be a mother twice. But I had assumed the pregnancy she was currently carrying was in that count.

Princess Amirah was closer to my height than Althea and showed more of her mother than her father, unlike her brother. Her hair braided in long locks down her back, cuffing in gold and tipped in charms. Her fingers and wrists clad in gold rings and bangles. Her ripe round belly was hardly noticeable from behind but when she turned to face us there was no mistaking her condition. She beamed up to Althea, who was wearing a her most relaxed smile.

"Cousin, I've missed you so much," Althea said as she held the Princess out before her by the shoulders.

"It's been far too long. I'm so sorry to hear about Cornelius." The Princess gave an exaggerated frown, "He was a wonderful man and would have made you very happy. Your children would have been beautiful."

Althea didn't speak, much like any other moment she had been offered condolences. Whether she didn't have the words or didn't find the sorrow sincere, I wasn't sure, but I knew she would have to be reminded of her losses for the sake of politeness for years to come.

"And losing your father as well," the Princess tsked, "Just awful."

"How are you feeling? Your father said you were deathly ill? But you don't seem to have a sniffle?" Althea said, changing the subject away from herself.

"Oh, he would say that. They have been hiding me away for months, starving me of attention and stimulation. I was supposed to travel to Arta fo your union." The Princess sniffed and turned towards the sitting area, "I suppose fate was looking after me on that inconvenience."

She lowered herself in to a large cushioned arm chair, missing the brief pang of grief shot over Althea's face. Althea paused, a conflicted expression preplaced the pain. I recognized that look. The instinct to run from what surely was to be an unpleasant visit.

"How far along are you?" I chimed in, offering Althea my hand which she squeezed tightly. Composing herself before sitting on the loveseat next to me, and across from the Princess.

"Almost to the end now. This little Duke will be here any time." She rubbed her belly in circular motions.

"A boy? Congratulations." I offered.

"Thank you, I have been forbidden to share the news or to celebrate him in anyway, of course." She screwed up her face in annoyance. "I've been so rude, I'm Princess Amirah," she held out her hand to me.

I reached over and gave it a halfhearted shake, "I'm Isa, a friend of Althea's." I glanced to Althea and smiled.

"It's so nice to meet you, Isa. I haven't met a Mortal in some years, you must be very special to be permitted on the grounds. Especially with all the new restrictions they have put in place."

"I'm sure it's for the best." Althea replied for the both of us.

"Is that why you have to keep your pregnancy a secret?" I asked, having the impression she was hoping that I would.

Her eyes lit up, their sandy storms whirled in excitement. "The father of my child was a hired hand. Unfit for the King's heir. So, my father sent him away, locked me up in this house, and swept all evidence under the rug." She gushed at her own scandalous misfortune.

"Aren't all Incubo fairly well off or hold a title? Why would they be so against your lover?" I pressed.

"Because he wasn't Incubo. He was Fata." She watched us for

the anticipated shock she was hoping to receive by spilling this unbelievable, and close to impossible secret.

Althea took a sharp inhale of breath and stared at the Princess who looked like a prim cat who'd eaten a juicy mouse. She relished our reactions and observed every bit she could. The conversation the Prince and I had on his balcony was starting to become more clear. He had known so much about Fata and Incubo's blood crossing because there was the possibility of one under the same roof. He'd watched the romance unfold, blossom, and crumble as the news of the pregnancy had broken the hearts of his parents. Like his sister, he'd wanted to bask in the heat of controversy.

"Are you positive it's his? That can't be true. Our kind can't reproduce with Mortals or Fata." Althea frantically grasping at what she believed to be true.

"This little blessing is proof that it is possible. I hadn't been with anyone else. At least, no one with the required equipment to contribute genetically." She winked to her cousin coyly.

"What will happen if the child resembles the father in his kind's abilities?" I asked, and she did not deflate like I had expected.

"I will love and care for him no matter what. I know what the treaty says but I love my baby. I won't allow anyone to take him from me." She wrapped her arms around her belly protectively.

"And what if it resembles a mix of the both of you?" She knew what I was asking whether she knew what I had been told or not.

"I will love and protect my son." She affirmed.

"Amirah, I don't understand how this could happen. We have always been told it just wouldn't work! Studies have been done to prove it!" Althea looked from her to me, "Isa, tell her what Talos said about Lawrence and his heresy."

"Althea, if the Princess says her son's father is Fata, I don't believe what Talos has said is relevant anymore." I held her hand in my lap, attempting to calm her.

Tears welled in Althea's eyes as they shifted from ocean mist to stormy night. She was being affronted by the realization that she may have been lied to by the one being she had held dearest her entire life. That in his quest to protect her and their kind, he had betrayed her trust. I felt for her, I truly did. She'd been confronting so many truths in such a short amount of time all while her world crumbled. Losing the love of her life, her father, and now the shroud of trust she had in Talos was shattering to bits. Althea didn't speak again all the while Princess Amirah told us of the way every Fata on the grounds was banished and since then, the Incubo hired in their place have been blundering idiots who created more messes than they cleaned up.

Althea bid her cousin a good night when dinner was delivered almost two hours later. The Incubo who dropped off the meal cart was surprised to see the Princess with visitors, and I had a feeling the encounter would have repercussions long after we said our goodbyes.

CHAPTER TWENTY-THREE

I went back to my room on my own as Althea was due to dinner with their majesties and needed to freshen up. On my way back to the west wing I caught Talos on his way up the stairs. The sun outside the large corridor windows was beginning to set but I had lost track of the time. I stood at the top step and waited for him to meet me, I thought it only fair to warn him about what he might be walking into if he was going to retrieve Althea for dinner.

"She's not going to be happy to see you." I said with a subtle shake of my head.

"What are you talking about? And what are you doing out of bed?" He began to usher me into the visitors wing.

"I'm fine. I have been out with Althea most of the day and we had a very intriguing chat with Princess Amirah. Seems that she also is with child." I confessed as we stepped into my room.

He shut the door behind us after looking down the hall with a huff. "Isa, I don't want to play games with you right now." He said as he spun around to meet my eye. "I have news about your brother."

My spine straightened and my eyes bolted to him. I waited

for him to speak, almost too scared to breathe too loudly that I would miss a single syllable.

"He is safe. Yamir and Amil tracked the trail and they are in pursuit of the bastards now. They had smuggled him out of the city and over the border of Meru. We will have to wait here until Amil and Yamir can locate and bring him back here. No more than two days."

A heavy sigh of relief crashed over me. The pounding in my head rang through my ears and I was almost certain I had misunderstood. "He's safe? He's alive?"

"Yes, Isa." He paused, allowing the words to sink into me. "I promised you that I would find him."

Before I even realize I had moved, I had wrapped my arms around Talos' waist and tears filled my eyes. I tried to catch my breath, I hadn't realized that I had given up a large part of my hope that Argo would be found alive. I wasn't going to stop until I had confirmed either way, and I certainly wouldn't have let his captures live long enough to allow my siblings to get their own retribution. A mix of sickening rage and relief whirled in my stomach.

Talos put a hand to my cheek and coaxed my chin up so our eyes met, "Isa, I—" his eyes were obsidian pools on his hard set expression.

"Thank you. I don't have anything else to say, but... Thank you." I stepped away and hugged myself. I stepped towards the seating area by the fire and perched on the edge of the loveseat.

The fire had been lit for me, warming against the brisk early Fall night. Talos stood planted where he had been, looking me over. Something hesitant in his posture.

"You saw the Princess today?" He slid his hands into his pockets and hung his head. We both prepared for the argument that was surely coming.

"She's carrying a son. The son of a Fata. Did you know?" I

175

wanted to give him the benefit of the doubt but as head of the royal family's security, I knew better.

"I knew the rumors. What she has been claiming but it has only recently become apparent that she may be telling the truth."

Maybe move the treaty conversation here

"If you want me to stay and risk my life for you and your kind, you need to be completely honest with me." Heat was rising up my neck as I watched him begin to pace the floor before me.

"I am paying you very well to do as I ask." He said in rebuttal.

"We are far and away from a boss and employee relationship, and you know that."

"Considering you climaxed in my lap upon our first true meeting, I suppose we never had a conventional working relationship." His sharp tongue lashed out, no amusement or enjoyment in his tone. A punishing judgment glazed over his features.

A flush of anger bruised my cheeks, "Screw you, Talos." I stood and made to walk to the bathroom door, embarrassed and hurt that he would throw our encounters in my face so crudely.

I was cut off by his firm torso in the way of the door, his hands pinning my arms to my sides to stop me from going any further. "You're more than welcome to do so anytime you'd like. But there is no use in pretending that our propinquity hasn't been venomous."

"That hasn't been my doing, or do I have to remind you of your indiscretions?" I pulled away from him a step but held my ground firmly.

"I am well aware of my actions whether they were known to you or not. But you will not demand more than you are permitted as my employee. There is information you do not have clearance to hear. I have been entrusted to protect the most vulnerable of my kind, even from the Black Banners. You don't think that the bit of information I have given you wouldn't be dangerous to the highest bidder? You hold more information than most living mortals and that is only to further protect Althea. If I thought you could fulfill your duties without it, you'd still be armed with useless trinkets and fawning at my feet." His tone not lifting, his eyes warning me of the storm to come.

"Amil was the one to teach me how to resist your influence. Don't take credit where it isn't due, it's petty." I said, crossing my arms and wishing I'd armed myself more thoroughly.

"Amil was weak. Distracted by the risk of consorting with a Black Banner and the challenge of luring you to bed without having to persuade you. The guilt he holds for his own abilities often outweighs his skills, if you were to ask me." He shrugged egregiously.

"You view him as weak for having a conscience? For only using his abilities when they are truly needed and not at every provocation. Or is it that you are intimidated that his power goes beyond what you are capable of? That he could, without tapping into that power, get me into bed when you didn't dare try?" I spat back, now more than ever appreciating Amil and his kindness.

"Intimidated? Are you such a rare commodity that I would feel in competition with one of my oldest friends and confidants for your attention? I merely amplified feelings you already held, Isa. Broke away the inhibitions you were keeping to give into what we both wanted. I have no use in courtship or taking my time with someone who would only quench my appetite for the time being."

"Whether you see it or not, Talos. You forced our relations. You manipulated my feelings and did so without explanation or caution."

"Is that so? Because I could feel what my touch did to you. I could sense each and every time your body reacted to the slightest brush of my skin against yours. The breath one look from me would take from you." He moved closer, gliding the back of his fingers down my arm, hair raising behind the stroke.

"Reactions. Not permission to invade my thoughts and feelings to twist into your own warped definition of consent."

"Do you regret any of it?" He took another step closer, towering over me.

"You took liberties and then throw the resulting actions in my face and dare to ask if I regret giving into your influence?"

"As your employer, it's still my place to remind you of where you stand here. I don't regret hiring you or any interaction we have had since. Desirable or not. I have not lied to you about who I am or what my intentions have been."

"Maybe not. But you've lied about plenty of other aspects of this assignment. Betrayed mine and Althea's trust in you."

"I can't change that and I wouldn't. If broken trust is what it takes to keep you and her safe. Then so be it. That is my job."

"You hide behind your duties but you're more scared of losing the people around you to death and act the martyr when those who feel betrayed look to you to take responsibility for your actions."

"And yet. Althea still breaths. You are still here to protect her. And the royal family will live to see another sunrise under my watch." The sultry silk of his voice tugged at the sensitive place behind my navel.

At the sensation of his request, I centered myself. Focused on the gleam of the fire light in his tie pin. The round surface orange from the glow dancing from the fireplace.

He dipped his chin down, the warmth of his breath met the flush of my cheeks. His hands smoothed up my arms, over my shoulders and rested at the base of my head. Pulling my face up to his, he brushed his lips over mine, testingly.

"I'm not asking for your forgiveness. But for you to accept me for what I am. See that I cannot offer anything more. It is not what others may want, but it is what everyone needs me to be. I have never promised you any part of myself. I only have the pleasure of my company to offer, and the promise of safety." Another reluctant brush against my guard from him. Asking to be let in. A suggestion of a physical apology.

"All I'm asking is that you are honest. I'm under no impression that you are more than what you appear to be, but if I am to stay here, then I need to be able to trust that you will answer my questions. I am at a disadvantage here and have already been attacked multiple times under your employment."

The hand holding my head took a tighter grip on my hair, pulling my body against his. Hot anger radiated from him at the reminder. "And when I find out who threatened your and the Princes' life, I will rip them to pieces with my bare hands." His warm breath filled the space between us. A ragged inhale doing little to calm his anger.

"Not if I find them first." I warned.

"Allow me to take out my vengeance and I will owe you a great favor." He retorted.

"If you let me have Argo's captures, then it's a deal." I said, the corners of my mouth perking at the exchange.

"You have my word." His tone pleading, his lips pressing to mine again. A new rippling tug at my middle, light but playful.

I knew what he was asking. For release. For a night of distraction and comfort, something that was appealing to me as well. To have every dark thought chased from my worried mind and replaced with his mouth, hands, and other tender appendages.

I leaned into him and that was all he needed. Hard and deep kisses mixed with hands moving over clothes. Loosening buttons and ties, zippers pulled, and shirts, then pants landing on the floor alongside briefs and panties.

Talos hoisted my legs up to wrap around his hips, the mattress meeting my back with a rush of air from my lungs on the descent. He wasn't going to be gentle, not after the words we'd said or the tension our arguments have built over the last week. No, this wasn't him needing or wanting me. It was stress relief. His own brand of conflict resolution. A reminder of where the power between us lie.

His fingers worked around my entrance, teasing and readying me for what he had in mind. Liquid heat flooded my core as his lips roamed my neck, and my breasts. Burning need left in the wake of his skin over mine. A rush of tension filling me as the familiar sense of his influence slithered into my nooks and stoked the fire of my own desires. Without hesitation, I let it happen. Let the control be passed on and let myself be pulled under. Anticipation quickened my pulse and nagged at my injured head, but a moment later relief washed over. Replaced by the smoldering fog he'd conjured to further relax me.

I needed him more than I needed to breathe. The density of the air around us imposing its presence down into my lungs, causing me to gasp for more. The intoxicating scent of his cologne mixed with the dampness of our hair and skin. A tightening gripped me deeply, his mouth taking the peak of my breast in and between his teeth. Gently rolling his tongue and sucking. Losing myself in his movements, a small wanting moan escaped me.

A throaty groan from him answered, sending a hum down through every nerve ablazened. I had either closed my eyes or he had suggested the lights around us to extinguish, leaving us with one less sense, but gathering me up into only what he wanted me to hear, and feel, and taste. His mouth trailed up over my mounts and valleys to my lips. The salt of my own sweat on his tongue.

"Is this what you want, Isa?" His words filled the creases of my lips, pressing down my throat and set fire to my belly.

Burst of pleasure erupted from so many places in my body at once, I thought I'd never feel pain again. Until his mouth reached the nape of my neck and his teeth met my flesh intimately. A mix of pain and pleasure coursed from the impact. A sharp intake of air was all I could muster as every one of my nerves sparked to life, electricity filling me to the tips of my fingers and toes. I called out his name and rode the wave of ecstasy until it waned.

The darkness of the room cleared enough for me to see a satisfied grin on his lips but a challenge hung on his brow and in his inky eyes. I squirmed under his gaze, he allowed me to shift out of his arms but tracked every movement. He got on his hands and knees, following me to the head of the bed. The muscles of his shoulders rippling as he prowled, glistening damp, and poised to strike again. In a blink he'd scooped an arm under my bottom and positioned me where he wanted me, nestling between my legs then looking over the conquest he'd liberated for the night.

"You don't make a sound until I tell you to." He warned, placing a hand to my belly as he moved to sit on his heels. He waited for my nod of consent before his eyes dropped between my legs, an eager bite of his bottom lip.

He grabbed my knees, his fingers dimpling where they landed before he spread my thighs wide open to him. The stubble of his chin drug down the tender skin, my back arching to guide him further. His moist breath scuttled over my highly sensitive core. When his chin dipped and tongue pressing into me, I bit my lip to stop the moan fighting to break through.

I tightened my grip on the pillow under my head as two of his fingers entered me, his tongue swirling around in rhythm circles in unison with my short heaving breaths. The pressure intensified with every stroke of his long fingers, hitting spots that he somehow had memorized.

I rocked my hips with his tempo, aching for the release he was coaxing. He added another finger, filling me to the brim and releasing a noisy breath. The moment the sound left my lips, he withdrew his fingers and hovered his lips over me. A husky voice cutting through my disappointment, "I told you, don't make a sound until I permit it."

I sucked in my swollen bottom lip and nodded eagerly, silently begging for relief. A gruff scoff rumbled from his throat but his expression was laced with a challenge. Whether to make another sound or warning me off from it. I wasn't sure which one would yield a more exciting result.

Not giving me a moment to catch my breath he replaced his fingers and mouth picking up speed and depth. I cupped a hand to my mouth to keep from calling out. The pressure mounting behind my navel and the sound of air rapidly escaping me over my fingers encouraging his pace. My muscles squeezed around his digits, and my thighs to his shoulders. I was on a steep cliff ready to plunge into crushing waves of pleasure but held back. Tilting my hips away to refute his effect, failing to retreat. He sensed my impending orgasm and hooked an arm around my hips to hold them still. Sharp hollow breaths were my only other point of focus. In and out. In and out. Air and fingers and hot, wet lips.

"Not yet." He spoke into me, a devilish teasing inflection.

I looked down to him, meeting his eyes as he watched me teeter on the torturous edge. Moments turning to agony. Tighter until my head fell back to the pillow and my back arched as high as it could. He pulled his lips only far enough away from me to give me direction. "You will remove your hand." He paused to draw his tongue over and suck between commands. "You will wait until I grant you relief." Another broad lap against my overstimulated nerve. "You will graciously thank me."

Another wave of excited warmth spread from deep behind my navel. Mounting the pressure as his fingers filled and stretched. My fingertips pressed into the mattress as I bit my bit to keep from screaming out, doing all I could to wait for his signal. His pace quickened, inching me closer to the edge.

Sounds of enjoyment and sadistic pleasure rumbled out of him becoming louder the closer I got to climax.

"Tora." He grunted.

I cursed and moaned his name as I burst and spilled over. Every muscle surrounding his fingers pulsed and gripped. A scatter of butterflies rushed through me as euphoria blanketed my vision. Talos had withdrawn his fingers but he kissed and licked softly sending jolts shooting into my fingers and toes. My pores opened and sweat pebbled my cool skin and dampening my hair. My lungs struggled to catch up with my needy muscles. Lead filling my legs and arms, pinning me to the bed further at Talos will.

He moved to lay on his side next to me on the bed and pulled my chin up towards him. His obsidian eyes peering down to me, watching me gather myself from the depths of ecstasy. With a quick scoop of his arm, I was lying on top of him with my head on his chest. A fresh tingle of electricity from our flush contact. Fingers caressing a trail down my back to my bottom, then back up to the middle of my shoulders. I looked to see his eyes closed, the glisten of my release still clinging to his pillowy lips.

I moved to sit and straddle him, his throbbing erection pressed hard against me. He opened his eyes, taking in the full sight and holding my hips still to prolong his view. "I'm supposed to show you my gratitude?" I breathed.

I made a slow figure eight with my hips, grinding down on him, causing his mouth to fall open. His wide hands held fast to my waist and pulled me down on to him harder. Gliding me over his tip, his head fell back as he groaned at the sticky friction between us. I wanted him to feel the tantalizing torture of being teased until he might burst. Ride his girth into another organism before he filled me fully. His impatience had already begun with his fingertips dimpling the delicate flesh of my lower back and bottom.

He let out a curse through clenched teeth. Taking in a sharp breath, his chest raised and lowered faster as his hips worked below me. If he was getting close, he didn't want to be because he was drawing his hips down into the mattress and lifting my off him slightly. I bit my lip to stop from smirking but very obviously failing as another guttural moan pushed its way from his tense jaw. Waiting for him to take in another gasp, I tilted my hips forward and impaled myself down onto him. An explosion of tension and pleasure surged up from my engorged nerves. He hadn't expected the move and let out a loud "Fuck! Isa!"

I raised up and slammed back down onto him. Again. Then once more before he reached up to my shoulders, pulling me down tightly to lie against him. His feet planted to the bed and his hips thrusting upward. Unleashing himself and plunging in and out; filling and pushing me to the edge once more. A deep pressure building to the breaking point. A wave of pleasure rolling through me and crashing followed by a gush of warm liquid pulsing from me, drenching him and the sheet beneath.

Shocked, I paused to look down but Talos was only encouraged by the effect. He tossed me to the side onto my belly which met the cool damp from my own excitement seeping the bed. He got to his knees and settled between my legs to enter me from behind. Rock hard and diving deep into me from the new angle, the sound of wet skin slapping together rang through the room around us. He reached up and tangled his fingers through my hair and pulled my head back, leaning down for his mouth to meet my ear, "I'm not going to stop until you soak the entire bed." Then released me.

The thought of the occurrence being a fluke hardly passed through my mind before he continued his relentless pounding. Dragging me back to a mounting pressure that first brought moans, curses, and his name from my tongue. I clenched the edge of the mattress above, my hands knocking against the wooden headboard with his every stroke. I gripped him deep inside of me and arched my back. I was close to the same breaking point and at any moment I was going to shatter. A loud noise followed by a painful sting on my bottom, then another to the other cheek and that sent me spiraling again. An explosion of fluid and electricity. The satisfied sound of Talos grunting behind me as he jerked and stilled at his own release.

He collapsed onto his back next to me, panting. His torso and chest covered in a slick sheen of sweat mingling with the dusting of hair. The dark clouds in his eyes clearing while he watched me attempting to catch my own breath. A chill clung to the beads of sweat converging at my temple and down my neck. His seed already collecting between my thighs and spilling onto the sheets. Rolling over, he kissed my temple and slid off the bed and walked to the bathroom without bothering to cover his bare skin.

The light from the bathroom flooding through the narrow doorway and filling the now evening dark room. Subtle thuds of cabinets opening and shutting before water from the shower splattered against the expensive marble tiles. Talos stalked out from the doorway and offered me a damp washcloth to clean up and a hand up from the bed.

I didn't bother try to mop of the mess but dabbed my face and walked to the steam filled bathroom. Talos trailed in behind me and opened the glass door and waited for me to step in to follow and close us in. The hot water washing away the sins from my hair and body. I took in a lung full of the humid air and turned to find Talos staring down to me, water pouring off the curves of his cheekbones and tip of his nose. His dark hair slicked back and his heavy brows shadowing his cloudy eyes.

"Why are you looking at me like that?" I turned and poured shampoo into my hand.

"Like what?" The corner of his mouth turning up into a wicked grin.

"Like I'm some sort of conquest that you just won and might possibly attempt again."

"I wouldn't dare look at you like that. I do find it thrilling to be an assistant in a new experience for you. By the look on your face, you haven't been so... stimulated by a lover before?" He perked a brow, further giving him a foxy expression.

My cheeks flushed but I had no come back or rebuttal to his assumption. I hadn't experienced anything like that before even with the more skilled lovers I'd had. Instead of responding, I massaged the rose and lemon scented shampoo into my hair. He pressed his abdomen to my back, water cascading over us from both nozzles. I turned into him and looking up to him. His features softening, focus roaming over my face. Eyes. Nose. Lips.

His hands smoothing up over my forehead and down the fall of my hair, pushing soap and water down my back and splattering on the tile below. The bridge of his nose meeting my brow in an unexpected show of affection. He cupped the base of my jaw, pulling me closer into him and kissing me. A sweet, foreign kiss. Far from any we'd shared before.

"I have to go. I'll send someone up with fresh linens." Another kiss and he let me go and stepped out of the shower, wrapping a towel around his waist and leaving the bathroom.

I grounded myself, expecting to feel the hollow we'll open up in my chest. The familiar pit that had cracked open in his wake but there was none. I probed my own emotions, examining them like raw gems but finding no cracks or blemishes. Talos' pull and influence had affected me in many ways since our meeting. He'd taken pleasure in his ability to manipulate my feelings. Had be done me a kindness and stopped tugging at me* to see how far he can push without my knowing. No debilitating aftershock of his presence. He'd looked at me as more than a distraction to chase away loneliness or intrusive entertainment.

Exhaustion set into my limbs, driving away the analytics of his intentions. Letting the water drench and cleanse me of my discretions. After several long minutes of allowing the scolding water to pinken my skin I shut the water off, wrapped an over-sized towel around myself, and went to find my cell phone. With Talos' men on their way to retrieve Argo, I needed to call my siblings and give them the update before I fell asleep.

The bed had been refreshed and made; erasing all evidence of our impassioned frenzy. An image of someone replacing the damp sheets flushed my cheeks. I cupped my hand over my mouth to stop the smirk spreading across my face but failing. With my phone in hand, I flung myself down on the bed, my wet hair spread over the silk pillowcase.

After dialing Zaida's phone number, the other line rang once before she answered, "We do not shy away from darkness."

"For we are the shadows. *double check this*" I answered

"Are you alone?" Her hushed voice volleyed back.

"I am, and I have news."

"Come to the Margaritári Hotel. I'll text you the address. Tomorrow. One o'clock." And her line went dead.

A moment later an address appeared on the screen notification. She seemed irritated, but was likely tired from searching and keeping the others from getting antsy. The hotel was only several minutes away from the hotel they had previously booked downtown. It wasn't unusual for us to switch hotels every couple of days while on assignment to keep anyone who might be too suspicious off our trail. They would likely move hotels after I came to visit tomorrow.

My eyes had closed sometime between setting my phone on the nightstand and the hundredth thought of where Argo was and if he was safe, whole, and unbroken. I slipped into a dreamless sleep only waking long enough to pull the covers up to my chin.

CHAPTER TWENTY-FOUR

Althea woke me the next morning with a nudge of my bare shoulder. I was wrapped in my sheets and duvet, hair wild and clinging to the side of my face where sweat had plastered it in my sleep. Her cheeks flushed and accompanied a teasing giggle as I attempted to cover my bare skin. The *helper Incubo* trailed in behind Althea with the breakfast cart. She waved him off and his eyes shot from her to my naked thigh, then bowed out of the room, closing the door behind him.

The heels of Althea's heels clicked on the wood floor as she went to the bathroom door and retrieved my bathrobe to toss on the foot of the bed. She then sat at the fire place to set out breakfast and waited for me to compose regain my faculties. An ache between my legs stung in a salacious way as I folded the wings of the robe around myself and tied the sash before joining Althea by the fire. She was pouring tea for the both of us and glanced up to me mid stream.

"Don't worry, I personally brewed the tea. No sneaky poison." She gave a lighthearted smirk across the table.

I hummed playful suspicion and reached to pile my plate

with fruit and pastries. I sat back with my cup in both hands to warm them up and breathe in the sweet aroma. Honey and crisp apple steamed the tip of my nose.

"You look much less pale today," Althea smirked into her tea cup.

"A compliment, I'm sure." I glowered with a roll of my eyes.

"Oh stop." She insisted as I stuffed the corner of an orange maple scone in my mouth, "I'm really glad you're feeling better because I have to talk to you about something that you may not want to get involved with further, but it is dire."

I straightened my spine and set my cup down, "I'm listening."

Althea adjusted the hem of her dress, then the sleeves at her wrists. She took a deep breath and met my eye, "Princess Amirah is getting closer to the birth of her child. She's said she has had some cramping and contractions. I would think she could be ready any time now."

"I'm sure she will be a wonderful mother. But what does this have to do with me?" I waited and watched her take another deep breath, fidgeting again with her clothing. "Althea?"

"I fear for the baby's safety. For her safety. Her baby and it's father would be the target of the royal family. They would view this as a stain on their reputation. A negation of the power in their position. A challenge to their reign." Concern and a plea strained her voice.

"I can't get involved. The Black Banners have to stay neutral in all political affairs. Otherwise, the playing field would shift and all balance we hold would topple. I can't be responsible for that."

"I'm not asking you to argue for or against anyone. I'm asking you to save the life of two people I care about. An innocent child and it's mother."

"I feel for her and her situation, Althea, but that isn't my occupation. I took your assignment under the guise that it would be quick and painless. Not to mention, Talos manipulated me. I don't regularly take on bodyguard positions. And now look where we are." I gestured around the room with a dramatic flit of my wrists.

She huffed an awkward laugh, "I know. I know what the Black Banners do. I know that Talos, and I have put you through much more than you signed on for but you're here now. And I'll pay you!" She grabbed my hand between our chairs.

"Talos has located Argo. When he retrieves him, I'll have to take him back to Cinder. There are protocols we have to follow when one of us is captured. I'm already going to be facing a shit storm of an inquiry for accepting help from an outsider."

A sinking feeling hit my stomach at the admission. I hadn't been brought in front of the Banner counsel in the past. I've had to give statements, been called as a witness, or give an account on a group assignment gone awry. The consequences for what I've done in accepting Talos' help could be detainment, or deactivation. A punishment worse than death. Exile from my organization. My family. I'd be given over to the Mortal police with every crime I have committed and forced to serve out the life sentence in a maximum security prison in an undisclosed location. No Banner who has been discharged has escaped their fate.

Althea poured herself another cup of tea, her brow stitched and her lips pursed. "I know what I'm asking is more than I should, there is more at stake here than I can fully explain. Talos will be bound by duty to the royal family. He can't help me."

Her gloomy grey eyes roamed over my face, hoping to read my expression or searching for pity. I stood and walked to the fire, my arms wrapped around myself. The soft flames licking up around the ashened logs. The fire had survived the night, leaving coals and piles of worn soot.

"You're the only being I trust."

And with that, she had me. She had lost her faith in Talos. Knew he would choose to follow the command of the King and Queen. He would uphold the esoteric treaty and maintain the social order to protect the Incubo.

"I have to talk to my siblings, but I will do what I can. That's all I can promise right now."

She sighed in relief, "Thank you, Isa."

I sat back down and offered her a weak smile. I would be leaving to meet with Zaida and the others soon and I was having a hard time finding the words to explain what had happened in the King's Chateau. My being poisoned, the head injury, and the treaty. I needed to know if any of them had heard of it and if they would be able to confirm anything that Talos had told me about it before.

Althea and I finished eating our breakfast together and I contemplated asking her about the treaty but I had the feeling that like all other beings, younger Incubo were given the same information as the new generations of Mortals and Fata. She had been caught off guard at the Princesses' claim that her child's father was Fata. The look of surprise and the pain of betrayal on her face still seared in my memory. A strange feeling of guilt washed over me that I may know more than my friend did about her own kind.

Talos often worked in half truths, discreetly skirting the veil between withholding information and speaking in need-to-know. I could only imagine being as close to him as Althea is wouldn't grant you any more insight. By their interactions, I could wager that he kept anything from her that he would deem damaging to the world he had helped build around her. Shielding her from any outside voice that would contradict the glitz and glamor of the Incubo's society.

His version of kindness was now putting Althea in a position to break every rule to protect her cousin and the baby. I couldn't help but admire my friend for standing up for her beliefs and choosing family over duty. Something I was currently facing myself. Even through our graphically different eyes, we were fighting the same battle. Yet another way we have grown in our bond. My only hope was that we both escape the threats that were chasing us.

CHAPTER TWENTY-FIVE

After Althea left me to dress and ready myself for my outing. Arming myself discreetly and hiding the Alexandrite dagger in my boot holster. Not the place I would typically keep the exquisite blade but for the time being, it would have to do. Another check in the mirror that none of my weapons were noticeable, I went to find Talos. I would need to borrow his car again and hoped he wouldn't insist on tagging along. He may have had more information since the night before, but I doubted my family would be so kind as to accept his word as freely as I had.

I found him in the library, reclined in a far corner lounging chair. He had several books stacked next to him on the floor and a cup of tea balanced on top as if it were a makeshift side table. The thick volume in his lap opened midway, the image of a family tree with names scratched in pen and pencil at the end of each branch. He glanced up to me momentarily as I approached.

"Good morning, Isa. You must be ready for another lesson if you are up and roaming about unescorted."

"I was actually hoping that after last night, you'd be inclined to do me a favor." My hands settled on my cocked hips.

He looked up to me with a wolfish grin, "Without sounding too confident, I believe I had already done you a favor last night?"

His silky voice was dulled against the stacks of books but the unmistakable air of satisfaction still lingered. I shifted my weight under the heat of his eyes, and cleared my throat.

"I need to borrow your car. I have to update the other Banners in town. I'll be back this evening."

He surveyed me, his grin dropping to a concerned frown. I watched as his mind worked out the logistics and more than likely an excuse to keep me from leaving or how to convince me to let him accompany me to the meeting.

"Talos." My voice shook him from his thoughts, "I need to update them that you came through."

"Which is against the Black Banner protocols, is it not?" He folded his hands in his lap, worry knitted his brows.

"They're not going to haul me off to the Banner Counsel before Argo is safe." I crossed my arms and sighed. Feeling almost childish that I was having to defend myself.

He studied me again, "This seems like an unnecessary risk after the attack on yourself and the Prince. And let us not forget that Lawrence is still in the wind."

"No one knows where I am going except for the Banners and I am not the main target after all. If you don't hear from me in three hours, you can send someone after me." I compromised.

A heavy sigh escaped him, sounding more frustrated than relieved. "Fine."

He stood and reached into his pocket taking out and tossed me his keys. "The garage is off the east wing. I'll walk you down."

I let him guide me down to the garage, rows and rows of luxury and sporty vehicles filled the windowless concrete terminal. The bright halogen lights above us shown off the polished bodies, enhancing the pristinely maintained cars.

Each one we passed more expensive looking than the last. Classics parked to one side that looked as if they had never been driven, even when they were the newest model of their year.

When we came to Talos' he propped his arm on the roof and looked me over, "You're sure about going in person?"

"You're being a little ridiculous, don't you think?" I rounded to the drivers side and opened the door.

"I am prone to protect my assets, Isa." He smoldered.

"I'll see you when I get back." I said as I slid into the seat and ignited the ignition.

He backed up and parted his lips as if to say something else, but I didn't give him the chance. I pulled away from the parking spot and drove out from the garage and rounded the front of the Chateau. The front garden was starting to show signs of autumn. Trees were beginning to turn orange, yellow, and red. The grass was littered with the early fallen leaves not yet raked up by the groundskeepers. But perhaps there weren't enough Incubo to perform those tasks with all the Fata being rejected from the grounds.

After hearing the Princess's story of conception, I had so many questions and wasn't sure who would be able to answer them. Were all Incubo-Fata born hard to kill or was it just Lawrence's special abilities manifesting? What would the Princess's child's abilities be, and could she somehow feel the power brewing in her womb?

Buildings passed overhead, lights and faceless beings passed by as I made my way to the hotel. Amples was becoming less foreign quickly, at least the side that I had seen so far. The main streets in and out of the metropolis were busy but easy to navigate. Not long after entering the city I pulled up in front of the white washed stone hotel. The tall polished marble pillars imposing against the grey buildings surrounding it. Carved in the archway that framed the double glass doors was a serpent wound around an olive branch. Each scale etched and polished to a lifelike shine.

The caller passed me a ticket in exchange for the keys as I rounded the front of the car. The cast lobby echoed with the footsteps of attendants and guests. Clacking of wheeled luggage carts distinguishable from high heels and leather loafers against the garnet floors. Carved serpents, matching their larger counterpart outside, climbed four pillars that divided the room into two seating areas on either side of the walk away and encouraged visitors to the front desk.

I bypassed the desk and headed to the elevator doors to the left, indicated by a narrow rug. The lift doors opened up with a sharp chime, letting guests out and leaving me alone on the assent. I illuminated the tenth floor button and gave the button to close the doors a couple taps to hurry them along. Not wanting to have to take a longer route to my sister's room.

When the doors opened again, I stepped out into a tighter hallway than I had expected, only enough room for two people to pass each other between rooms on either side. The wine red and black carpet harsh against the pure white walls and doors. Only the black room numbers on the doors gave the walls contrast. Even the sconces blending into the bright white interior.

I waited a moment for any sign that the elevator would return to this floor, if someone was attempting to follow me, they would have waited to see which floor I had gotten off on then come after me. It would have surprised me if I were followed that it would have been by Talos, I had no doubt he had a tracker planted on his car for situations just like this. But the lift did not stop on the tenth floor so I proceeded down to Zaida's room.

I knocked once, paused, then knocked twice, paused then one last time. A simple code but one that hadn't failed us yet.

She answered with a takeaway cup in her hand, extending it to me, "Nectar of the Gods?"

"Solute', sorella amore!" I greeted, and took the paper cup in my hands.

She ushered me inside, and I followed her to the foot of her king sized bed. I took a long, hot sip of the sweet latte, bitter notes clinging to my tastebuds as the liquid warmed my chest on its way down. Zaida retrieved her own coffee from her side table, then sat next to me. Watching me carefully.

"Glad to see you're still in one piece and not a mess like most other Mortals when they spend too much time in the Incubo fray." She took a sip of her drink, a smug look on her gorgeous face.

"Any day now, they'll melt my mind and trap me in their world." I huffed a sarcastic laugh, but Zaida wasn't amused.

"Any time is too much right now. Have you heard about the attack in *Small city near by*?" She waited a moment for me to shake my head, "Three Fata cornered an Incubo and all three Fata were found with their necks and spines broken in several places."

"What was the motive to attack the Incubo? Were they provoked?"

"The Mortal Police is being tight lipped. Trying to sweep it under the rug as self defense. I'm sure Incubo money and power has louder influence than anything else."

Her eyes bore daggers into me, waiting for my response. Which I didn't have anything coherent to add or reason. It was suspicious that Fata would openly commit a crime to an Incubo, and even rarer still the incident wasn't causing more of a stir at the Chateau. I wriggled under her gaze, and cleared my throat.

"Where are the others?" I asked to change the subject.

"Markus went back to Cinder. Called away to assist Renee' on a tech consult. Derek is upstairs resting. He was out all night chasing down a lead on Argo, but came back empty handed again. I called him and left a voicemail that you'd be here to give us an update. He'll be down when he wakes up."

"And Talia?"

"She's still weak from her injury. I sent her home with Markus. She didn't want to leave you here, but even at her fittest, I could kick her ass."

We both laughed, tension splintering and lifting from both of us. Our relationship had its ups and downs, but we'd always found ways to accept the others views and push through any awkwardness. This was new territory for the both of us.

"You said you had news?" She took a long pull of her cup.

"Talos' men have tracked Argo and his captors down.They should be back in soon from Meru." I gave the condensed version of what Talos had told me.

"Why would they have taken him across the border? We didn't get that intel at all. Derek was checking out the shipping yard on the other side of city last night."

"I don't know but I'll find out when the culprits are brought to me at the Chateau. When Argo is released to me, we'll take him home. You, me, and Derek."

"I wished you'd stay with us. Talos could have Argo delivered to us and this whole mess would be over." She stood and walked to the window, glancing down to the street before turning back to me.

"It's more complicated than that. There are things going on within the Incubo community, in the royal family. Althea is more terrified than before, I can't leave yet."

"Have you changed your profession? Are you the new companion to the royal Incubo?" She said, her tone prickly.

"They do pay well." I joked, eliciting a reluctant smile and a shake of her head.

"You're taking this all too lightly. And the Banner Counsel will be sniffing around any day now. We've been here too long.

Argo's situation is going to bring a lot of suspicion to your door."

"If I stay, I'll have more leverage when they do."

"What do you mean?" She narrowed her eyes to me.

"The Incubo Princess is heavily pregnant. Another secret child. But even more surprising, the child's father is Fata." I could see the realization wash over her at what I was saying.

"Isa, you are not a spy for the Counsel. No one has hired you to obtain this information. This is a very risky attempt to get out of the trouble you've already gotten yourself into. A distraction at best."

"Distractions are one of our last resort when complications arise. Isn't that what Mr. Green taught us?"

She sighed and rolled her eyes but, I had her there. Many strategies we were taught during our time at the Banner House were how to avoid being caught or killed. This was one of those situations, even if it was from my own organization.

"Alright. Fine." She shrugged her shoulders in surrender, "I regret encouraging you to take this assignment, even if Talos is a good lay."

"Without him, we wouldn't have gotten Argo back. I don't regret that, or sleeping with him."

Zaida snorted at that, wiping the coffee spray from beneath her nose. I laughed and reached for the box of tissues on the side of her bed, passing them to her.

"So, now the Queen and Princess are with child," she clarified, regaining herself, "Who had passed in their ranks? This isn't like their kind to reproduce so freely."

"That is the other part of the leverage I would have to bring to the Counsel. What do you know of the Treaty of Life?"

She blinked at me, no response being loud enough for me to go on with what I had learned.

"Talos told me that there had been a Great War between the

Incubo, Fata, and Mortals. Thousands were killed on all sides, but the Incubo were losing hundreds daily. Their numbers were dwindling and they were looking at quick extinction so they called for a treaty. They would promise to keep their numbers low, stay to themselves, and only reproduce with their own kind as long as the remainder of their kind were protected. The secret as to how to kill them would be buried for future generations."

"This sounds like some sort of fairytale. Something to tell young children to keep them from fighting on the playground." She sat back down next to me and waited for me to go on.

"Mortals and Fata went on to forget the treaty and war. All history of it erased to protect the Incubo as they maintained their mysterious society. They kept their lands and titles, spreading rumors that they could not procreate with the rest of us. To keep their bloodlines pure and powerful. But this has become an old restriction, many of the younger Incubo have been raised to believe that they are incapable of reproducing with any being other than their own kind and this has led to Incubo-Fata crosses dotting their family trees."

"This can't be true." Her dark brown eyes roamed my face, looking for any indication that I was lying, but finding none.

"These offspring have been kept secret in the families they most resemble. Passing for one side or the other, and living out their lives as shadowed as possible. But, like Lawrence, some have possessed features of Fata and Incubo. I'm not sure how yet, but these children have been disposed of, families ravaged to make the deaths look like an accident. Or they have been hidden away to save them from their gruesome fate."

"Are you saying that they kill their own babies and children in the name of keeping their bloodlines seeming pure?"

"I'm not sure. That's what it would seem but as far as I know, the children of Incubo and Fata are very difficult to kill. Which is what I'm trying to find out now because Lawrence may still be alive."

"Lawrence? The same man who almost killed you even after you slit his throat?" Her eyes widened, and mouth agape.

"His body wasn't accounted for at the Manor in Arta. I have no explanation for it, but Alexandrite didn't work and neither did Talos beating him to a bloody mess."

"Remind me again why it is safer for you to go back to the Incubo and not stay here? Or go back to Cinder?"

"I don't know if it's safer. But I can feel something is stewing and when it all comes to light, we will need to know how to defeat any new enemies."

"Which new enemies? The Incubo or their secret offspring?" She asked, but was left waiting a moment for my response.

I wasn't sure who would be the highest bidder when the Fata and Incubo tension came to a head. It was no surprise that Fata were fed up with being treated less than Incubo when they possessed abilities that Mortals didn't but were seen as employees or play things by the Incubo elite. At least that is what Mortals had been led to believe. I was still sorting out what made sense and what was fed to all beings as a false truth. Unsure I could trust Talos' word in what the treaty held and what was social construct of older Incubo generations.

"Isa?" Zaida's voice shook me from my thoughts.

"I don't know who the next threat will be, or who will be looking to the Banners for help. But either way, we'll need to know how to kill either one most effectively, right?"

She nodded and pursed her lips. I wanted her to come with me, help me navigate through what I would be facing when I returned to the Chateau to wait for Argo. The first thing I was going to do was make a visit to the library and find a written copy of the treaty for myself. Verify what was the truth or Talos' version of it.

I didn't wait for Derek to wake. Partly due to being emotionally exhausted and partly because I wanted to get back to the Chateau in case Amil and Yamir returned with Argo early.

Zaida walked me out to the vallet and eyed Talos' car, passing silent judgment on me with a smirk.

"How else was I supposed to get here?" I joked with a shrug.

"I didn't say anything," she laughed and put her hands up in a mocking defensive gesture.

"You didn't have to. But it's the least he could do after dragging me into this mess."

"I don't disagree with that. Be safe and call me the moment they bring Argo back to you."

"I will." I promised. "I love you." I wrapped my arms around around her and she embraced me. Both of us unsure of what would come next.

"I love you, sorella."

CHAPTER TWENTY-SIX

The drive back to the Chateau was calm, silent. The interior of Talos' car void of color or city sound. Only the clicking of the turn signal and the occasional vibration of revving of the engine against the shadowed windows. I could have kept driving, away from the Incubo and conflict bubbling under the surface. Meet Amil at the border and take Argo straight back to Cinder. The thought trickled through the forefront of my mind. I could imagine Argo sitting in the seat next to me, the scenery passing us by as the sun sets and a blanket of stars accompany us back home.

My hands on the wheel and feet on the gas pedal took me back to the gate entry of the Chateau, negating all other scenarios that had projected in my head on the drive back. I drove back into the garage and parked Talos' car in a vacant spot near the garage entrance. I wasn't ready to go inside yet. I wasn't ready to be pushed further into the cloaked truths and silencing expectations.

I locked the car and headed out to the path that led around the Chateau to the gardens to the south of the compound. The sun was hanging low, each day it seem to set earlier and earlier as autumn settled into the changing leaves of the forest surrounding the property. A haze of evening light cast a golden light across the lawn and crept up the stone walls up to the crest of the brick shingled roof. The ivy that wound its way up towards the top floor balconies like gold leaf spindled web.

Bright orange and yellow flowers lined the cobblestone path which carved a path that weaved through the garden beds and shrubs, looping back to the rear French doors of the Chateau. Each step along gave a slightly different view of the grounds and many fruit heavy trees dotted around. I rounded the last corner and came into full view of the back of the Chateau. Each window set ablaze with the setting sun. I knew I had stalled long enough and began up the inclined walkway to the doubled doors, shadowed by tall shrubs.

It wasn't until I was about five yards away from door when I noticed a shadowed figure lurking behind the bush. Ice flooded my veins and my hand shot for the blade at my belt. A shift of gravel from under the forms feet as they began to crouch low, either unaware that I had seen them or that I was there at all. I held the throwing knife in my fingers firmly. The muscles in my calves tensed and readied to strike. The bramble obstructed a clear shot but I waited for the figure to shift. Just a little to the left and I would be able to aim through a thinning spot in their hiding place. I lowered myself slowly to gain a better look but it was no use, they would have to make the first move.

My pulse was quickening as my heart fluttered in my chest, it had been so long since I'd been filled with adrenaline from a proper fight. I took a slow, deep breath to steady myself. The shadow stood, a branch snapping under their foot causing them to startle and leap to the left. I let my blade loose, and heard the wet thud of it burying itself in to a thigh.

A grunt of pain followed by the crunch of gravel as the man went down hard to the ground. I grabbed the Alexandrite dagger from my boot and lept towards them. Yanking them beneath me by the scruff of their neck, landing my knee to their chest, and holding the blade to the soft flesh of their throat.

"Please! Don't kill me!" The man pleaded but didn't struggle against the blade or the weight of my on top of him.

He was young, possibly in his early twenties. His ears gave away that he was Fata before the smell of fire and warmth caught my nose. His scent reminded me of a kitchen, an undertone of yeast and bread wafted from him.

"You have thirty seconds to convince me to do otherwise." I answered, the pulse against my eardrums dulling.

"I need to see the Princess. She's expecting me, I swear." He gulped for air between his words.

"And why would she be expecting you when all other Fata have been relieved from their duties on these grounds?"

"I can't tell you, they'll kill me and her."

I knew who this was. The poor idiot was going to get himself killed by sneaking in to see Princess Amirah. He had to know this was a suicide mission.

"You're the Fata that fathered the Princess's child. Do you have a death wish?" I didn't allow him to get up or release him but lifted myself off his chest enough for him to catch his breath.

"My name is Mikal, and Amirah sent for me. She doesn't want to be here, she wants to leave with me. Tonight. Before she gives birth to our son, and they take him from us."

"Who would take your son from you? If he resembles the Incubo, they'd allow her to keep and raise him as one of their kind." I recited what I had been told, waiting fo his confirmation.

"The King and Queen aren't going to let her keep our child and they haven't made arrangements to transfer him to my care. This boy is a stain to their name and they hid her away during her pregnancy to not raise suspicion when they get rid of him."

"That is a dangerous accusation you've just made, Mikal." I raised a brow to him.

"You're Mortal, you know there is something wrong here. If you're here, you know what's coming. She isn't safe. Our son isn't safe here." He put a hand to my knee, "Please. Please, you have to believe me. You have to help me."

My heart constricted in my chest. When did I become the savior of Incubo and Fata. It would have been much easier to kill him and take the accolades for protecting the royal family, but instead I gave a great sigh and stood up to offer him my hand to stand.

His leg was bleeding, the trail of blood wetting his jeans and pooling at the heel of his boot. He ripped a strip from the bottom of his shirt, pulled the blade from his leg and tied the cloth around the wound with gritted teeth. When he was done wrapping his wound he stood favoring his injured leg, he passed my bloodied blade back to me. I had to give him that he was brave, not that he had any sense of self preservation.

"What will happen to the child if the King and Queen take him?"

I looked him over, he was taller than me by several inches, thin and lanky. His arms a bit more defined, likely from working in the Chateau kitchens.

"I don't even want to imagine it." A mix of grief and anger hung in his expression.

"You couldn't have expected to leave this place in one piece with the Princess. She's guarded by Incubo heavily and from what I've heard, close to full labor. I wouldn't be surprised if she were pushing as we speak." I folded my arms over tucking both blades to my sides, and cocked my head.

"I had to try. He's my son. She is the love of my life."

I shook my head and huffed another sigh, "Where is your vehicle?"

"In the woods," he said, turning and pointing behind him to

the tree line beyond the gardens. "There is a clearing not far from the edge of vineyard, it's used as the hunting trail."

"How fitting."

"Please. I can protect her and our baby once we are out of here." He placed a hand to the center of his chest.

"And how will you do that? Every Incubo in *this country* will be looking for the three of you."

He gave me a dry smile and closed his eyes tight. At his will, his features began to change. His skin lightening from dusky brown to olive, his cheekbones sharpening, and jaw becoming more square. My brows raised and my mouth fell open at the sight. I'd never met a Fata who would change their appearance so rapidly. It typically took long periods of time for their skin to take on the characteristics of their surroundings or duties. I wouldn't have been able to recognize him if it weren't for the shape of his eyes and the point in his ears.

"Where would you go? They'll still be looking for Princess Amirah and a new born baby."

"West, far far west into Meru. I have family there who will let us hide there for a couple years while the child grows and we are forgotten or presumed dead."

"Do the royals know you have family there? It wouldn't be difficult to track you down there by a familial connection." I argued.

"No. I have no paperwork stating that I have family there. My parents passed away many years ago and most of my family records were lost to time. My mother was born here and my father wasn't permitted to be on my birth certificate."

I squinted my eyes to him, waiting for more of an explanation or a plan. But before he would utter another word, a sound of footsteps up the path came from behind us. I pushed him into the bush that he had been hiding in before and pushed his shoulder down to crouch low. I stepped out from the doorway and waited to see who would had been roaming the gardens as well.

Althea's long blonde hair bobbed as she peered around as she prowled the gardens stone walkway. When she caught sight of me, she straightened and looked around for a moment before stepping closer.

"Isa! What are you doing out here?" Her sweet voice chimed through the last light of the evening.

"I could ask you the same question, Althea. Where's Talos?"

"He's entertaining their majesties in a private dinner. I wanted to take a stroll before having dinner myself. Would you like to join me?"

The corner of my mouth pulled into a coy grin at the tember of her voice, the hint of guilt and a lie laced through every sentence.

"You looked like you were expecting someone?" I mused.

"Hmm? Who would I be expecting?" She shifted her weight back and forth, and placed her hands to her hips.

"Althea. You're a terrible liar." I took a few steps back and pulled the Fata from the bush by his arm. "You called the Princess's lover, didn't you?"

Her eyes widened at the stranger, "I don't know who that is, and I didn't call him."

"The Princess sent for me, Lady Althea. She told me that you'd help us."

Althea's misty eyes darted between Mikal and me. Her chest rising and falling in panic. She cleared her throat and looked at the windows above as several began to light up from the inside. She worried her lip and wrapped her arms around her, hugging herself.

"It's ok, Althea. Where is the Princess now?" I asked, trying my best to do so in a calming tone.

"She's waiting in her room for my signal. Is he bleeding?"

"Well. I did find him first, he's lucky it was just his leg."

She smiled and her shoulders sagged in relief. "I had to do something, and I couldn't put you at anymore risk than I already had."

I nodded in understanding, she had come to me for help and I couldn't promise my fealty. She did the next best thing she could think of: remove the Princess and her son from the royals before it was too late. A dangerous attempt but I respected her and the Princess for it.

"Isa, I have to get her to safety and this is the only chance we have. Tonight."

"I know." I turned to Mikal, "Can you walk?"

"I would walk over broken glass and burning coals if it meant Amirah would be safe." He stood on both legs, wobbling slightly with weight on his injured side but steady enough to drive.

"That's very romantic but for this mad plan to work, you'll need to be able to get to your vehicle without passing out from pain." When he didn't respond, I went on. "When you get to to the clearing, be ready. Althea and I will bring the Princess out to meet you. I hope you're prepared to drive very quickly for a long while. Once the royal family realizes she's missing they will be on your trail. Very quickly."

He raised his chin and puffed out his chest, but faltered, falling to one knee with a painful groan. Althea bent to help him up and when he stood up again, the pool of blood at his foot was spreading across the stones of the walkway. Pooling in the grout, winding around the large stones. We needed a new plan and fast.

"Althea, can you bring the Princess out? Mask it as a walk to help with her labor cramps? Meet me in the garage."

"We'll be down in five minutes." She dashed past Mikal and I and into the double doors.

I hooked my arm around Mikal's waist, letting him lean on

me for better support. We stuck close to the side of the Chateau and made our way to the garage entrance.

"How did you change your appearance so quickly?" I asked, partly to distract him from his wound, and partly to gain answers.

"I've always been able to do it. No one else in my family can do it. My mother always told me it made me special."

His answer didn't satisfy my curiosity. I'd met many Fata over the years and as far as I knew, they weren't special abilities like his.

"You said your father wasn't on your birth certificate, was he Incubo?"

"No. He was Fata as well. I don't know why he wasn't named at my birth." He was breathing heavily, laboring against the pain in his leg and loss of blood.

We got to the edge of the garage and I set him down to sit on the ground the garage door. He leaned against the wall, letting his head fall back to rest. Sweat trailing down from his dark hair and brow. I took Talos' keys out of my pocket, unlocked the car from outside and watched for any movement from inside or around us.

"Wait here." I spoke to Mikal but didn't break concentration.

I made a start to the car and opened the door to climb in to pull out of the parking spot. I left the engine running but got out of the car and headed to the door that led inside, waiting for Althea and the Princess. There was no noise beyond the door, no footsteps or bustle beings passing by. I cracked the door, peeking to see down the long hallway that opened up into the foyer at the bottom of the main staircase. I closed over the door and looked back into the garage. Talos' car was positioned to easily exit once the Princess made it down. I would drive the car out of the garage, pull Mikal into it and then drive them both down to where his vehicle was waiting. I didn't trust that Talos' didn't have his car bugged so I couldn't let them leave in it. But to make the journey off the grounds easier would increase the chances of the two of them making it out alive.

I looked back through the crack in the door and saw Althea and the Princess coming towards me. Both laughing like giddy school girls as they walked arm and arm down the hall. As they got closer, I saw that Althea was more holding the Princess upright than just walking together. Princess Amirah clutched the side of her stomach, and winced. She choked back her pain and only paused for a moment before continuing.

Althea pushed to door open and I took the Princess' other side to help her down the couple stairs onto the polished concrete floor. Together we led her to the passenger side door and she reclined back. Breathing in deeply. Exhaling slowly.

"She isn't going to make the trip to Meru without having the baby." I looked up to Althea, who was catching her breath.

Althea's eyes shifted to a dark, stormy blue haze. "She has to try. We're too close to turn back now."

"Please, I need to get out of here. I have to save my baby." Amirah's glassy grey eyes begged.

"Ok, lets go then." I said and closed the door. I turned to Althea to give her the next instruction, "I need you to get Mikal ready to jump into the car."

"No, I'm going to take him down to the edge of the forest. I can carry him and get there quickly."

"I don't think that's a good idea, Althea. If they come looking for the Princess, they'll need an excuse from the person who saw her last."

"You said it yourself, I'm a terrible liar." She gave me a wary smile, "Come on. Follow us down the side road."

I hopped into the drivers seat and waited until she was at the mouth of the garage and had hoisted Mikal up into her arms. He clung to her, looking slightly more pale than when I had left him. I eased the car out of the drive away to be mindful of the Princess who was clutching the handle of the door for dear life.

"We can still turn around. You could have your baby safely here."

"I would rather give birth in a car and keep my son safe, than hold him for mere moments before he's snatched from my arms forever. No. We have to go now. I'll be fine." Tears fell from her eyes.

"Ok. Hold on tight."

In a blur, Althea ran down the dusty road off the side of the fence lined property on one side and a wall of bushes on the other. Her speed rivaled Talos'. I had never seen her move like this before, or the strength. When we made it down to the edge of the forest the path had ended. We would have to move the Princess on foot.

Mikal hobbled to his van and started up the engine. It looked to be one he used to catering. Solid white, no windows aside from the front and back for visibility. He jumped stumbled out to the back to open the doors and tried to help us ease Princess Amirah into the cabin that he had prepared for them to travel in. A bed had been fashioned to the bed of the vehicle, braced by brackets that raised the bed enough for storage compartments to be fixed underneath. The floor had also been carpeted and looked to be cushioned for comfort. They would have to sleep in the van for several days on their journey and it seemed he had thought of everything.

Althea and I held onto the Princess as she took deep breaths to calm herself before climbing into the back. The slope of the clearing made it a little more difficult to push her up onto the high step but once inside she settled onto the bed. Mikal sat down on the back bumper and leaned inside to open one of the storage compartments. He pulled out a zipped pouch and handed it to me, turned back to the compartment and handed a luxury bag to Princess Amirah. She opened it up and riffled around as if to check that all its contents were what she expected.

Mikal turned to me, "I need you to stick up my leg before we go. Otherwise, I'll bleed out before we hit the border."

I unzipped the bag he'd given me. A fully stocked medical kit. I nodded and set it down on the vans floor to get what I needed. Needled, stitching sutures, a pair of scissors and a pair of forceps. He pulled his pants down and turned so I could see better by the vans overhead light. Not ideal but nothing about this was but it would have to hold him over until they got to Meru. I took out a small bottle of alcohol and dampened some gauze to clean the area.

"Althea, I need you to take Talos' car back up to the garage. I'll come up when they're clear. Take the Princess's coat and place it on her bed, then turn her shower on and lock the door. Distract anyone who comes looking and call me if anyone catches on." I instructed and handed her Talos' keys.

Princess Amirah took off her coat and tossed it to Althea and she was gone. There was no time to waste on goodbyes, she would probably never see her cousin again or ever meet the baby, but they would be alive and together.

I went to work stitching up the knife wound on Mikal's thigh. I'd landed the blade only an inch away from a major artery, he was ouch to still be alive. Each stich I made came with a grunt of pain. A wince and heavy breathing. Princess Amirah cooed and shushed him, attempting to calm him and slow his bleeding. The cut was deep but quickly stopped bleeding once I'd finished. I poured some more alcohol over the wound, patted it dry, then taped a padding of gauze over it for the drive.

He pulled his pants back up and stood, supporting himself on the door of the van. "Thank you. Not for the knifing, but for helping us."

"Getting out of here safely will be thank you enough. Now, go." I looked between their pained but grateful faces, then shut the door closest to me.

Mikal looked inside to his precious cargo, a tight smile

cracking over his expression. Hope that they had done what seemed impossible. He nodded to the Princess then shut the door, moving to the driver's side door and getting in. I moved out of the way and he backed up into the woods, a worn drive etched into the dense trees. The road, if you could even call it one, was dark and narrow but he maneuvered back through it with ease. By the way he was able to drive in reverse and with very little light, I had the impression that he had driven it often.

I watched the nose of the van disappear into the darkness and waited for the sound of the engine to die away before I started to make my way back up to the Chateau. It would only be a manner of time until someone realized the Princess was missing, but I hoped that we were able to give them at least a half hour head start.

CHAPTER TWENTY-SEVEN

The path back to the Chateau was much longer than it had seemed, what had felt like seconds to drive down took ten minute walk. The garage door was still open, and Talos' car was parked discreetly towards the middle of the parking lot. It didn't seem that any other vehicles were missing but I couldn't be certain.

I reached the door that led to the hallway to the foyer. There was no sense of urgency yet. Absent of pounding footsteps down the stairs or halls looking for what has been lost. No worried beings prowling the doorways for any sign of intrusion or escape. I stepped lightly up the staircase and crept up to the second floor.

When I opened the door to the darkened room, a wave of ice through my veins hit me first, then the skull splitting pain to my temples. I gasped for air, my lungs ached against the strain of the thickset room. My hands groped the walls around me looking for the light switch, I needed a visible target for my blade. I pulled a throwing knife from my hip and aimed for the closest chair landing with the sound of ripped fabric. He was there somewhere waiting in the shadows and flickering low fire in the fireplace.

My fingers found the switch, throwing bright white light around the room. Blinded by the sudden brightness, I let loose another blade to the next chair. The impact another cushioned thud. My muscles burned from the lack of oxygen with each movement. Focusing on what little air I could squeeze down into my lungs, my eyes darted around the room searching for Talos. A moment later landing on his figure casually leaning in the bathroom doorway.

"It took you a long while to get back. I was beginning to worry." He lazed.

I choked, and reached for the Alexandrite blade at my boot. The handle warming in my palm. I focused on each groove of the handle. The sheen of the polished stone blade. The shift from violet to emerald at the slightest movement and quake of my wrist.

I looked back to Talos and the curve of his cheekbones, and the brush of facial hair on his tense jaw. His eyes pitch black, and deadly. The blood pumping in my ears began to slow and dull as fresh breath filled my chest. The tensity low in my stomach remaining like a stain he left after letting the bond break. He pushed off the doorframe and swaggered towards me. Stopping a few feet away and sliding his hands into his front pockets.

"Do you have any idea what you and Althea have done? What danger you have put all Incubo in by your rash actions?"

I shifted my weight and adjusted the dagger in my hand, assuring that the threat to him was still visible. "I don't know what you're talking about."

He dipped his chin and a wolfish expression broke over his face. "You don't." He huffed a laugh.

The silky sound of his cool voice sent a tingle down my

spine, pimpling my skin on its way. The air beginning to thicken as Talos' inky black voids barreling down into me. I swallowed hard at the knot in my throat, feeling as though the tension was coming from a pair of invisible hands encircling me. Taking a step closer and holding the blade ready to strike by my side. Dark amusement played at his features and in his posture. A powerful jungle cat sizing up his opponent. I was no longer prey.

"The Princess is missing from her room. It would seem that she has vanished into the shower drain. You don't have any knowledge of this?"

"I have been gone most of the day in your car. Not to mention, I wasn't hired to serve the Incubo Princess, that is unless you'd like to give me a raise?"

"As of the moment, I can only offer to spare your life if she is found within the next few hours."

Every muscle in my body went rigid at his words. They wouldn't find the Princess with their lack of manpower. Yamir and Amil were still gone and the Chateau was sparsely employed and without Fata to care for the King and Queen. Talos would have to go after them himself. That thought pulled at the corners of my lips.

"Don't make me force you to speak. We've moved far passed that, you and I." His insinuation spoke to admiration he held for me, but how quickly he would abandon it to get what he wanted.

"You're welcome to try." I shifted my eyes to the blade in my hand.

He took a sharp inhale, a pleasurable hum from his throat as he stepped closer, meeting my challenge of his assertion and turning his palms out open to me. "I'm unarmed, Isa."

A warmth brushed my cheek, accompanied by a thrum of sensation between my thighs.

"That's the second mistake you've made this evening." I took another half step to ease our distance but he held his ground this time.

"I suppose the first was accusing you of treason?" He quipped.

"I'm not loyal to any being outside of the Black Banners, Talos. Even if I had anything to do with the Princess' disappearance, I haven't committed treason."

He cocked his head, the gleam of the firelight behind me reflecting in the far corner of his eyes, reminding me of Amil for a moment. Guilt in that memory snatched at my gut.

"There it is. The ice in your veins heating for possibly your only weakness outside of your family. I was foolish to believe I had a carved out a place within you to share with him."

Pressure slithered around my chest, a pounding beginning in my ears, and the twinge of pain prickled at my temple. He was getting ready for another attempt to subdue. "Have I ever told you how beautifully venomous you are when you threaten my life?"

"A third mistake. You're getting sloppy, Talos." I lunged, the dagger tearing his jacket and not reaching his skin.

His feet caught on the rug and he landed hard on his stomach. I planted my knee into the middle of his spine, pinning him and grabbing at his jaw. Pulling his chin up and giving the dagger's blade a wide field. Holding it's cool smooth side to his skin, the tip angled to the rim of his jaw.

He swallowed, the blade making the wave of motion along the cartilage of his throat. His hands pressed to the ground beneath him, arching his back to escape my grip. I pushed down against him, the edge of the dagger digging into his sensitive flesh until he stilled. His eyes clearing to their normal storm clouds as he reeled in his emotions with every heave of his chest. Adrenaline pumped through me. Pouring into my lungs, and pumping into every strand of muscle held tight by the hold I had on him.

"What now, Isa?" Even with certain death pressed to his artery, he goaded me, "Spill my blood. Let every last ounce drain onto the floor. Then what? You'll surely never see Argo again. If you made it off the property, you'd be hunted down and dragged back for a trial." He paused, hushing his tone, "I will wait for you at the gates of Sheol. We can face what awaits us both, together. Hand in hand."

He smiled mockingly, and gave a throaty chuckle at his own imagery. "We could spend eternity together paying for the treacherous things we have done."

"What a pair we would be." I gritted out between clenched teeth.

I leaned down to meet his ear, his ragged breath straining against the pull at his neck, "But I don't need to spill all of your blood to get out of here alive. Do I?"

His eyes widened and his shoulders clenched beneath my knee but his movements were for once too slow. I drug the dagger through the rip I had made and pulled up against his side and along his ribs. He screamed in pain as the gash flowed and pooled against the fine fabric of his shirt, then jacket. I got to my feet and made to dash to the door but Talos reached out to catch my ankle. I crashed down onto the floor, knocking the wind from my lungs. I yelped in pain as the force of the fall sent a shooting pain through my side. I knew that at least one of my ribs had cracked but couldn't pause to check.

The dagger was flung from my hand and slid across the smooth floor just out of reach. I winced, holding my side to turn onto my back and kicked down against the crook of Talos' arm but his grip tightened as he pulled me towards him. I kicked again, smashing my free foot into the side of his face. He grunted a curse. My foot landed once more, this time I heard a bone crunch under my strike. His hand released me and I scrambled away, the heels of my shoes scuffing against the polished wood floors.

Talos groaned. His hands cupping over the bridge of his nose and mouth. Blood was gushing from his broken nose, the trail threading through seams of his fingers and down his wrist into his sleeves.

I reached back, feeling for the hilt of the Alexandrite dagger. Gulping down as much cool air as I could before he healed enough to repay me for his injuries. My side throbbing with every movement. The side of my palm bumped the cool handle of dagger and I quickly sheathed it in my boot. Hoping he didn't see the motion through the blood and rage covering his face. Stabbing jolts sent bright spots across my vision making focusing on Talos' movements all the harder. His wounded torso dampened his shirt and jacket.

"You're hurt, Isa." He spoke thickly. "You won't get far in your condition."

"I could say the same about you." I gritted out through shaky breaths.

Talos pinched his nose and got to his feet, bracing himself on the closest armchair near the fireplace. The pulse of adrenaline thinning and allowing the dull ache to give way to a roar of deafening pain. I reached the wall and pulled myself up by the edge of the dresser, wincing at the pull of muscles over cracked bone.

Talos took slow, leaded steps towards me. One hand to his wounded side, the other pinching his nostrils together to slow the bleeding. A blush of a bruise had already begun to surface beneath his eye. A dark proud smile tugged at the corners of his lips as he looked down to me.

He opened his mouth to speak but before a word could escape him, the door to my room flung open and Anisa stood in the doorway. She looked to Talos, then to me, assessing our wounds before rolling her eyes.

"How did a simple question turn into the both of you

becoming wounded?" She spoke to Talos who's smug expression had been washed away by her scold.

"Banner, it is in your best interest to follow me freely. If you'd like to be escorted, that can be arranged." She stepped aside and both *her henchmen* stood behind her practically drooling at the chance to man handle a Black Banner.

"Lead the way." I answered, propping myself up on the side of the dresser. The stabbing pain at my rib intensifying with the last bit of the rush of our fight leaching from my blood.

"Can you walk?" Talos asked with a hint of a gloat.

I didn't answer but shot him a deadly warning look. Anisa cleared her throat then stepped out into the hall, waiting for Talos and I to exit and follow her. Dorian and Sandros flanked us. They didn't speak but gave each other telling glances as we trekked down stairs and into a small room off the foyer. It looked to be an oversized pantry or utility closet but it was empty all except for two plain wooden chairs. Lit by recessed lights along the edge of the ceiling, the bright crisp light only made the space more out of place for the elegance it was hidden in. This wasn't a room that saw guests or even the royal family. It was clearly meant for storage or, at this moment, interrogations.

Anisa swept to the back of one of the chairs and waited. Talos stepped inside and indicated to the other two Incubo to plant me in one of the chairs. My arms and legs bound to the bare wood with plastic zip ties. The pull of my arms caused me to wince at the tension on my ribs. Once their silent instructions were complete they left the three of us alone, shutting the door behind them.

The edges of the restraints dug into my ankles and wrists at my slightest movement. I didn't doubt that I could snap them but I was outnumbered. A situation I had come across many times but those had been Mortals, and Fata. I could have easily taken on four Fata while injured. Mortals would have been dispatched long before cornering me in a room. But with my broken bones and lack of an arsenal, I had to comply. I only had three throwing blades and the Alexandrite blade in my boot. It would have to be my last resort, I could be overpowered by one of the Incubo guards.

I sat quietly and waited for one of them to make a move.

"Do you know where Princess Amirah has fled to?" Anisa started, her tone even.

"Why would the Princess flee?" I countered, keeping my expression neutral through Talos' huff of discontent at my answer.

"She is a very unhappy young woman and believes that she and her child are unwanted by her family. This isn't true and we only want to bring her home where she belongs. Safely." Anisa didn't take her eyes from me.

Talos shrugged off his jacket and let it fall to the floor without picking it up, sweat beading at his forehead. Blood had dried in patches down his rugged features. His nose had stopped bleeding, but the stain on his grey silk shirt trailed down to the waistband of his black slacks. He untucked the shirt and unbuttoned the first few to expose the sparse patch of hair at the bow of his clavicles. I tracked his every movement, he would be the one to attack and pry the information from me if I kept resisting.

"Where is she, Isa?" Talos' rough voice cut thickly through the inflammation of his injuries.

"I don't know. My answer has not changed from before I broke your nose." I smirked, rolling my eyes up to his to see that he was watching me in cunning amusement.

He chuckled and proceeded to roll the sleeves of his dress shirt up his forearms. His tattoo exposed on his forearm, untouched by blood or bruises. "I don't want to hurt you again, Isa. Please. For the sake of us both, tell us where Princess Amirah has gone."

"The fall injured me, not you. But I'm ready to see you try."

"*Inatosha!*" Anisa's shout rang between us. "Talos. You are only here for one purpose and if you can't do that, then you are useless to me."

She turned to me again, "If you do not give us the information I want, we will get it by other means." Her ash smoke filled eyes scanned me.

"It seems that you know she is missing and you're wasting your time on me, when you could be tracking her down."

Anisa took a seat in front of me, leaning forward and before I could see her hand move she lashed out. The sting of the blow to my cheek almost toppled the chair over. The burn of the zip ties bit into my wrists as I struggled in my restraints. My cheek burned from the impact of her assault. A metallic taste filled my mouth as my lip and inner cheek split open. I blinked away the bright spots from my vision and looked back to her. She didn't show any trace of hesitation or fear of the murderous being that she had struck. Talos began a slow pacing of the room, keeping his distance but watching us both closely.

"Your sass isn't as appealing to me as it is to Talos." Her voice was low and lethal.

Blood mixed with the rush of saliva in my mouth. She glowered, watching for my reaction. I held her gaze and with a slight turn of my head spat the mouthful of copper to the floor, the smell of my blood quickly filling the cramped room. From behind me, Talos' throaty sound of levity sent a chill up my spine.

"You aren't used to being the one strapped to the chair." He moved to my peripheral, but I didn't look away from Anisa.

"I don't mind switching roles on occasion. Not having all the power can be exhilarating." I let the spiteful smile spread over my blood stained lips and raised a brow.

Anisa rolled her eyes and stood, turning her back to me and bringing her hands up to massage her temples. She was

K. ELLE MORRISON

tired, over exerted by the role she had to play in this kingdom while her sister's family was in shambles. An attack on her kind, and threat of war spreading over *continent* was weighing heavily on keeping the secrets of this Chateau under wraps.

"*Kwa miungu...* The games of Mortals are tiresome." She turned to and spoke to Talos, "I told you that I wouldn't kill her if she was helpful, I suggest you make use of her if you would like for me to keep that promise."

Talos' eyes plunged into darkness and he took the seat across from me. He leaned over resting his forearms on his knees and clasped his hands together in front of him. He took a deep breath and a heat boiled in the pit of my stomach. A raging inferno engulfed my every sense and sweat poured from every pore. The sound of my screams bounced off the walls and caged me into the hell he was creating. A burning of my flesh and tightening of my lungs began to spread a consuming panic. I pulled against the ties at my wrists, the thin skin raw from the tension.

He released his hold and leaned back in the chair, his hands slack on his thighs. "Tell us what you know and we will end this."

I slumped in the chair, my nerves still sizzling in the aftershock.

"I don't know anything." I panted, my throat raw and dry from screaming.

"Do you know that Amil and Yamir will be back any moment with someone very dear to you? It would be a shame if they went all that way to retrieve him just so he would die right here in front of you. It wouldn't take long considering the state he was found in."

"You bastard!" My blood began to boil again, but from my own anger.

"I wouldn't touch him. Not a finger. Not a thought. I simply would leave the both of you here in this room. A few hours would be plenty of time for the reunion to become mourning."

Acid crept up my throat. Argo was close but still in grave danger. Anisa watched from the corner of the room, her focus flitting between Talos and I in slight confusion. He hadn't told her why I had come or stayed around since Althea had settled in. One promise he had kept but was close to breaking any moment.

Sweat ran into my eyes, masking the tears that had found their way to my lashes. Althea would be furious but she would understand my position, I knew, but Princess Amirah, Mikal, and their child would be found and brought back. Argo and I would still be held and likely executed by the Incubo royal family for the conspiracy. Scenarios rang through my pounding head. No hopeful outcome except being able to hold Argo before we were killed for my actions.

I swallowed hard, drawing in a breath to inflate my hollowed core, "Meru. They're headed to Meru." I choked on my own betrayal.

Talos angled forward and cupped my cheek to tilt my face up to his, "*Kalό korítsi.*"

He kissed my lips and a spark shot through me, a feeling of calm nestled in my chest when he pulled away. Anisa sighed in disgust and rolled her eyes before she pushed away from the wall and stalked out of the room without addressing me. Talos grabbed up his jacket and folded it over his arm before turning towards me one more time, "Sandros has seen to it that your room has been cleared of any suspicious items. You'll remain here until the Princess and her child are found. Argo will be tended to until a decision is made on whether either of you will live or die for your crimes against the crown."

"How convenient it must be to have brought your own scapegoat. The Princess runs away to save her child, and to cover for the embarrassment it'll be passed off as a kidnapping done by a Black Banner. You're going to sentence me to death and let my brother suffer for good measure." The realization of his plot falling from my mouth as it came to me.

"You'll see a fair trial, Isa. I wouldn't deny you that." He winked and followed Anisa out of the room.

The door shut behind him with the click of the lock. His muffled voice on the other side gave instructions but I wasn't able to make any of them out. The nugget of peace that he had given me was beginning to wane and crushing panic was stretching open through me. Argo was close. Amil and Yamir were bringing him back here and I had no way of warning him that the Incubo who had orchestrated his rescue was now both of our captor. Yamir would likely follow Talos' directions, he would have to, but Amil. The pit in my stomach bottomed out at the thought of what Talos would do to Amil if he refused to follow orders.

It wasn't difficult to imagine Amil challenging Talos and dying in the process. He would allow his heart to overrule his better judgement. He's more useful to me alive than dead but would he be able to hold himself to rational headspace once he heard what Talos and Anisa had done?

I was strapped to the chair for what felt like hours when Dorian came in and cut the ties off my wrists and legs, blood staining the plastic from me readjusting for too long. He hoisted me up by the shoulder but my knees protested and gave out. My legs had fallen asleep from the hardened chair and little room to move. He gave me little choice but to be marched upstairs. The swelling at my side pulsated through each step I took back to my room. My clothing and belongings tossed about the floor and bed. Sandros came out of the bathroom with a duffle bag in his hand. He held the bag open when he reached the doorway and waited. My knives and electronics exposed in the opening of the bag.

Dorian held my shoulders and wedged his leg between my

feet, spreading them wide and allowing Sandros to pat me down. He glanced up at me when he reached my inner thighs, a pig like expression on his face. When he got down to my boots he found the hidden throwing blades and the Alexandrite dagger. He tossed them into the bag and slung it over his shoulder with a cocky smile.

"We'll keep these safe for you, gorgeous." He said with a stormy grey wink.

After shoving me into my room, Dorian and Sandros shut and locked the door. I went to the bedside table and searched through it. Every weapon gone, along with my phone and laptop. The balcony door and windows had been locked from the outside. The glass of the windows would be easily broken but would cause alarm. I would have to move quickly even if I broke them gently.

I went to the bed and began pulling the blankets and sheets off of it and ripping them into strips. A desperate plan of escape taking form. If I could make it out of the Chateau, I might be able to get to the road leading here and stop Amil and Yamir before they brought Argo here. I would then have to find Zaida and the others in Amples. They would have moved on to another hotel, but if it took days of searching for them, it would be a better chance than waiting to see if Anisa would wait to pass judgement before any type of trial.

I began tying strips together when a knock sounded at the door. I tossed the wad of linens under the bed and stood waiting for the visitor to enter.

CHAPTER TWENTY-EIGHT

Talos' swaggered into the room. He had changed his clothes and his nose already healed and perfectly aligned. He was wearing a more casual clothing; jeans and a black t-shirt. This constructive look made me more uneasy than finding him lurking in my room uninvited. Dorian held the door open for him and waited for Talos to give him a wordless instruction to leave us. He slipped his hands into the pockets and looked down to the floor. I held my ground, not sure what he was waiting for but ready for another round of mental onrush.

"I'm sorry." He said, not meeting my eye.

I didn't give him the relief of a reply, he had now exposed me, my organization, and my family. He didn't know how sorry he would be if I made it out of here alive.

"I can feel how much you hate me right now, but if you give me a chance to explain—"

Another knock on the door cut off his words. The door opened and an Incubo with salt and pepper hair walked in. A smile pulling at his short cropped beard. King Idris. I wasn't sure what to make of his demeanor, he didn't hold himself like a man who had just learned that his only daughter had been abdicated from his home with no word on if she or her child were safe.

"Talos, I'm not surprised to see you also wanted a word with our guest." He clapped Talos on the shoulder as he came up next to him.

He was about a head shorter than Talos and heavier set, with broad shoulders. He was still wearing a dark blue suit emblazoned with gold and bronze leaves at the cuffs and lapels. An elegant ring of gold sat in the waves on his head. I hadn't noticed if he wore his crown on our first meeting or if he adorned it when he had duties that demanded he be seen as the unopposed regent of his kind.

"Isa is wounded. I was going to assess her before bothering the doctor." Talos assured him. His muscular frame rigid at his King's attention.

"It's not a bother at all. Go and fetch the good doctor. I only have a quick matter to speak with Isa about and I will be out of their hair."

Talos looked from him to me, then back to King Idris who gave him a nod. "Yes, Your Majesty." He inclined his head in respect and left us.

"It seems you are more injury prone than other Black Banners I have met." Idris said upon turning his attention back on me. "Not that I have met many in my time."

He looked me over, then behind me to the state of the room. I stood breathless, my hands clenched to my side. He wasn't here to chat about my injuries, we both knew that, but his tone was calm and diplomatic.

"I've already told Anisa where the Princess was headed, at least to my knowledge." I said, hoping to cut to the chance and relieve him from my room.

"I appreciate your cooperation. If it becomes fruitful, then you will surely be rewarded with our sincerest gratitude. A missing member of the royal family during the new threat to our kind is most troubling." He spoke as casually as if he were telling me the history of his home. His words that would seem urgent held no inflection of urgency.

I didn't respond. He wasn't here to hear my explanations or gratitude that I was still breathing. He was bringing me further warning and what the threat of my knowledge would bring me if I spoke of the events that had happened here to anyone out side of these walls.

"Lady Althea is very fond of you. I met her in the hall on my way here. It seems many Incubo are willing to sing your praises, that is very rare for a Mortal." He walked over to the chair nearest the fireplace and turned it with ease before he sat.

He crossed a leg over a knee and put his hands in his lap. His misty eyes casually flitting over me. "My son was also taken with you before the poison almost took his life. I would dare to say that if it weren't for you that night, he may not have made it to the hospital in time to receive the antidote. Your connection to Talos and Amil seems to have saved you and others a few times now." He knew much more than I had given him credit for. "He has requested that he see you again, you know? Wanting to finish the lovely chat you had started."

"If that is what he wishes, I have no objections." I said, trying to steady my breathing.

"Kind of you. My son can be a bit nosy and bored at times. He will grasp on to anyone who is mildly interesting." He attempted a smile but it looked foreign against his eyes.

"Is there anything else?" I said to break the long silence between us.

"No, that will be all. But I think it only fair to warn you that if you plan to leave without my permission, you will not succeed. The lax in our security has been rectified now that Talos' men are back from their retrieval assignment. Such a prize they've brought back too." He stood and straightened his jacket, then left my room without another look to me.

I was too late. Argo was here somewhere and I needed to get to him. I looked through the remaining objects in the room, hoping to find a makeshift weapon or distraction. If I would lure the Incubo at the door inside and incapacitate them, I would give myself a few minutes headstart to find him. If he were stable enough, we could fight our way out. I looked through every drawer and closet but they had taken everything obvious. The iron fire tools had been taken out, clothing hangers, belts, even toiletries were removed. I had to acknowledge they were not underestimating me, whether it was under Anisa's orders or Talos, they were going to make any chance of escape a feat of ingenuity.

The sound of the door unlocking tore me from my search. Talos walked through the door, followed by the the royal doctor who was carrying a bag of medical supplies. The doctor blinked around the the disheveled furniture then to me, "Uh, Talos said you may have fallen and hurt yourself?" He said and moved to the low table near the fire palace to set his bag down.

Talos didn't move from the door, he was there for the doctor's protection. My hands went to the hem of my shirt and lifted it over my head, exposing a deep purple bruise that had spread over my rib and side. Talos swallowed hard and flint he'd at the sight of my painfully damaged bare skin. I held his gaze as the doctor palpated the area gently. I winced in pain but didn't allow Talos a reprieve from the hot daggers shooting from my eyes. If I couldn't pierce his skin, I'd bore into him until he relented.

"Oh yes. I would say at least two of your ribs are broken, young lady." The doctor cleared his throat and told me what I had already suspected. "You'll need to rest and limit your movement until you heal. I can give you something for the pain but stay off that side for at least six weeks."

He busied himself in his bag and pulled out a bottle of pills, turning to hand them to me but Talos snatched them out of his hand.

"I will ensure that she gets them in a timely manner. Wouldn't want you to be in too much pain, would we?" He said, popping the top off and holding out two oval white tablets.

"Yes. Yes, of course." Replied the doctor in a wary tone, he watched us both uneasily.

I took the pills and stuck out my tongue. I dropped the pills down into my open mouth and swallowed them, knowing there wasn't a glass in the room to use for water.

"I'll be on the premises for the rest of the night. If you need anything, please call for me." The doctor said as he backed to the door.

He looked between me and Talos one last time before knocking twice to be seen out by Dorian on the other side.

"Your brother has already been seen by the doctor. He is dehydrated and malnourished but otherwise unharmed. He's been given an IV for fluids and a sedative to rest." Talos moved to the chair that the King had turned and sat, crossing his ankle over his knee.

I was hardly breathing, whatever the doctor had prescribed was already starting to spread a numbing warmth over my aching body without food in my stomach to cushion it.

"You don't have to thank me. I know I don't deserve it now, but you have to understand that you have put me in a rather unenviable position. Princess Amirah is gone and one of my own assisted in the foolhardy plot."

He waited for my response but the thickening of my tongue wouldn't allow the words of defense to come. It didn't seem that he knew that Althea had been involved and I wasn't going to put her in the King's path. I had already betrayed her in confessing where the Princess and her child's father had been going. He pursed his lips and subtly shook his head at my silence.

"We will find them, Isa. I am doubtful that they will have the same reticence as you do. I would think that you would want to secure yours and Agro's safe passage by ensuring that the Princess and her child make it back here as quickly and safely as possible." His smooth voice slipping over his words and pressed heavily in on my ears.

"Am I only a weapon for Incubo safety when the enemy is Fata or Mortal?" I paused to catch my breath, "The Princess and her child were in danger and asked for my help. Would you have wanted me to deny a request from the royal family?"

I crossed my arms over my bare torso, a chill starting to settle over my skin. Talos stood before me in a blink of a slowed eye. Placing a hand to my shoulder and pulled me closer to him. A spark trickled down through me from his touch.

"As I've said, you have put me in a compromising situation." He raised a hand to my jaw, smoothing his thumb over the ridge and pulling my eyes up to his.

"I could make it less complicated if you let me." I gave a malicious grin and grabbed his belt. "I just need ten minutes and Argo and I will be gone. Never to meddle in Incubo business ever again."

He smiled down to me, cupping the base of my head in his palm, and pulling me up to meet his lips. "You're going to be the death of me."

His lips feathered over mine, and I drew him in closer by the clasp of his belt. I parted my lips to welcome him inside. He wrapped an arm around my shoulders to deepen the kiss. The room around us became foggy and far away as the drugs coursed through my blood faster as my heartbeat picked up pace. I hooked my thumbs into his waistband to encourage him to hurry. The front of his jeans tightening with his excitement.

He pulled me away, a pit black abyss peering down to me. The air in my lungs filled with his exhales and scent. A mounting tension filled my chest until ready to burst when his lips crashed over mine once more. The heady sensation of him all around me mixed with the medication and dragged me under. My body fell back onto the soft mattress as all the light in the room dissipated from my vision. I wrapped my legs around his waist as he drove his hips into mine.

His heavy breath breaking over my neck and chest as he dragged his lips over the sensitive crook. I let out a whine of need and gripped his belt tighter. In response, he increased the friction between my thighs and bit down on my neck. My fingers coaxed him closer, begging him to undress.

He pulled away and looked down to me, a night sky piercing through my clouded mind. "Close your eyes." A thick darkness pressed down into me through his words. "Rest now, you'll need your strength for what I have planned for you later."

"Argo?" I managed to pass through my dry lips.

Talos only shushed me gently.

His lips pressed to my brow and pure bliss washed over me. All the pain from my muscles melted away into the depths of sleep. No images of a bloodied Argo impeded my dreams. In the place of nightmares there were only the voices of calm and sweetheart voices of Amil and Talos lulling me to an inexplicable place between sedation and sleep. A state of rest I could have never imagined possible, one only possible when enacted with outside manipulation. If it weren't for the volcanic fury I could feel bubbling under the surface for when I woke up, it would have been nirvana. But Sheol awaited me when my eyes opened.

CHAPTER TWENTY-NINE

When my eyes cracked open, sunlight spilled across the floor of my room. Sometime during my slumber, someone had come in and cleaned the torn linens and put my belongings away into the drawers and closet. I wasn't sure what woke me, but I looked to the door and realized it was left open ajar. I threw the blankets off of me and padded over. The floor holding onto the chill of the night without a fire lit in the fireplace. I placed my hand to the solid mahogany and pulled the knob slowly towards me, careful to not open it too quickly. I tipped my eyes to peer down the hallway.

No one guarded my room that I could see, I turned my ear to the crease. The hardwood floors were covered with a cream colored runner rug but it didn't deaden footsteps completely. I had at least several yards of free hallway to attempt to escape.

Acid in my stomach tumbled over as the sensate at my ribs came rushing back to the forefront of all other faculties. The piercing pain felt like white hot blades being driven in between each rib and reaching them wide open. I slapped my hand over my mouth to keep from screaming and alerting whoever had left their post that their prisoner was aware they had been left alone.

I stumbled backwards, guiding myself down to the ground and holding onto my side trying to apply counter pressure to relieve the overwhelming gnarling of agony. A muffled disembodied chuckle of amusement echoed around the room. Spots of light danced across my vision as I searched for the owner. I rolled onto my back and looked straight up to the torso of Dorian standing over me. A disturbing smirk streaked over his face, his eyes were burning ash. Flecks of molten red and orange filtered the pitch black smoke overlay.

"Thought you'd have a walk, gorgeous? Sorry to disappoint you." He reached down and hauled me up to my feet by my shoulders.

The ensnaring pain replaced by a nagging ache as he released his hold on my shoulder and senses. He walked me over to the sitting area and roughly dropped me into one of the velvet lined chairs. Sandros' back pushed against the door behind Dorian and a cart from the kitchen came in to view next. Sandros wheeled the cart over and looked from Dorian to me, then to the cart.

"Is our guest ready for breakfast?" A lilt of sarcasm rang from his voice.

"I'm sure Isa will be a good girl and eat." Dorian turned to me to speak again, his eyes clear from his previous viciousness. "Talos will be up in a few minutes to prepare you to his liking."

They shared a grotesque snicker at their misogyny. I was aware that the both of them would be able to influence me, likely try to use their pull to torture me into cooperation if they felt I wasn't appearing docile enough while they watched over me, for however long that would be. Anger simmered in my chest, and I bit back threats on their throats. They had already shown they would use their abilities and the advantage of two of them against me.

Sandros looked me over, his misty veiled pupils settled on my breasts a moment then flicked to my face. I narrowed my eyes in a warning scowl. The pleased expression falling from his face before he nudged Dorian's arm then gestured his chin to the door. Dorian looked back to me one last time and followed Sandros out, the click from the lock sounding behind them as they secured the door shut.

I braced myself against the arm of the chair as I pulled the dining cart in front of me. I took the silver dome off the top of my plate and noted that I was only provided a spoon for my scrambled eggs and toast. The plate reinforced to not shatter into sharp pieces if dropped or broken. An impressed smirk pulled at the corners of my mouth at the thought they had put into keeping me alive and comfortable. Like a wolf being held captive by jackals. Respectfully admiring the other's deadly nature.

I ate quickly, then showered. Allowing myself as much time as my nerves would allow under the scalding water. I examined myself in the mirror. Dark circles had formed under my eyes despite the long sleep I had the night before. I pulled open the drawer and took out my makeup bag, the thin blade I had stowed away inside missing. They hadn't missed a single weapon during their sweep. I took out my concealer, eye makeup, and a light red lipstick. If I were going to be killed in front of the royals, at least I would look presentable for such a monumental occasion. It wasn't everyday that a Black Banner was put to death at the hands of the Incubo King.

After my skin took on the glow of a being not awaiting their sentencing, I smoothing the red glossy stick over my lips. The chapped skin snagged and burned where it had been split open. At least the blood would be lost in the color of the rouge. I walked out in a towel and waited on the end of the bed for Talos to come. Tapping my bare foot on the ground and wringing my hair dry into a second towel. The drugs they had given me last night had done my muscles a world of good. I hardly ached anywhere but at my side where the bruising of my ribs was spreading towards the middle of my stomach and down to the crest of my hip. My back was sore, likely from taking the brunt of my fall and holding the tension of my broken bones.

I tested my own pain by breathing in deeply until a sharp pain began to warn me. I doubted I would be able to run if I found the chance. Wherever they were holding Argo would be far enough away from my room that it would take much of my strength and wind to find him. Leaving me exhausted and unable to carry him out. Whatever Talos had planned for me today would give me time to plan out a strategy to get Argo into Amples for my siblings to take back home. Whether I was with him or not.

A knock at the door pulled me from my thoughts and Talos walked in with a garment bag over his arm. "Good morning, Isa. I trust you slept well?"

"I suppose drugs and Incubo influence are the solution to insomnia." I quipped.

He smiled to himself as he hung the bag over the nearest chair. He was wearing a dapper suit, resembling one that I had seen Amil wear. Navy blue with black floral embroidery at the cuffs and lapels. Silver dashed about his wrists in small bursts like flowers or stars. He wore a black shirt and tie underneath the jacket, a vision of the mystic cosmos. A smoldering essence perfumed from him, earthier and richer than his usual cologne.

"I would have put you to bed with my preferred method, but I didn't want to aggravate your injury." He said, turning to face me fully.

I let the towel fall and puddle around me. His brows raised as his eyes roamed over me, lingering too long at my bruised ribs. The nudity of my weakness flushing my cheeks. I cleared my throat and his gloomy eyes trailed off back to his hands with a subtle shake of his head.

"What's in the bag?" I asked, pulling his attention further away from my side.

"This is what I would like for you to wear today. I have arranged a meeting with the royal family to discuss your further cooperation in the matter of bringing the Princess home from her... excursion across the border."

He unzipped the bag and pulled the dress through the canvas. The burnt orange dress hung loosely around the bottom of the bag it had been sheathed in. I ran the fabric through my fingers, and pulled the long sleeves out to admire the full extent. It was rather plain but fashionable for the changing of the season. He reached in and pulled out black strappy heels to be worn with it.

"Why would you want to dress me up and parade me in front of the royals? What are you planning?" I narrowed my eyes to him as I took the dress from the hanger.

"Today you will need to call upon all of your previous acting skills. To fool the King into believing that you are solely under Incubo control, you'll have to be the perfect puppet."

He sat and watched me dress. I turned over his words in my head, pulling the soft fabric down my body. Raising my arms too far above my chest caused me to wince. I smoothed out the small wrinkles from the bodice over my breasts, feeling his attentive gaze following my every move.

"I want to see Argo." I looked up from the dress to Talos. "Prove to me that he is here and safe before you walk me into the lion's den."

"Do you remember when we first arrived at the Welp manor? How Cornelius hadn't met us at the station and his father was rather interested in you?" He said, crossing his leg over his knee.

I watched him, waiting for him to continue. We both remembered that moment clearly, even after all other tribula-tions that had come from that greeting.

"You gave him a false name. Isabella." I recollected.

"I need you to be Isabella again. Be the young Mortal that took my lead and allowed me to protect your identity."

"Every member of the royal family knows that I'm a Black Banner. Calling me by another name won't change their feelings towards me." I shifted my weight and stepped into the first shoe.

"But if they believe that you have slipped completely under my influence, like many Mortals before you, they may let you live long enough to allow me to hand Argo over to the safety of the other Banners. He has not wronged the Incubo and will be spared any wrath brought upon the Banner who gave their daughter passage out of the country." He swallowed hard, the knot in his throat bobbing.

He was trying to save my life. Not just my life, but Argo's as well. He had promised he would but I had expected that those terms had changed as did the circumstances of my stay at the Chateau. I was no longer a guest, but he was attempting to remove the status of "prisoner" from my name by changing it. He wanted me to become Isabella, the sweet friend that Althea had brought to help with her wedding plans. To give the illusion that he had penetrated my consciousness and alter it to fit the needs of the Incubo royal family.

"This sounds like an immense risk for you to take. If they find out you haven't scrambled my brain to that of a sex-drunk Mortal playtoy, they'll be furious."

"Oh, they'll punish me harshly." He stood and came to stand behind me to zip the back of the dress up to the middle of my back, "But you are worth each lashing."

"What if they don't believe this charade you've created?" I crossed my arms beneath my chest, the dress hugging my curves tightly.

"I will do my best to make it seem believable, but you'll have to use your skills to stay just above the full effect. Do you think you can do that for me?"

The way he spoke sounded as if I were doing him the favor by not getting executed or found a fraud. The warm tone held no bitterness but there was something else that felt off. Whether it was his eyes that were clearer than they typically were when we were alone together, or the soft touch he had when his fingers lingered over the zipper. Something in his demeanor had changed. When he came around to stand at my front to inspect the doll he had dressed, there was pain in his eyes.

The curves of his cheekbones less ridgid, his hair loosely combed to the side instead of slicked back in it's normal style. His silky black waves less restricted by product than the night before. Each lock more inviting to my fingers that were itching to rake through them and bring his lips to mine. A trembling in my core to thank him or to hurt him, I wasn't sure if there was a distinction between the two emotions when it came to Talos. I cleared my throat and looked away from his shadowing gaze, I had been staring too long.

"Well?" I held out my arms and turned in a tight circle.

"Exquisite." He gave me a hollow smile and took my hand in his to lead me to our meeting.

CHAPTER THIRTY

I followed Talos through the Chateau down to the basement. This level of the great home resembled every other sans windows along the walls. More wall and ceiling lighting was provided to offset the reduction of sunlight streaming in from outside. A long cream colored hallway of doors separated by art hung on the walls, tables with vases of flowers, and tricked boxes lined the way. Disguising what the basement was used for. Placards over the doors read: Infirmary, incinerator, electrical, and numbered holding rooms.

We had been walking for what felt like a mile until we reached the end of the wing. Two Incubo stood guard outside the door at the left across from another utility closet. I hadn't met them or seen them before and neither acknowledged me in Talos' shadow. He silently commanded them to open the door, then stood back for me to enter before him.

The room was fully furnished but like mine, was missing key elements that someone with extensive knowledge would use as weapons. There were no windows but several flush recessed lights surrounding a bed. The body in the bed shifted under a pile of cream and yellow blankets. My heart froze in my chest and clenched at the tuft of black curly hair peeking from the pillow. Tears welled up in my eyes as Argo rolled over and his eyes met mine. A labored breath shook my shoulders, and streams of relief flowed down my cheeks. He pulled himself up to sit on the edge of the bed.

Argo had always been thin but his face was more gaunt that the last time I had seen him. Dark circles had settled under his bloodshot eyes and his brown skin pallid, either from his ordeal or the shock hanging from my face. I blinked away the obstruction of tears from my eyes and we collided. Our arms wrapping and holding around the other desperate to confirm the other was really there. I wasn't sure either of us was breathing.

"Isa." He said, his voice hoarse and cracked in pain.

"I know." I held him out in front of me to better examine him.

He was wearing a pair of dark sweatpants, white tshirt, and socks. He had rings of indented dark bruises around his wrists. Black and purple smudges on his cheeks and neck but I didn't see any cuts or blood. He had bathed or been cleaned since being brought to the Chateau and smelled of the same shampoo that had been provided in my room.

"Where are you hurt?" I asked, lifting the him of his shirt to better see if he had any internal bleeding, but saw nothing.

For a being who had been held against his will for ransom he was well cared for. "I'm fine. A little banged up from the transport vehicle being blown off the road but no worse for wear." He smiled, his chapped lips stretching over his intact teeth.

"They must have taken your threat seriously." Talos' voice interrupted, reminding me that we weren't alone.

Argo looked to Talos, the muscle in his jaw tensing at the sight of him looming in the doorway. I squeezed his shoulders where I was still gripping, fearful he'd fall away if I let go. "Where are the beings who took you? Who were they?"

"They didn't survive the extraction." Talos answered.

I turned my head to see him, anger flashing through my eyes and heat rising up my neck. He had promised Argo's perpetrators to me to do with what I saw fit for their transgressions. I knew he couldn't have predicted what had happened, but disgust and betrayal coated my throat like bile. One of the Incubo outside the door leaned in to Talos, speaking low for only him to hear.

I refocused on Argo, "I'm going to get you home safe. I promise." I vowed.

He pulled me in close, wrapping his arms around my shoulders and turning his face into my hair. The sound of air passing through his lungs easing long aching tension but I knew I would have to leave him in this room to play my part in Talos' plan. On his warm exhale he whispered into my ear, "None of this is as it seems."

My body tensed as he pulled away and Talos' voice came from behind me, "It's time for our appointment, Isabella. You will be able to visit with your brother soon."

Argo's fingers dug into my arms, his grave expression screaming for me not to leave him there but I had no choice. No weapons to defend us with, and no way of knowing an effective escape route if we did make it past the three full grown Incubo at the door.

I took a deep rattling breath, "I will be back soon." I turned to the Incubo out in the hallway, "If one hair on his head is harmed by either of you, I will personally see to it that you die a painful death."

They both looked between Argo and me then to Talos who only gave me a nod of understanding. I turned to Argo one last time and swallowed hard at the sight of tears brimming on his thick black lashes. Hopelessness weighed heavy on him. He had already endured his previous captors for days then to be brought into a new prison. One that I was also trapped in with only fragments of what could be seen as fabricated truth. The trust I had in Talos wavering on each new move he made. From moment to moment our rapport shifted with his actions.

"We do not shy away from darkness, for we are the shadows." My tongue carefully slipping over the words of our family's words. "We do not have fear, for we are the terror." One last tear fell from my eye, the last of the phrase catching in my thickening vocal cords.

"We know no danger, for we are vicious." He continued for me.

"We are the Black Banners." We finished in harmony.

Talos walked me upstairs from the basement to one of the receiving galleries. I paused in the hallway to wipe the streaks of makeup from my cheeks before we entered. He looked me over but didn't speak. He hadn't said a word on our way to what he said was just a show of good faith that he had me under his control. Every question that formed in my mind would stop short of my tongue. What I needed most was for him to reassure me that my cooperation would see to it that Argo be released. But instead I was only given anxious butterflies in my stomach threatening to release themselves on the polished floor of the spacious room Talos was leading me into.

The King and Queen sat on a raised platform towards the far wall that overlooked a semicircular arrangement of tables and chairs. Each of the ten chairs was taken up by an Incubo of the royal court. Amil, Yamir, Althea, and Anisa turned their eyes to us when we entered. The other Incubo shuffled their paperwork in front of them. Dorian and Sandros were standing on either side of the diasis the King and Queen sat upon, both allowed their eyes to wander but didn't turn their heads.

"Your majesties, I have accomplished what we had discussed and would like to introduce you once again to Isabella."

I bowed my head to each of them and plastered a doe-eyed expression on my face. Althea's jaw dropped at his announcement but I didn't look to her or Amil whose jaw was clenched.

Talos placed his hand at the small of my back and encouraged me gently to step forward for the King to get a better look at me. The sense of Talos' pull coiled in my stomach, keeping me from over acting or under selling the lie. A slight nudge from within to keep the blissfully toxic smile on while the King looked me over. He squinted and pressed his thumb to his lips. My heart raced as the King took a step closer, then another to get a better feel. Talos pulled harder, my pulse slowing as he sent a radiating warmth through my limbs to loosen my muscles. My shoulders slacked against his will, allowing my chin to rise slightly under the King's gaze. The room dimmed as Talos took me deeper. The far away sound of the King's shoes on the floor came closer but dulled at each new stride.

I pursed my lips, spreading the smooth red lipstick I had applied before Talos arrived across my lips. The pressure pinching at the broken skin that hadn't healed over yet. I blinked, my eyelids heavy from the haze of Talos surrounding me and enveloping me. A drunken relief washed through me and I could feel my vision glaze over. The light coming in from the windows casting rainbows across my field of view, until I realized I was looking directly at Amil who was watching me intently. His eyes pure black. I searched for the spark of his dancing flame but only darkness stared back at me. He sat silently and unmoving, for a moment I thought I was imagining him there. Until I heard a voice come from the being standing in front of me.

"She certainly seems to have given into your influence." The King spoke to Talos, his misty eyes not leaving me.

The brass button on his jacket glinted against the sun pouring in from the large window. The curves of the crest stamped on it's surface vibrated as I focused on each edge and line. The thick air that had taken up residence in my lungs became lighter and more fluid as I took in a deeper breath and let out a sigh. Talos pulled me back against him, his arm wrapped around my shoulder and hung lazily down my front.

"She is as calm as a kitten." Talos answered the King then urged me to confirm, "Pur for the King, my pet."

A shiver ran down my spine at his request, and my teeth chattered behind my tight lips. I took a deep breath and looked to Talos who raised his brows in encouragement for me to play the part we had agreed on. I parted my lips and let out the closest thing to a pur I could muster then plastered the sticky sweet smile back onto my face, avoiding Amil's gaze.

The King looked to Talos, then turned to the rest of the room. "We would love to see a demonstration of how you were able to tame such a magnificent creature. A Black Banner who has previously been able to ward off the abilities of Incubo was sensational, and now it seems that was nothing but a parlor trick by the behavior we see here."

Talos tensed behind me, the tightening of his muscles gripping low in my stomach. The residual pull he had laxed began to pull tout at the seams of my insides. He reached up and held my chin firm in his fingers. I allowed him to pull my face to the side and expose my neck to him. His lips trailed down from the lobe of my ear to the top ridge of my collarbone. The trail of moist kisses and warm breath setting my skin ablaze.

My chests rose and fell harder with each press of his mouth over my nerves. He spoke into the nape of my neck, "Who do you belong to, Isabella?"

His sultry voice floated around in the darkening room. I gulped at the soupy air, trying to push the words up my throat. My lips parted "Talos," I croaked out.

"Yes, pet. I'd say you earned a reward." He groaned, his voice thick with desire that felt all too sudden and all too familiar.

A plunging pleasure gripped low in my belly. My knees rebelling against the weight of my body, they buckled and I crumpled against the wave of intense heat coursing through me.

Talos' arms held me up on my feet but sent me over the edge again. I reached up and cupped the back of his neck to steady myself through the loud moans escaped me. He released his hold over me and let me fall to his feet to catch my breath. I looked up to the others around the room. Each of their faces held pity or grotesque embarrassment for what they had just witnessed. My thighs were slick with my own release causing the dress to cling and dampen.

Shame and anger filled my stomach. A gentle tug from Talos reeled me back to focus. He stretched out his hand for me to take and tsked coolly, "It looks as if my dear Isabella needs to retire to her room to tidy herself up."

"That was quite the show!"

A burst of laughter from behind me startled me to my feet. I turned to see the King doubled over in amusement. Talos pulled me tight to his side, the contact of his hand to my back pulsed with a ripple of calm. He fought against my impulse to lunge towards the King and rip his vulgar throat out with my bare hands. Pressing into my sore ribs to remind me that I was injured and supposed to be pretending to be the unaware Mortal.

Talos inclined his head to his King and turned to lead us back out of the room but before he was able to take his second step a new voice rang out to stop us.

"You mean for us to believe that you screwed her into submission?" The clear, feminine voice countered.

Talos turned us back around to face the Queen. She hadn't stood from her seat but her overwhelming presence came down all around the room.

"Are you suggesting that Talos is being fooled by a Mortal, my darling?" The King asked his wife, puzzled.

"She is not the first Black Banner we have had roam these halls. We know they are raised to deceive their targets. Lure them into a sense of comfort before they mount a full attack."

She admired the ring on her finger as she spoke. Though her posture would suggest she was bored of the whole display, she spoke in an accusatory tone commanding everyone's attention.

"Hm, she has a compelling argument, Talos. If you have subdued the Banner, show us that she would not react on her instincts when provoked." The King trailed back to his seat next to his wife and sat on the edge of it waiting for Talos to put on another show or call their bluff.

I squeezed Talos' arm gently, urging him to do as the King said. A silent agreement that it would be for show. He stood me up on my own and took a step back, I held out my hands to him in mock need. I hoped a show of desperation would convince the Queen I was as I appeared. I let out a small whimper at the distance Talos had put between us. He lifted his chin and puffed out his chest, ever demonstrating he was the dominant being. A sinister veil falling over his eyes. I held my ground at first but then laxed my body. Welcoming the pain he was about to inflict on me.

I was plunged into darkness at first. Then my lungs were cut off from precious oxygen. Deprivation attacking every crevice of my being. A scream slammed against my ear drums a moments before a solid mass crushed to the side of my face and body. My injured ribs splintered at the pressure of my lungs constricting to take in a sip of air. I realized I was on the floor, the hard surface cold to my skin. A flood of ice rushed through my veins attacking my nerves like needles.

Red and white lights flashed across my eyes as what was arguably the worst part of Talos' attack began. Blood pulsed thickly in my ears as a skull splitting pain streaked across my temple. The vision of my bones fracturing into thousands of pieces blurred into nothingness. For a brief second, nothing hurt. I thought for a moment that I had passed out from the torture, but knew that wasn't possible for me to comprehend. Then I felt my body lift from the floor and be hurled into the open air. Shouting and curses took the place of the pounding in my head, but before I could focus on where in the room I had been tossed I was being scooped into a pair of strong arms.

Talos' voice came from somewhere in the room but not from the being that had gathered me up off the floor. I nestled into his chest, the buttons of his shirt curing into my fingers. Bergamot and persimmons laced with sweat, and rage.

Amil.

CHAPTER THIRTY-ONE

The thunderous footfall of Talos behind us on the stairs was the only sound I could hear over my own wheezing breath. Amil's hold tightened up the last few steps into my room. He pulled me in close before he laid me down on the bed then rounded on Talos, his voice venomous, "You bastard!"

I sat up, regaining my composure from the scene downstairs and watched the both of them take a guarded stance. Amil had turned his back to me and taken two threatening steps back into the middle of the room. Talos shut the door before turning back to face Amil and I, but focused solely on Amil's vehemence.

"I warned you, and you swore to me that you wouldn't do this." Amil lashed out, the soft fabric of his shirt stretched tightly against his shoulders.

"You had your opinions but I had to make a choice." Talos' voice steady and brooding.

"A choice. You choose to betray my trust and dazing her within an inch of her life? You were killing her!" Amil lunged, his fist colliding with Talos' jaw.

The impact toppled Talos to the floor, his yelp echoing off the walls. I held my hand over my mouth as I watched Talos stagger back to his feet but didn't retaliate. Blood trailed down his lips and when he spoke, blood stained his teeth.

"Amil, don't lose your head. If I didn't act, they were going to kill her and call it retribution for treason. Never mind that she has no claim to our laws."

"Your solution was to screw with her mind until she was a senseless rag doll?" Amil countered, "I told you what I would do if you hurt her again. She isn't your pawn like Althea."

Amil knew what that comment would illicit in Talos, he was ready for it. The muscles in his legs coiled and when Talos rushed towards him, he bent over for his shoulder to take the brunt of the attack. Amil hammered Talos back onto the ground this time Talos brought his hands up and landed a hard blow to the middle of Amil's back. I rushed from the bed when the both of them began pummeling the other, a mass of rolling fists and fury. I caught Amil's arm in the air and pulled at him to stop his attacks. Talos jabbed at Amil's ribs, knocking the wind out of him with a thud.

"Stop! You're both idiots!" I set my foot on Amil's shoulder and pushed until the both of them fell over and separated.

Amil's eyes flew to mine. Realizing that the display in front of the royals wasn't real, he stood and took my face in his bloodied hands. His eyes shifted from pits of rage and fiery anger to soft soulless blackness. Talos shakily got to his feet, leaning on the nearby chair for support. Blood trickled from a cut beneath his clouded eye, mouth, and nose. The previous break I had given him refreshed by Amil's hands.

"I am still a being of my word." Talos spoke to Amil, his breathing rigid and shoulders slacked from exhaustion.

"Are you alright?" Amil ignored Talos, refusing to look away from me.

"I've been worse. But I'll be fine." I assured him.

He brought my brow to his lips and breathed me in deeply.

He looked over my head to Talos and pulled me behind him, "You could have at the very least told me your plan."

"And risk you not reacting so harshly?" Talos smirked, wiping blood from his scruffy chin.

I rolled my eyes, "You deserved that." I gestured to his swelling nose.

"I deserve swingeing damnation." He gave Amil a dark mischievous grin, humor in his tone despite the beating Amil had inflicted.

Amil repressed a smile to his comment, and his hand still clinging to my arm, "What's your next move? I'd rather not rip your head off in front of the King and Queen next time you put on a performance."

"I believe the King and Queen have been thoroughly convinced that Isa is under my control. This will give us the opportunity to allow Argo to be delivered to her association in Cinder. Once that operation is complete, we will evaluate the best course of action to get her to safety."

Amil scrubbed his hand over the scruff of his chin, and looked back to me from over his shoulder. "You're willing to go along with this?"

"Do I have a choice?" I asked, knowing what his reply would be.

"No. You don't." Talos answered for the both of us.

I looked between the two of them, aware that we hadn't been alone together in a room since the night before Althea's wedding. It felt like a lifetime ago that we were concerned about the way I had been honing my skills on the premise that if the occasion came, I would be able to protect myself. Not being able to fully grasp how I was able to fend off Incubo advances at the time was a hindrance but it had likely saved my life in front of the King and Queen.

My head was still pounding from Talos' earlier invasion and my body was aching. I needed to sleep. I needed to get the dress

Talos had given me off my skin. I pulled at the flowing sleeves, but they held tight to my swollen wrists. I'd been on my hands and knees at some point during the purposeful torture that it felts as though I had thrashing my arms and hands against the hard ground.

I fumbled with the buttons at my cuffs. Amil reached out and took my hand in his, pulled the smooth circle through the loop, releasing my hands and arms.

"Let me help you take your dress off." Amil pulled the sleeves down over my arms, freeing them.

Talos was suddenly behind me, "Here." He whispered while unzipping the back of the dress and letting it melt to the floor around me.

My breath hitched in my throat at their gentle hands. Amil's eyes traveled down to my bare breasts, and when they returned to my face they were black as coal. A dancing flicker igniting in their surfaces. Talos' ran a hand up and over my back, slipping his other hand around to my stomach. I wanted them both but never imagined they would be willing to acknowledge the need I knew they both could feel.

Amil's fingers trailed down up to my chin, tilting my face up to his and pressing his full lips against mine. Talos kissed the top of my shoulder, and pressing his front to my back. His tight slacks presenting his excitement against my bottom. Amil pulled away, his heavy lids cressening his eyes. I reached behind me to Talos' hip to pull him closer, his lips making their way up my neck to behind my ear.

I took Amil's hand and lead it down my chest, over my stomach, and into my warm center. Two of his fingers gliding in with little resistance. Talos' fingers smoothed down my stomach and started soft circles around my navel, then lower, and lower until he was caressing my eager nerve slowly. Amil watched Talos' pace to keep time, his jaw slack and his breathing quickening along with the movement of his fingers. Talos increased his pressure but not his speed, allowing the pressure to build to the precipice. I laid my head back to Talos' as he took on the weight of my torso on his chest.

Amil's husky deep voice hung between us, ringing through me "I can't wait to taste you."

I let out a moan, the strain pulling at my broken bones at my side. Talos slid a hand to the spot, a warmth spreading from his hand to smooth the ache. My gratitude for his act of kindness expressed with another louder sound of pleasure.

Amil plunged his fingers deeper, more determination in his wrist movements. My chest heaved with each stroke as my muscles began to spasm around his fingers. He gave a throaty approval, "That our girl.*Change this but MOVE ON*

Talos' pace slowed to allow me to savor each constriction. His warm lips pressed against the ridge of my cheek, and the bulge in his pants pressed hard enough for me to feel each pulse. He took his hand away from between my thighs and brought it to my lips, damp from my release he coaxed me to open my mouth. Amil leaned into me, his mouth hovering over mine. His tongue gliding over my lips, then joining Talos' fingers against my own tongue. Amil took Talos' fingers into his mouth then let them fall, his eyes intent on me.

Talos stepped back to unbutton his shirt, untucking it from the waist of his pants. The tight corded muscles of his stomach and chest rippling as he shrugged his shirt off his shoulders and down his arms. He laid it over the back of the nearest chair and began taking his belt and shoes off.

I stepped back to admire him, stepping against Amil's solid frame. His hands smoothed up my arms and pulled me back towards the bed. The cool surface of the duvet licked the back of my legs. Amil guided me up to the middle of the bed, then began undressing. Talos came from the other side, his knees sinking into the mattress. I got to my knees and took his shaft into my hand, pulling my wrist up and down.

Amil sidled up behind me

My heart raced in my chest watching Amil's lips working over Talos' tip.

"Take what you need, Isa."

"I hope you're ready for us."

His and Talos' fingers working together to bring me to climax.

Maybe the Queens sister offers Isa a job to kill Talos or the King who is the reason that all these ridiculous rules are still in place and mixed Fata-Incubo are swept under the rug. She had a son take from her and killed by beheading and the body burned. She shows Isa a locket or charm made from her sons ashes on one of her bracelets. If Isa kills the King, she will be able to take Argo away without worry. No one in the Incubo community will stand by her. There is an uprising within the Incubo ranks and in the Fata ranks. In exchange for her freedom and aminitity

The prince comes home from the hospital and comes to see Isa to thank her for saving his sister. The Prince tells Isa that Talos was behind the kidnapping and gets more in depth about the treaty. He leaves the right book in her room with the treaty in it. She also finds out that the easiest way for Incubo to mate with Fata is when past Fata-Incubo crosses are involved and likely Mikal is a crossbreed.

Something has to happen to cause a huge attack on the chateau so that Talos can die by Isa hand. And the king too. Maybe they catch the princess and Mikal and drag them back to be put on trial. Isa is present and acts on instinct when the King sentences Mikal and the Princess to death. Isa, Amil, Yamir, and Althea jump into save them and retch the baby from the Queens sisters arms. Isa and Talos have a row. She finally beats him mentally and plunges the Alexandrite blade through his heat. The king lunges at Isa and she kills him too (before or after). The queen goes into distress and flees with her sister to their homeland. Althea claims the throne as their bylines call for whoever claims first gets it. Idk. Maybe she just steps in and Marries the prince so they both can change their world but don't have to deal with each other.

Last Chapter:

It had been two days since Talos died and I came home to Cinder with Argo by my side. He hasn't slept or eaten, and hasn't let me leave his sight for more than a few minutes. Zaida and Markus were on their way to my house to help me debrief and care for Argo. They had returned to Cinder a few days earlier to check in with the council and tell them about the events that happened in Amples. The Incubo King is dead and by my own hand, but I had no choice. It was either him or Althea and for the first time in my life, I chose to pick a side and not linger in the grey area in between. Althea and the Prince will be married and she will become the new reigning Queen. If she manages to stay alive. Yet another wedding she has to stay alive long enough to see, perhaps this time she would have a chance to cut the cake.

I'd only been home a few hours when a call came from the buildings front desk. A currier had dropped off a parcel to the doorman. I thought it would be a note from the Banner council, they had on occasion called for last moment meetings that way. But to my surprise a plain brown paper wrapped package waited for me. No return address but the name scrawled in pink ink read "Althea of Amples". I tucked it between my arm and stomach, nestled perfectly against my forearm. It sat the length from my wrist to my elbow.

I waited until I was back upstairs to open the wrappings. The black velveteen box lid lifted to reveal a familiar sight but with a new addition. Light rippled off of the Alexandrite blade adorned with a new golden handle. A delicate vine wrapped around from the hilt to the new raw gem sitting at the pommel. It was jagged and rough with a darker hue than the blade itself. I took it out of the box to admire the almost perfect curve to my palm. The weight of it slightly heavier than before it broke. An inscription on the new shining hilt read "A piece of my heart" and caused a catch in my throat as I set it down on its pillowy cushion.

A note was pressed into the lid in the same color and lettering of the paper it had been wrapped in:

He wanted to be with you, always.

A tear fell from my cheek and left a small splatter on the simple but powerful note. The time we had spent together was tumultuous and toxic but I had cared for him. I'd admired his love for Althea and his selflessness for his kind and the family he had created. He'd saved his brothers in the end and befallen to the blade his grandmother had predicted would be his demise.

Guilt and pain strained the back of my throat as visions from that night flooded and tears flowed down my cheeks. The last conversation we had panged through me:

"I may have needed you in more ways than I could have planned/imagined/thought." He had said.

If I could have known that would have been our last moment of intimacy, I would have held him closer, kissed his lips longer. There had been times when I wanted to beat him bloody but the scar of being the one who took his life will mar me until my last breath. Another envelope fell out of the brown wrapping, this one pearl white with sage green lettering. It was an invitation to Althea's wedding. This time only as a guest with a place to mark if I'd be bringing a plus one. She had asked me to be her maid of honor before I left Amples but I had to refuse. One botched wedding was enough for my lifetime and probably hers as well.

I had promised I would attend but we didn't discuss who I

would bring with me. The thought whirled around my brain for an answer. Amil? Yamir? If Yamir would even speak to me after what had happened. I did accidentally murder his boss and close friend, I don't think I would want to attend a wedding with me either.

I knew my siblings wouldn't be going near another Incubo for the foreseeable future. There were many things I didn't have answers for. Would we even see that wedding day without more attacks or a full war breaking out between the Incubo and Fata? Banners have been instructed to stay out of it. To not take employment from either side or risk punishment by the council.

ACKNOWLEDGMENTS

I want to give credit where it is due. I wouldn't have been able to continue on this journey if it weren't for the amazing support of friends and readers.

First, I'd like to thank my

ABOUT THE AUTHOR

K. Elle Morrison lives outside Portland Oregon with her husband, children, and two cats. She is a podcaster, novice gardener, and avid watcher of tv shows and movies she's seen a hundred times.

You can find her on social media, Amazon, and goofing around on Tiktok.

ALSO BY K. ELLE MORRISON

Under The Black Banners

Coming soon

Blood On My Name

CPSIA information can be obtained
at www.ICGtesting.com
Printed in the USA
LVHW041540120122
708314LV00005B/159